# AMINA

# *AMINA*

## A Novel

**Mohammed Umar**

Africa World Press, Inc.

Africa World Press, Inc.

First Printing 2005



Book design: Sam Saverance
Cover design: Ashraful Haque

Library of Congress Cataloging-in-Publication Data
Umar, Mohammed, 1958-
Amina / by Mohammed Umar.
p. cm.
ISBN 1-59221-403-7 -- ISBN 1-59221-404-5 (pbk.)
1. Nigeria--Fiction. 2. Women--Nigeria--Fiction.
3. Muslim women--Fiction. I. Title.

PR9387.9.U445A82 2005
823'.92--dc22

2005028522

This novel is dedicated to my late mother
Halima – for everything;

to my wife Sonja van Mansvelt
and our children Salim, Karim and Nafisa
for their love, support and understanding;

to all those who taught me over the years;

and all those who made me what I am
today!

*We are realists. We dream the impossible.*

—Ernesto Che Guevara

*Our lives begin to end the day we become silent about things that matter.*

—Martin Luther King Jr.

# 1

It had gone midday and the sun was high in the sky as the two young women walked calmly out of the women's university hostel. In the carpark outside, they leaned on a white Mercedes saloon and continued their light-hearted chatter for a while. Eventually, one of them adjusted the red beret on her shoulder-length hair, the other rearranged her headscarf.

'I'll see you later.'

*'In Sha Allah'*

Amina sat in the back seat of the car as it moved slowly out of the university campus and headed towards the town, turning over in her head the forthcoming event at her house. This gathering would differ from others organised by her husband, Alhaji Haruna, in that it was a women-only party to celebrate his recent election to the State House of Assembly. The guests were to be mainly highly placed women in the town-wives of legislators, government executives, privileged civil servants, contractors, army and police officers, businesswomen and the like. At the centre of this party was to be his newly wedded wife, Amina. In short, this was to be her party. Her husband was organising it as a means of introducing her to the 'women's circle.'

The car passed the Government Girls Secondary School, turned left, and entered a wider, newly constructed road. The driver reduced his speed as they went past the military headquarters, then he turned right, sped past some government ministries and reached the town centre. The road was a confusion of cars, motorcycles, bicycles and pedestrians, all of which came to a standstill at the traffic warden's signal from the roundabout. While they waited, Amina peered through the tinted window at the traders locking up their shops in front of the central market, hawkers packing their wares away, shoppers leaving. On the other side of the road, hundreds of men in turbans and prayer caps crowded in front of the newly built mosque to offer afternoon prayers.

Another signal from the traffic warden, and the driver engaged the gear and zoomed forward. Amina sat back and pictured the party. She saw herself receiving the guests as they walked into the compound, took their seats and began the usual chatter. They were the richest and the most influential women in town. She knew her future was to become one of them, to start her own business, make money, buy expensive clothes, jewellery, cars…she might even become one of the richest women, not only in the state, but in the country. By the time the party ended she would have been ceremonially introduced to the upper echelons of society.

The car sailed smoothly into the central part of Bakaro district and came to a halt in front of the only two-storey building in the area, Alhaji Haruna's house. Conscious of being under scrutiny as she alighted from the car, Amina pulled her headscarf forward and tried to instil dignity into her walk. The band of praise-singers which habitually hung around the gates drummed and sang her praises, extolling her virtues and her beauty and calling her 'the best gift of Almighty Allah to Alhaji Haruna.' Amina smiled and gave the bandleader some crisp 500 naira notes from her handbag.

Upstairs in her room at last, Amina was not surprised to see her first guest already waiting for her there. Kulu was the wife of the local government secretary, a successful businesswoman and Amina's friend. A middle-aged woman of average height with an expansive bosom, she was dressed as always in the height of fashion. They exchanged greetings and Kulu helped Amina to change from her street clothes into an immaculate white blouse with gold embroidery, with a matching white shawl and headscarf. As Amina added golden rings, silver bracelets and diamond earrings to her outfit, Kulu enquired where she had been.

'I went to the university to invite Fatima.'

'That useless, irresponsible girl!' Kulu hissed.

Amina made no comment. She knew there was no love lost between Kulu and Fatima, but thought it was nothing to do with her. As she and Kulu stood side-by-side in front of the long mirror admiring themselves in their formal attire, they heard the first guests arriving and Amina went downstairs to welcome them. As she stood in their midst, with her regular features, exquisite figure and smooth dark skin, she presented the perfect hostess figure: elegant, beautiful and poised. Only when Fatima and two other girls from the university arrived and headed straight for her did she relax slightly, and her expression softened into a genuine smile.

When most of the guests had arrived, Kulu came downstairs, accompanied by Alhaji Haruna. It was Kulu's role to welcome everyone formally and invite Alhaji Haruna to speak. As she spoke, he stood at her side, a tall and bulky man who towered over her, his flat, square forehead, flat nose and clean-shaven chin offset by an immaculate white gown with green embroidery on the front and back. He wore a short red cap and shiny brown shoes.

As Kulu introduced him and stepped aside, Alhaji Haruna cleared his throat gently and adjusted his gown. He thanked Almighty Allah for His help and guidance and the guests for responding to his invitation. 'As you all know, our religion, Islam, permits the Muslim man to marry up to four wives. Amina is my fourth. My principle is: "New success, new wife."' There was a rustle of gowns and a murmur from his audience, and he beamed around proudly. 'When, with the help of Almighty Allah, I was appointed the local government storekeeper many years ago, I married my first wife. When again, with the Almighty's help, I was promoted to the post of accountant in the State Ministry of Finance, I married my second. When Almighty Allah showed me the way into business, I married my third. And now that, with His help, I've won a seat in the State House of Assembly I've married my fourth.' He looked directly at Amina as he said: 'You are my fourth; the last but not the least.' Some guests clapped; others smiled or laughed. Alhaji Haruna waited for silence and quickly added, 'In strict compliance with Islamic rules, I can assure you that I love all my wives equally.'

After his speech the guests broke into groups, and talk became lively. As Amina wandered through the crowd, exchanging compliments and receiving congratulations, snatches of conversation on familiar topics came to her—recent political successes and setbacks, economic prospects, who had won what contract, who had the latest model of car or electronic equipment. The compound was packed, and hostesses served the guests soft drinks, biscuits, roasted and fried beef and chicken. As Amina made her way towards a group of student friends, she heard Fatima say: 'He's a cheat. What if he's elected or appointed into a higher office in the future? He'll just divorce one of his wives to marry a new one.' Arriving at the group, Amina simply smiled and chatted serenely with some of the students.

When the party ended, however, Amina sighed with relief and went upstairs to rest. 'Thank God it was a success,' she said, as she threw herself onto her king-size bed. Lying there, she contemplated the room, allowing her eyes to travel over the colour television, the video recorder, the fridge, the radio cassette player, the cupboard filled with numerous sets of plates of different colours and sizes; and the wardrobe, sheltering countless outfits for different occasions. She had supper brought to the room and changed into her night-gown.

Much later, Alhaji Haruna entered and locked the door behind him. Sitting on the bed and pulling off his shoes, he said as if it were an afterthought: 'Amina, I forgot to announce during the party that as my wife you are entitled to a house and a piece of land. Also, I met Bature today and he's expecting you soon.'

Amina thanked him, genuinely surprised at his generosity. She did not expect such gifts, though her husband was at pains to assure her that while he was still alive and still rich, she could have anything in this world she wanted. He switched off the lights and joined her in bed. 'The house is not far away from here. The piece of land is not far either. It's near the river, opposite the primary school.'

'Thank you,' Amina said again.

'How wonderful Allah can be,' Alhaji Haruna said after a short silence, 'only some months ago we were strangers, today we are husband and wife. Although it's dark, I can feel your beauty. It radiates.'

The next day, Amina got up early and offered her morning prayers. She put on some of her smartest clothes, and left the compound at about ten o'clock. Outside, a dark blue Range Rover was waiting, and as she approached, someone opened the door for her, singing her praises. 'Take me to Bature's house,' she told the driver as the door closed.

Bature's house was on the outskirts of the town. The car stopped in front of the metal gate, and Amina lowered her window a fraction. 'Amina Haruna, wife of the Majority Leader in the State House of Assembly, here to see Bature,' she said. The guard spoke briefly into his radio, the gates opened, and they rolled towards the compound car park. From here, one of the guards escorted Amina down a tree-lined pathway towards the house, passing a swimming pool and a tennis court.

'I am very happy to meet you at last,' Bature welcomed Amina at the door. 'Please come in and make yourself at home.' He ushered her into a reception room where a man was already sitting, and begged her to excuse him for a moment while he finished some business. He resumed his conversation with the man, who, Amina later found out, was called Mohammed Idris. She was not interested in their conversation, but allowed it to drift over her as she looked around at the lavishly decorated room with its marble floor and spectacular chandelier.

'Your father invested in shares that have fallen in value,' said Bature.

'I'm interested in what is left in his bank accounts,' Mohammed said.

'The money I helped your father deposit cannot be withdrawn for many years. I gave him many options and that was what he chose. I can show you the original documents with his signature on them. You can only withdraw twenty-five percent in the next ten years.'

'But he said he had millions ...'

'In theory the money is his, but in practice no one, not even if he was alive, could take out more than twenty five percent over the next ten years,' Bature explained.

'I don't understand. Do you mean we can not transfer this money back into Nigeria?'

'You are right. It is almost impossible to bring this money back!' Bature said, looking straight at Mohammed. 'But I'm afraid I'm busy right now. My son will explain how it works. Lucas, Lucas,' he called. 'Please take him away and explain how the business works.' Having dismissed the supplicant, Bature's demeanour changed as he turned smoothly to Amina. 'You are welcome. Please come with me. I want to introduce you to someone.' Amina followed Bature to the swimming pool, where a white woman in a bikini was lying in the shade, sipping wine. Amina felt very uncomfortable, not knowing where to look, but Bature introduced her as Paula, a London-based florist, who had flown in specially to arrange the flowers at the swearing-in ceremony of the State Governor to mark the return of civilian rule in the state.

'I'm delighted to meet you,' Paula said, removing her sunglasses. 'I've fallen in love with your country and its people. Fascinating place. Extremely nice people too. Lots of business opportunities here,' Paula said, sipping from her glass. 'I understand you'll be in business too. That's great. Maybe we should work together.'

'I've not really made up my mind,' Amina replied. 'Anyway, it is a pleasure meeting you.'

Amina felt relief as Bature led her back to the reception room and left her with his son, who had apparently dispatched the earlier visitor. Lucas called for bottles of cold water and glasses, sat next to Amina and filled two glasses. 'I understand from my father that you're interested in doing business with us,' he said, arranging some brochures and papers on the table. 'Why don't I explain the services we offer? Basically, these range from managing funds, to advising people where to invest their money. If people want to buy a house anywhere in Europe, we can get very competitive rates. We set up appointments for medical checkups, arrange holidays and get children into the best schools.' At the end of their brief meeting, he gave her some brochures and files of documents on various services.

Amina thanked him. 'I'll get back to you after studying the materials,' she said.

Lucas called his father, who walked in with his mobile phone in hand. 'I understand you're Fatima's friend' he said, as he took his leave of her. 'Perhaps you could do me a favour. I'll be out of the country for a few months, so when you next see her, please tell her I accept her invitation to join a debate at the university. I'll be in touch when I get back, energised and ready for the intellectual duel.' He smiled ironically, and again Amina felt uncomfortable; but Lucas was the soul of chivalry as he escorted her back to the car.

# 2

Several weeks passed. Amina's daily routine of praying, eating and sleeping continued peacefully, and she enjoyed her idle but comfortable life. Because her husband was rich, she had almost all she wanted, and so far had no cause to complain about life as a lady of leisure. Despite this, however, she viewed it as a transitional period, believing that as time went on, she would find something interesting to occupy her mind.

On a beautiful sunny Saturday, Amina attended the inaugural meeting of the Legislators Wives' Association. It took place at the Assembly premises where she recognised some of the guests from her party. At the end of the meeting, she was elected Assistant Secretary General of the association, and went home delighted. Alone in her room, she locked the door, removed her blouse and moved close to the mirror to admire her features—a long-standing habit of hers. She touched her smooth face. 'I thank God for creating me beautiful. I am blessed with all the qualities a woman needs. I think God must have spent extra time in creating me. I am more beautiful than all those women at the meeting ...' A gentle knock disturbed her meditation. She quickly put on her blouse and opened the door.

'Hello Queen. How are you?' Kulu asked, with a broad smile.

'I'm fine, and you?' Amina replied, showing her guest into the room.

'Excellent. I won't be long. Just came to tell you that I'll soon be travelling to Europe, and then to the Holy Land to perform the lesser Hajj.'

'Lucky you,' responded Amina with a smile.

'My new company has been registered.'

'Which one?'

'The Travel Agency. This sort of business is very lucrative these days, especially when pilgrims are travelling to Saudi Arabia.' Kulu paused for a moment. 'I hope you haven't forgotten my offer to take you to the Holy Land?'

'No I haven't. I'll tell you when I'm ready.'

Just when Amina wanted to have a rest, Mairo, the second wife of a popular Arabic and Koranic teacher walked in. She was a fat, talkative woman with bow legs, popularly called 'Radio Bakaro,' as she was always armed with the latest news.

'You're a lucky woman,' Mairo began, making herself comfortable.

'In what respect?' questioned Amina.

'You live comfortably compared to most women here.'

'That's the will of Almighty Allah,' Amina rejoined.

'You're right ... do you know Larai?'

'No. Who is she?'

'A young mother who's been in hospital for a while. She was admitted for the delivery of her first baby some months ago. She had a very difficult delivery. She's now suffering from the ailment that afflicts underage girls when they give birth.'

'What's that got to do with me?' Amina asked with a frown.

'Nothing. I just pity her and women like her. Most of them live the rest of their lives in poverty and neglect. I thought as a young and educated woman, you might be concerned about their lives.' Mairo regarded Amina penetratingly.

Amina reacted with indifference. 'I'm not. We all have our separate lives and separate destinies. I didn't force them to marry so young. I'm not a medical doctor and I'm not rich enough to take care of them. I would advise you to see the Emir of the town or the Governor of the state, or some other influential person.'

Mairo was not to be put off. 'They're all men and would not understand the seriousness of the ailment,' she explained seriously.

'There's nothing I can do. It's the will of God.'

With a shrug, Mairo moved on to other local issues. When Amina felt she had listened long enough for politeness, she said she was tired after the events of the day and needed a rest, and Mairo left. As Amina started gratefully loosening her plaited hair, she heard a familiar voice in the compound. It was her friend, Fatima, chasing Abdullahi, the ten-year-old son of the first wife. She loved to tease him, and always jokingly called him her reluctant bridegroom. When she caught him near the guava tree in the centre of the compound, Fatima said loudly, 'You have no choice but to marry me now.' Releasing Abdullahi, she picked up Jamila, the three-year-old daughter of the second wife, who patted her face admiringly, and lisped, 'You are beautiful, so you'll be my brother's wife.'

'Is this Gambo, the woodcutter's son?' Fatima asked a woman in the compound referring to a bow-legged boy of about five.

'Yes,' his mother replied.

'Then this is the future president of our country,' she joked.

'That's impossible,' his mother replied with a smile.

Fatima went upstairs to Amina's room. 'We've been very busy on campus,' she said still standing, by way of apology for not visiting her. 'The student union elections have just taken place and I was elected vice-president.'

'Congratulations!' Though uninterested in politics, Amina was sincere in her endorsement of her friend.

'Thank you,' Fatima said. She sat on the sofa, removed her red beret and tied her long hair at the back.

'Can you can help me plait my hair?' Amina asked her friend. 'Also, I have a few things I'd like to talk about with you.'

'That's all right. I have time.'

Fatima went downstairs and got a carved wooden stool to sit on. They went outside onto the small balcony, and Amina sat on the floor at her feet while Fatima parted her hair into sections. 'Amina,' she said, 'the elections were interesting and I learnt a lot from ...'

'Listen,' Amina interrupted, 'you know I'm not interested. I fear and hate politics.'

'Whether you agree with me or not, every human being is a politician. The only choice is whether to be active or passive. If you are not prepared to exercise power and control over the things that affect you, others will do it for you.'

Abdullahi's appearance on the balcony interrupted them. He shyly offered Fatima some kola nuts, and she seized him by the arm and drew him closer. The women watching in the compound below laughed. Abdullahi struggled, freed himself and ran away.

'So where do you belong?' Fatima resumed.

Amina was nonplussed, and replied uncertainly, 'I would say I belong to the group that steers the middle course.' Fatima pulled roughly at a bunch of Amina's hair, and Amina protested. Apologising, Fatima nonetheless continued her harangue. 'I must tell you that in politics there is no middle road, no sitting on the fence. You are either for or against the existing order. You either support it or you think of how to change it for the better.'

Amina was silent. She knew Fatima was deeply immersed in political issues and could speak about them for hours, and that once started, it was impossible to distract her. Despite this, Fatima's warmth and directness appealed to her, and she regarded the rhetoric as the price she had to pay for her company.

'You look more beautiful with this hairstyle. It really suits you,' Fatima commented after finishing the last bunch of hair. She stood up and stretched.

'Stop teasing me.'

'I'm not. Anybody who has eyes can see you are a rare beauty. Even a blind person who touched your face would say the same. However, beauty is just part of what a woman needs. She also needs intelligence and strength of mind.'

'Thanks for plaiting my hair,' Amina responded, offering Fatima a cold drink as she inspected her new hairdo in front of the mirror. There were things Amina wanted to talk to Fatima about, but she judged that Fatima was not in the mood for personal issues and decided to wait. Instead she asked:

'Okay. Accepted that the conditions of women require reform; what should be done?' Fatima's face lit up at once.

'A lot must be done,' she responded with enthusiasm. 'For a start, people in positions of privilege need to get involved.'

'Okay, I'll talk to my husband and ask whether the State House of Assembly can look into the conditions of women,' Amina offered.

'Rule that out!' Fatima countered. 'They'll never do it.'

'But he loves me,' Amina insisted.

'Yes he does, but he loves his interests more.' Fatima paused. 'On the other hand, the Legislators' Wives' Association could be used to improve the lot of women. How organised are you?'

'Erm, well, our association is still young and we discuss mainly how to take care of our husbands, to press for better amenities for our husbands in the Legislators' Estate and other issues. The next meeting is to be held here and if you like, I'll draw the attention of the other members to your concerns. Perhaps we can influence our husbands to enact laws that create more favourable conditions for women.'

'Listen, they'll never initiate changes out of goodwill,' Fatima contended. She bit her lower lip and continued thoughtfully. 'One of the main causes of female oppression is our own ignorance. We need more schools and free compulsory education for girls, but that's a plan for the future. Meanwhile, we should set up special adult education programmes to eradicate illiteracy.'

'What do you mean?'

'We need first to teach women how to read and write, and then about their civic duties and human rights and how to defend them. Most women don't even understand Islam. They just accept what their husbands, brothers or other people tell them, and they confuse traditional values and norms with those of Islam. If women are given the correct basic education, they'll understand society and their place in it better.'

Despite herself, the more Fatima spoke, the more interested Amina became. Although she did not necessarily agree or understand, she respected Fatima and struggled to follow her thoughts. Since they had met and shared a room at university two years before, Fatima had been the most reliable and honest of all her friends. Although her outspokenness sometimes got her into trouble, everyone in their circle admired her simplicity and sincerity. It was virtually impossible to know her well without responding to her warmth, and politically she was one of the most articulate defenders of human rights and justice at the university. Though Amina had liked Fatima immediately, when Fatima had, on various occasions, tried to draw her into politics, Amina had withdrawn. On one occasion, fed up with her diatribes, Amina had threatened to change rooms. Despite this, they had remained very close friends, and Amina was glad that they had stayed in touch after she left university. Their views, however, were no closer together than before.

'Why do women need education?' Amina asked firmly. 'Look at me. Despite my being educated, I'm a full-time housewife. I tend to agree with those who say education for women is a waste of time and money.'

'Just because you're not using your education, that doesn't mean women don't need to be educated. You're not worthless, you're just idle. You can, and will, be useful.'

Amina excused herself and prepared for last prayers. Afterwards, still sitting on the prayer mat, fingering her prayer beads, she remarked: 'It's dangerous to walk at night. I'd rather you made your way home before it gets dark.'

'Don't worry, I can take care of myself,' Fatima assured her. 'I can face a rapist or even an armed robber. Don't you know I've a black belt in judo and I'm learning karate?'

'I know,' Amina said, nodding her head. 'By the way, I went to Bature's house and he asked me to tell you that he has accepted your invitation for a debate. What's it all about?'

Fatima smiled and after a long pause explained: 'I've known Bature for some time. He's very close to my father, so I've had the opportunity of discussing various issues with him, and I had the idea that students would benefit from an open debate between the two of us. So I proposed that we set it up, with a jury to decide the winner. The princess of the savannah will not need to cover her head with a beret any more if defeated by Bature in an intellectual duel. Also I promised that, should I lose the war of words, I would be willing—once and for all—to be at the service of imperialism. However, if Bature loses, he'll put pressure on the politicians to free political prisoners and pay for a certain number of students to study. In other words, he will use his power and wealth for the benefit of the people. I look forward to this debate and I suggest you come. I'm sure you'll learn something.'

'Tell me more about Bature. I honestly don't know a lot about him.'

'Where do I start?' Fatima said and paused for while. 'Bature first came to Nigeria during the civil war as a mercenary. He was said to have fought with the secessionists but fell out with the leaders and left via Cameroon. Months later, Bature came back to Nigeria as a military adviser to the Federal Government, although he was not involved in fighting during his second stint. It was believed that the rebels got in touch with him and promised him control of the oil sector should they succeed. He changed sides again and became a leading supplier of arms and sophisticated radio equipment to the rebels. During the battle of Umuahia, he was injured and was first flown to Ivory Coast and then to a European capital. He was there when the war ended. After making a full recovery, he came back to Nigeria as a general contractor and adviser to the Federal Government on reconstruction and state building, with his company, Fortuna International Limited.

'So astute is he at taking advantage of opportunities that he was soon providing a wide range of services to the ruling classes in the new environment created by the oil boom. In the 1980s he was also busy in many other African countries, and was a close friend of Mobutu Sese Seko, Jonas Savimbi and a few other dictators. He advised the rebels during the civil war in Angola. On one of his visits there, Cuban soldiers ambushed his entourage killing several aides, but he survived, was arrested and detained in a hospital in Luanda. A special commando unit from the apartheid regime rescued him in a daring operation one night and took him to South Africa. So now you know why I call him a freelance imperialist!'

Amina was amazed at her friend's easy acquaintance with a world she was only dimly aware existed. She stared at her, wondering how Fatima had such knowledge, and why she cared so passionately. She looked at Fatima more closely and though it was getting dark, she noticed how young she looked, how neat and smart in her simple clothes.

All she said, however, was: 'I think it's time you went home.'

Fatima regarded her seriously. 'Amina, tell me the truth. Deep down, are you satisfied with your idle and dependent life? You're young, healthy and capable of being productive, but someone keeps you for life in his house just because he wants you there, just because you're his wife, because he's a man and you're a woman. Is that what you want?'

Amina was touched at her obvious concern, but could only stare at Fatima, who let out a sigh. 'My suggestion to you is this: try and organise the women in this area. Educate them in the broadest sense. Open their eyes so that they can see the world they are living in clearly. Someone once said "Once a person can read, then that person is forever free." You can show them how to live better, healthier and happier lives. But listen, Amina,' Fatima took a deep breath, 'before you can do any or all of these things, you must open your own eyes, broaden your knowledge; in short you must study hard. Going on what I know of you, let me advise you honestly; if you don't read widely and engage yourself in work, you will die of boredom under this roof.'

Fatima stood up and walked slowly and silently towards the closed window. She stood there fingering the lock.

'Aren't you afraid?' Amina asked.

'Afraid of what?' Fatima asked, turning. 'This is what I believe. I think women's lives can be improved and I'm certainly not afraid to try.'

After a pause, she continued quietly. 'You know I was married and lived as you're now living. My former husband was very rich, and we travelled abroad on our honeymoon. My first months with him were blissful and exciting, but as time went by, I got the real picture. I was his third wife. When I realised domestic violence and tyranny, inexplicable brutalities, backward beliefs, isolation and idleness were my future, I left the house. Yes, I walked out with my daughter. I accepted the dissolution of the marriage with joy. That's how I was able to go back to university, where we met. As a result of that experience, I resolved not only to study the conditions of women but also to do as much as I could to change them. That's why I chose to study law, to fight for and defend women's rights. I was at the top of the social ladder, but I see no joy and happiness there. I decided to slowly descend the rungs to the class where I felt I belonged. It's the base of society that interests me now.'

There was a slight noise in the compound, followed by footsteps climbing the stairs and a gentle knock. Alhaji Haruna entered with a broad smile. 'I can see you've been gossiping all day,' he said after responding to their greetings.

'Discussing,' Fatima corrected him.

'Women gossip, men discuss,' he said with a laugh. 'Okay, so what have you been discussing?'

'Women's issues,' Amina responded.

'She means, the conditions of women, how they are being exploited and dominated by men in this society,' Fatima elaborated.

'What about it?' Alhaji asked smoothly. 'Men are born to rule; there's nothing you can do to change what is ordained by Allah.'

'I think it's time for me to go,' Fatima said, standing up.

Unexpectedly, Alhaji Haruna asked Fatima to sit down because he liked talking to her. He switched the topic of discussion to his brother, Lamido Dan Bakaro, a lecturer at the university who was in detention for having criticised the ruling party in a newspaper article. 'I know you're actively campaigning for the release of Lamido. But as his brother, I say he's not a political prisoner, he's a traitor.'

'Lamido is simply exercising his right as a citizen. He hasn't committed any offence. He simply described what is happening: the recent elections were rigged; there is corruption, nepotism and sycophancy in the state. Everybody knows that! As a political scientist, it's his duty to describe and analyse ...'

'This is Nigeria,' Alhaji Haruna interrupted. 'Why would anyone in his right mind criticise the ruling party? Why would a brother criticise his brother's party?'

'In a democracy, we all have freedom of thought and speech.'

'But democracy doesn't mean disrespect and lies.'

'I read the article and there is nothing offensive in it at all. So, does this mean you will incarcerate anyone who criticises you and the ruling party?'

'Yes, if my son criticises me I'll send him to jail. I'll make sure he suffers ...'

'When is Lamido going to be released?'

'He'll be there until he repents.'

'But it's against the law to hold him like that.'

'I'm above the law.' Alhaji Haruna said, laughing mischievously.

'What about Dan Habu?' Fatima asked, referring to a close relation of Alhaji Haruna also in detention on his orders.

'He's another traitor. He campaigned for another party and they lost. He protested and had to be punished. There must be law and order.'

'But it's within the law to protest.'

'This is Nigeria and this is how politics works here.'

Fatima stood up. 'I think it's really time for me to go,' she said firmly and walked out of the room.

# 3

Amina spent the next weeks alone in her room. She lived quietly, each day a replica of the previous one. Even as she tried to adapt to the idle life of a young housewife, she was starting to worry about being inactive and the boredom irritated her. However, she could not complain. This was the life of most women in her society, brought up to believe that the main duty of a woman was to stay at home and care for the husband and family. Her husband, the owner of the house, controlled her and decided what she would do and when. According to his plan, she would probably only be allowed to go into business after having her first child. 'If you count the months of pregnancy and those before you can leave the child at home, that's roughly two years,' she thought with desolation. She longed for something to do to relieve the monotony of her life.

On one such boring day, Amina was in her room, thinking of nothing in particular, and playing with Isa, the young son of Alhaji's third wife, when Fatima arrived. As usual, she wasn't wearing any make-up. She looked disturbed.

'What's wrong?' Amina inquired, after the usual greetings.

'So many things. Our movement has been banned indefinitely, and six of our leading officials have been expelled from the university—Danbaki, Aremu, Jibril, Bagu, Rachel and your friend Muktar.'

Amina knew the organisation, which was called the Progressive Students' Movement. It was the only revolutionary organisation on the campus. 'What will you do?' she asked quietly.

'There's nothing we can do, really, except to condemn the authorities and work to strengthen the movement.'

'Aren't you afraid?'

'No! Why?' Fatima responded with bravado. 'I've taken over as leader and pledged my commitment to the movement.'

'You should be thankful to Almighty Allah that you were not one of those expelled. Why do you have to take such risks?'

'I would have been expelled if I'd been on the campus when the clash occurred,' Fatima agreed, and fell silent for some time. She resumed thoughtfully: 'To succeed in anything you have to take risks. We've got to if we're to continue.' As if frightened by her own voice, Fatima swiftly turned to Amina. 'Listen, I have an idea.' She came closer, with her fingers crossed and a bright smile now on her face. 'Some female members of our movement will meet in your room, here, for some hours on Saturday. Just a few of us-about six or eight of us—agreed?'

'No,' Amina replied, shocked.

'Why? We've been pushed underground. Please help us.' Fatima pleaded.

'I'm afraid of the consequences,' said Amina, shakily.

Fatima was disappointed, but wouldn't give up. She looked Amina in the eyes and explained: 'We'll only be an hour or two. You don't need to get involved in anything. The boys will meet somewhere else. Security men and informers are watching us closely on the campus. We have to be discreet. Please Amina!'

'No! Not here,' Amina insisted. 'I'm afraid.'

'Okay,' Fatima said in a relaxed voice, fingering her long hair. 'In that case, when we come, you either throw us out or call the police.' She picked up her handbag and headed for the door. 'To remind you, it's on Saturday at ten o'clock in the morning. Goodbye till then.'

Amina was left feeling very uncomfortable. She couldn't understand why Fatima would not leave her alone, or why her room had to be used as a venue for clandestine meetings. She didn't know what would happen if her husband found out she was even in contact with a movement that agitated for fundamental changes in the system and propagated revolutionary ideas.

On Saturday, Amina woke up earlier than usual. The cold harmattan wind was seeping through the cracks in her door and window, and she stayed in bed for a long time under the thick bedspread. Later, as she bathed and tidied her room, she felt relieved that her husband had gone to Abuja, the federal capital city of Nigeria. She opened the window and soft rays of light brightened the room. Just after ten o'clock, as she returned restlessly to the window, she saw six girls get out of a white Peugeot and walk towards the house. Nervously, she rushed downstairs, where she recognised two of the girls with Fatima: one who had accompanied her to the party, and Bilkisu, the daughter of the State Deputy Governor, who had been her classmate at secondary school and university. Amina forced a smile and welcomed them as they greeted her and the other women in the compound and played with the children. They were simply dressed, as though for a casual visit.

Upstairs in her room, Amina served her guests tea and biscuits while Fatima started the meeting: 'I'd like to thank Amina for allowing us to be here. The purpose of this meeting is to discuss the condition of women in northern Nigeria. As we know, a girl in traditional society in our part of Nigeria, domesticated from birth and seen as a burden, is prepared only for the role of housewife and mother. She is brought up to see her own brothers as better than she is, her husband as master and men in general as superior. Deprived of all opportunities for individual and collective development, she experiences a feeling of injustice and has to make a choice—whether to accept her fate or rebel against it.'

The topic was not new to Amina, who had heard Fatima holding forth many times in similar words when they shared a room. But here there were other voices adding to the discussion.

'It seems to me,' Bilkisu cut in, 'that the degree of oppression and discrimination against most women in Nigeria is very high. When a woman is pushed to the wall by a ruthless and exploitative system with callous and irresponsible leaders, life itself becomes meaningless.'

'There's no discrimination in suffering,' Fatima cautioned. 'Let's not be carried away. Men suffer too.'

'But women feel the pain more than men,' Bilkisu argued. 'The ordinary Nigerian woman is living under terrible conditions where she's forced to struggle for survival for herself and her children. In this situation, we women can't be mere observers as our rulers are always advising us, because we too are directly affected by their mismanagement of the economy. We're daily denied our basic needs. Our main providers—fathers, brothers, husbands—are facing a constant threat of being sacked or having their land seized by unscrupulous landlords.'

Amina suffered as the meeting dragged on, the discussion taking its predictable course. 'The cunning and parasitic behaviour of our rulers makes it easy to identify them,' Fatima was saying. 'Wherever you go, you see gross inefficiency, massive corruption, political deception and, to crown their dirty tricks, the recent general elections were fraudulent.'

'Last year there was drought,' Gloria said, with a concerned look. 'This year there may be famine and many people may die, especially children. At the same time, the rich are buying flashy cars, building expensive houses, travelling abroad on questionable missions and marrying more wives. I think it's the bourgeoisie that should be held responsible for the mess we're in. In developed countries, they have at least played an important role in developing the economy and in nurturing stable political systems, where people are given the freedom to contribute to the development of society. Unfortunately, the reverse is the case in Africa. It's difficult to find one patriotic bourgeois here. They're lazy, crafty, ignorant, dubious, arrogant and irresponsible. They deliberately block all avenues of progress and instead propagate backward ideas.'

Amina quietly removed herself downstairs to the kitchen to inspect the food her maid Hauwa was having prepared. When it was ready, she served it into seven dishes, and Hauwa helped her carry them upstairs. Here, the meeting had degenerated into an argument, with everyone talking at the same time. Amina told them food was ready and brought water. As always, she wondered where they got the energy and enthusiasm for such a discussion, and after eating, she went downstairs again to wash the plates. Hauwa rushed to help her, and they were amicably at work when Kulu walked in briskly. As they were exchanging greetings, they heard a peal of laughter from Amina's room. Kulu looked perplexed. 'It's Fatima and her friends,' explained Amina.

'Oh, her again,' Kulu said dismissively. 'I've come to tell you I'm going to Kano soon. I've found out that my goods have been impounded at the airport. Later, I hope to travel to London on business and then on to Switzerland for a short winter holiday.'

'That's fantastic,' Amina said warmly.

Kulu smirked. 'You'll soon start your business and we might be competitors. Just ignore those girls upstairs, tune your mind to business only.' With that, Kulu left hurriedly.

Back upstairs, the meeting was preparing to break up. Fatima was telling them about the beauty contest and fashion parade coming up at the university that evening, imitating the stylish walks of models in beauty contests.

'If you enter, I'm sure you'll win,' Bilkisu mocked.

'No, she'd be better in the fashion parade,' suggested Gloria.

'Will you participate?' Rebecca questioned.

'No. I've no time for such things.' Fatima replied and after a pause added. 'Maybe! Girls need good bodies and beautiful wings too.'

They all laughed as they got up to go. In the compound, Fatima tiptoed up to Abdullahi and grabbed him from behind. 'I've the honour and privilege to introduce to you my husband, Mallam Abdullahi,' she said to the other girls, and to him: 'I'm ready for the marriage. Look, my friends are here. Are you ready?' Abdullahi was silent and shy. The girls laughed and filed out of the compound.

'Why does Fatima say I'm her husband?' Abdullahi asked Amina.

'Because she loves you.'

'But she's older than me, very old ... I don't love her. She plays too much and she'd be a troublesome wife anyway.'

'I'll tell her to change,' Amina said with a smile.

In her room, Amina noticed Fatima had left some books and pamphlets on the bed. Moving closer, she saw a note was attached to a copy of Abubakar Tafawa Balewa's novel, *Shehu Umar*: 'The worst form of cruelty to other people is slavery. For centuries African societies were raided for slaves, our economies were plundered, our towns and villages destroyed, our development retarded. As Fanon once said: "Each generation must out of relative obscurity discover its mission, fulfil it or betray it!" Before we can fulfil our mission we have to liberate our minds. Abubakar Tafawa Balewa wrote this novel to illuminate this problem. I hope this book will help in decolonising your mind. Fatima.'

# 4

Amina woke up very early. The weather had changed, and it had suddenly become very warm, so the room was stuffy. She opened the window and a cooling early morning breeze blew in. She lay in bed with only half of her body covered and thought of the meeting scheduled to take place in her room later that day. It would be a different type of meeting from the last one, and she had to participate in it, but what would they discuss? The role of legislators' wives in society ... Rubbish! The wife of a legislator is still just a wife.

The meeting was supposed to start at one o'clock but members of the association didn't start arriving until half past two. Asabe, the president of the association and the third wife of the Speaker in the House of Assembly, was the first to come. She was about Amina's age, with various rings on her fingers and chains round her neck. She walked haughtily into the room, inspected it and said nothing, though she seemed unsatisfied. Once the meeting started, Asabe led a discussion centred on the duties and role of a legislator's wife. Amina found it dull, but sat listening quietly.

During the break for refreshment, Asabe invited Amina downstairs for a private talk. Amina agreed, although there was something she didn't like about Asabe. Was it arrogance or pomposity? 'Asabe is too proud just to be the wife of a legislator,' she thought, watching Asabe as she looked for a shady corner. Asabe sighed: 'It's too hot. Because

I bleached my skin I can't tolerate the sun.' When Amina made no comment she continued: 'I can see that you're not comfortable here. You need privacy. If I were you, I'd get Alhaji to rent a flat or build a house for you in the Government Reservation Area. After all, he's rich and can afford it, but you have to take the initiative. I live in GRA, and believe me, it's wonderful. It's a secluded area, quiet and natural. In the evenings, if I don't stroll to the golf club, I usually take a walk in the nearby woods.' She paused, adjusted her bangles and continued. 'We're trying to form the women's wing of the Circle International Club. The wife of the State Chief Judge, who's also a Magistrate, will contest for the post of president. I want to contest for secretary, and Kulu is going for vice-president. But the wife of the State Commissioner of Police, and a lecturer on the campus, are also vying for the post I'm after. It'll be an exclusive club for rich women or wives of influential men in the town. Membership will be restricted and very few wives of legislators will be invited to join. But how about you? Would you like to stand for a post? If so, we can start campaigning or form an alliance.'

'No thank you,' Amina answered with a smile.

'That's good,' Asabe said, with a sigh of relief. 'You'll of course be a member and because you are educated and look enterprising, we'll invite you into the inner circle.'

'Why do we need such an organisation?'

'Well, you see, it will unite us wealthy women under one umbrella to protect and defend our common interests. Through it we can get our own share of the cake, while also helping the poor.'

'Understood. I'll wait and see.'

When the meeting finished and Amina was alone in her room, she compared it with that of the students. Participants of the earlier meeting had raised wider problems facing society and related cordially to others in the compound, while the legislators' wives were focused on their own interests, and kept aloof. Asabe had even advised her to leave the compound. She was so engrossed in her thoughts she didn't notice Alhaji Haruna coming in.

Amina quickly knelt to greet him. She had not seen her husband for several weeks, as since his return from Abuja, he had stayed at the Legislators' Estate. He did not reply to her greetings, and she noticed with concern that he looked annoyed and was behaving coldly towards her. 'How was your trip?' she asked respectfully. When he remained silent, she repeated the question, twisting her fingers. 'I've got a very serious issue to iron out with you,' Alhaji Haruna said with a frown, 'but I haven't got time now.' A frightful coldness seized her and she trembled. 'Don't go anywhere,' he warned and turned towards the door.

Amina wondered what had caused his strange behaviour, and could only think of the students' secret meeting. But no one had listened to it. Maybe the information had leaked out on campus and he had been informed, she thought. Throughout the day, she remained restless and nervous. It was only towards evening that Hauwa told her what she had overheard in the compound: that Amina was having a secret love affair with Bala, one of Alhaji's private drivers. She bit her lower lip until it almost bled and shook her lowered head gently. 'How on earth can he think I would do such a thing?' she asked? She didn't even know this Bala. Who could have come up with such a malicious story? And why? Her thoughts turned to Jummai, Alhaji's third wife. Although they had not quarrelled openly, Jummai had recently been showing signs of hostility. It was to be expected in a situation where there were four wives in the same compound, and Amina hadn't let it bother her.

But now she was concerned about the effect of such a story, not only on her dignity and integrity in the family but also in the district. In a place like Bakaro such news would spread like wildfire among the women and inevitably a lot of lies would be added. She tried to anticipate the worst reaction Alhaji might have: If he divorced her, where would she go? To whom? What sort of life was it where she could be accused like this? As the minutes ticked by, she sat sunk in thought, like a criminal on the eve of judgement. 'Well, God Almighty is not asleep. He will help me,' she said to herself with resignation.

Late that night, she received a visit from Alhaji Haruna's first wife. The older woman looked concerned, and asked for her reaction to the story.

'I don't understand. It's totally false,' Amina said at once. 'God knows I'm honest and innocent.'

'Have you gone out alone recently?' the old lady inquired.

'No. I don't even know who Bala is.'

'Then it's a lie,' the first wife said, nodding. 'As you know, I've been with Alhaji for years and I can tell you that he is terribly short-tempered and can be violent. He's very jealous too. Oh my God, I remember our first years; he couldn't even stand me talking to my male relatives!'

They both knelt down as Alhaji Haruna walked in. His eyes were bloodshot. Standing in the centre of the room, he again accused Amina of an immoral affair. She could only look at him, her eyes shining with tears, and deny it. She suggested that witnesses should be called. As Amina tried to convince her husband she was innocent he remained furious and uncompromising. When she appealed to Talata to intervene, the first wife looked concerned but remained silent, and Alhaji ordered her out of the room. She obeyed. He held Amina's left ear very tightly and screamed into it, 'Next time I hear that you're seeing someone, I'll kill you. Do you understand?'

Amina managed to nod forcefully. She was soaked in her tears. Still holding her left ear, he threatened her again: 'If I hear that you even admire another man, I'll not be as lenient as I am now. I'll beat you up first before throwing you out into the streets.'

When he left, Amina lay on the sofa, buried her head in her hands and sobbed uncontrollably. She cried for love and protection, and for the way the strength on which she had prided herself had vanished. As she obsessively relived the whole incident, she felt deprived of love and understanding, alienated, lonely and angry with herself.

Next day, she woke with her heart heavy and her head fuzzy. She needed someone to talk to, confide in, advise and console her, someone close to her who would be honest and reasonable. She wanted someone to tell her not to worry, that it was the will of God and that she should take consolation in the Almighty. 'Oh! If only my mother was alive, she would have been my best adviser,' Amina cried to herself. She longed to pour out all her troubles and pain and gain some relief. She got out of bed, walked to the window and looked out, but saw nothing. Her torments followed her like shadows, everywhere she turned. Then she thought of Fatima. She wiped away her tears, got dressed and asked Hauwa to accompany her to the university.

The sun beat down from a cloudless sky as Amina left Hauwa in the car and headed towards the women's hostel. She found a note pinned to Fatima's door: 'BACK IN TEN MINUTES. PLEASE WAIT—FATIMA.' She stood on the balcony for what seemed like a hour, feeling dizzy and sick, until Fatima appeared. Despite her own state of grief, she couldn't help noticing that Fatima's eyes were red and she looked tired.

'It seems a year since I saw you last,' Fatima said in surprise. 'How's life with you?'

'Terrible,' Amina admitted.

'Why?' Fatima asked, in concern.

'Sit down. I'll explain everything to you.'

Amina sat there in front of Fatima, her eyes filled with tears, hands shaking, head bowed, and recounted everything that had happened. 'God Almighty knows and He is my witness, I was and will remain honest and faithful. I just don't know what to do,' she concluded, sobbing.

Fatima was silent for a while, but when she spoke, her voice was sympathetic. 'My dear Amina,' she said, 'I feel for you, but you have to stand up for yourself. I suggest you inform your father immediately. He must know what's happening to you. He's the only person who can talk to Alhaji Haruna on his own level and make him see sense.'

After the visit, Amina went home somewhat consoled, but still miserable. She had been given some advice but no solution to her problems, and realised she would have to live with them. She was tired and weak and when she tried to eat, she had no appetite. 'God!' she cried alone in her room. 'God help me! God Almighty please protect me!' She lay awake and afraid until sunrise.

# 5

Months later, Amina went to listen to the debate between Fatima and Bature at the university. She went early, hoping to have a chat with Fatima, and sat in the front row. As she waited, she saw Lucas Danfulani, the son of Bature, coming towards her with a smile, 'Nice to see you again,' he said, and sat down next to her. 'I've not heard from you since you left, I hope all is well?'

'I'm fine. Thanks.'

'I've been wanting to see you to let you know that my father has got a proposal to put to you.'

'Really, what is it?'

'He's trying to get the state government to set up a company to manage its mineral resources and he wants you to be the Managing Director. We want to show the world that a Muslim woman can be in a responsible position. This state is rich in mineral resources, and we think you have the vision to manage those resources.'

Amina was taken aback. 'That's a surprise. I don't think I have the skills and knowledge for such a job.'

'It doesn't matter. I'll be around to guide you. I strongly suggest you enrol for an MBA course immediately. By the time you complete the course, the company will have been set up.'

She was still trying to take in his proposal when Lucas got up and went to meet his father, who was entering the assembly hall. At the same time, Fatima arrived, and came to greet Amina, looking very excited. 'I'm sure you are going to enjoy the debate. Pay attention to what Bature has to say. Do you want to be one of my judges?'

'No!' Amina laughed, 'I've got to leave early to cook for Alhaji.'

There was a hush as the debate moderator, Taj Rahman, a political science professor, stood up and waited for silence. 'It gives me great pleasure to introduce Mr John Kingfisher, the man we all know as Bature. Ever since he came from Great Britain, Bature has worked tirelessly for the development of his adopted country. His contribution has been immense, but not everyone agrees with his methods. Today, Fatima will present a challenge and demand a response. A jury of nine people will decide who wins. First, we will hear from Bature.'

Bature stood up to speak accompanied by an attentive silence. He looked around the room, and then addressed himself directly to Fatima. 'I've spent over thirty years—the best part of my adult life—in this country, thinking, sweating and working for its betterment. It hurts when some people, especially the younger ones, do not appreciate my efforts. I welcome this opportunity to hear the allegations levelled against me by Fatima. I want to ask her: Why do you hate me? Because you see success, wealth, influence? Or because to you I represent the West? And why do you hate the West? Because of our colour? Our technology? Our freedom? Our religion? Why do you only see the negative in everything I do?'

Bature sat down and waited for Fatima to state her case. Fatima was ready for him.

'Bature, this is not personal but political. I don't hate you as a person. I've lived in the West and I adore your freedoms, I admire science and technology. I have nothing against your religion. I'm comfortable with the colour of your skin. What I hate is the capitalist system and the way it exploits people worldwide. In particular, I hate the way the West connives with our rulers to deny us the very freedoms that you cherish. I hate the way you encourage our leaders to systematically destroy our institutions and I hate you because you promote a culture of corruption and violence; you promote a system of exploitation; you destroy our values; in short, you cause death, destruction and destitution …'

Dr Taj Rahman indicated to Fatima that she should sit down, and Bature rose again.

'Listen Fatima,' he said, 'first of all there is no alternative to the capitalist system.' He repeated the sentence slowly but loudly, 'THERE IS NO ALTERNATIVE TO CAPITALISM! This is not the time for ideological fantasies. If you genuinely want to develop, there is only one path and that is the capitalist way!'

Fatima leapt to her feet in dissent: 'There is an alternative!'

Bature laughed. 'I'm interested in knowing the alternative. For any African country to develop, the International Monetary Fund and World Bank conditions must be strictly followed. This is the only way to achieve prosperity in the long term.'

'That's hypocrisy! Why aren't these policies applied to Western countries? Are the pills too bitter for your system?'

'There is no hypocrisy here. There are different medicines for different ailments. In any system, there are winners and losers. Your view is one-sided. I've made many people in Africa rich, including your father and your former husband. I've guided and still guide many African countries towards meaningful development. The problem with Nigeria, as with all African countries, is not money but how to spend it, and the problem is not that you do not have the resources, but that you don't know how to manage them. In almost all your analysis, you blame colonialism and imperialism for the parlous state of affairs in Africa. You cannot blame these historical elements for what's happening today. Most African countries have been independent for decades, yet you still blame the distant past for the present malaise. When will you take responsibility for your own mistakes?'

'Colonialism and imperialism are part of our history. We need them in our analysis to understand the present. We need them for historical clarity.'

'You accuse me of stealing your resources. Of course Africa is blessed with all the resources in the world. Nigeria is also blessed with many resources.' Bature opened his bag and brought out six small bottles. He placed them on the table carefully. He gestured to Fatima to come forward. She obliged. Turning to the audience, he said, 'Here are samples of mineral resources found in this state. Not a single scientist in the university could identify or analyse them. I paid scientists to come and explore and exploit them. I wonder if you can name even three of the resources?'

Fatima smiled.'This is not my field and I must admit I don't know what they are.'

'There you go. The truth of the matter is that you cannot accuse me of stealing what you do not even know you have,' Bature reasoned. 'This is gold, this is copper, this is bauxite, this is iron ore, this is aluminium and this is yellow cake, do you know what that is?

'Uranium,' Fatima said, 'I'm aware that half the state sits on uranium!'

'It's one thing to be speculative about what sits where. It's another thing to know what you have and how to exploit it.

'You accuse me of discouraging education. That is unfair. I helped draw up a new school curriculum but your leaders turned it down. If your respectable leaders want me to import books, scientific equipment, computers, I'll do it. Instead, the State Commissioner for Education has just given me a contract to import twenty-seven cars into this country for his ministry, buy him a house in London and build a mansion for him in Abuja. What is strange but true is that your leaders don't even educate their children!

'Let us now turn to health. You have on various occasions accused me of scientific genocide. Let me seize this opportunity to set the record straight: three years ago, two Western pharmaceutical companies carried out trials of two drugs with the approval of the State Governor. Of course, he was paid for agreeing to these trials being carried out. Unfortunately, one of the trials went disastrously wrong and many people died, especially women and children. Of course I deeply regret it, but I cannot be held responsible. The trials were done with the knowledge and consent of the Governor. He is a Western-trained medical doctor and knows the risks very well. So it was not genocide, because there was no intention to kill.'

'Why weren't the victims' families paid compensation if that's the case?' asked Fatima.

'I'm in the final stages of getting the firm responsible to pay up. Very soon, compensation will be paid for each and every victim,' replied Bature.

'Why didn't you carry out the trials in Europe using Europeans?'

'The drugs are for tropical diseases,' Bature said, looking straight at Fatima. 'Again, you accuse me of supporting repressive regimes. That is not true. I support regimes that promote stability. Africa can develop only when there is peace and stability, when military regimes are equipped to provide a healthy climate for investment and development.

'Look; there is famine, drought, and yet, what have I been told to buy for the Governor for his sixtieth birthday? A new jet, although the one I bought three years ago is in perfect working condition, and he hardly uses it. But it's not for me to dictate to him. I only carry out his orders. He also wants me to build a new mansion for him, the third in two years! Each of the Emirs and traditional leaders in the state will have a new limousine and new palaces built for them soon. These are the priorities of your leaders, not mine. These are the hard facts, and no amount of idealism is going to change them.

'Fatima, I honestly admire your courage, creativity and intelligence. Unfortunately you have decided to join the wrong camp. Nothing is going to come out of your ideological fantasies. Join us and you'll enjoy the fruits of your labour. My dream is to see Fatima putting her talents to use in the real world. The ball's in your court. Show us what you can do apart from sloganeering!'

Fatima laughed scornfully. 'I concede that you're strong, but that doesn't mean I'll join you. I have a mission, and one thing I'll never do is compromise my principles. I'd rather drink water and sleep with my dignity intact, than eat caviar in the service of capitalism.'

Amina looked at her watch and saw that it was time to go home and cook for her husband.

# 6

Days and weeks of inactivity passed. Amina continued to live her life in the women's world of idleness, always waiting for something that might never come. Confined to the same small district of the world where she was born and raised, she felt she was decaying, mentally and physically. She wondered what was the point of living and yearned for something to do, but could not identify what it might be.

She resolved, however, not to attend any more Legislators' Wives' Association meetings, as she found the other wives a useless bunch of gossips. She also rejected an invitation to become a member of the women's wing of the Circle International Club, seeing it too as an aimless band of cheats and braggarts. Her plan to go into business was put on hold when Bature was involved in a road accident. Meanwhile, she had still not made up her mind about the students, because though she was at ease with them, she was not interested in their discussions. She saw very little of her husband and they hardly spoke intimately to each other, especially once she had informed her father about what had happened and he had directly criticised Alhaji. She had lost interest even in her appearance, and had stopped wearing expensive clothes and make-up, even on visits. She no longer spent hours in front of the mirror, praising God for creating her beautiful. Apart from the third wife, whom she had discovered had been the one who had slandered her, Amina was on good terms with everyone in the compound. However, sometimes she felt isolated and would eye everybody suspiciously. On these occasions, she would lock herself up in her room and cry. In desperation, she turned to some of the books Fatima had given her.

On one such weary day, she went downstairs and joined the children playing under the guava tree. Thick dark clouds soon covered the horizon, and a strong wind raised the dust and dried leaves. The children ran inside while Amina followed slowly. She went upstairs and stood on the balcony looking out at the horizon, with its slowly gathering clouds, before going back into her room. She was lying flat on her back, staring blankly at the ceiling, when she heard voices and steps on the staircase, and Fatima and five girls burst in. They were still out of breath as Fatima introduced the excited bunch to Amina. 'These are the new members of our movement. We've had a series of meetings on campus ... but the security men almost caught us yesterday, so we decided to meet here today. I hope we're not disturbing you.'

'You're always welcome,' Amina said and invited them to sit down.

The initial chitchat soon gave way to more serious topics. 'Let's continue our discussion on Man and Society,' Fatima suggested, and stood up prepared to launch into one of her lectures: 'If we look back in history and see how states have risen and fallen we must accept what a philosopher once said: "All is flux, nothing is stationary."' As Fatima spoke, Amina wondered what was wrong with these girls. Although the movement had been banned, they still met, secretly, to talk about Man and Society? To Amina, these were not the most burning issues. She walked out silently and stood on the balcony. The clouds had passed and the sun was shining brightly. She heard Fatima's voice: 'As people have acquired new experience and knowledge, they started asking certain fundamental questions. It became very important for people to understand social change, to know why things were happening, and who was responsible. That's where religion comes in. Religion claims that everything in this world was created by God, that all actions are predestined.'

Though Amina was disturbed, she listened attentively to what Fatima was saying. 'Religion claims that God has ordained that some people will be idle but wealthy, while others will toil all their lives and live in abject poverty, some will be powerful and others weak, above all, that men are superior to women. He also decrees that only those who accept His decree will go to paradise, while those who disrespect or disobey Him will go to everlasting hell.'

A heated argument erupted between Rebecca and Fatima. Amina went to the kitchen where Talata, the first wife, was cooking. 'Don't worry about cooking. I thought you'd be busy with your guests, so I'm doing the cooking for you,' she said.

'That's very kind of you,' Amina replied.

'Is it Fatima and her friends?' Talata asked.

'Yes. They're here for a short visit.'

'That's all right,' Talata said, stepping closer to Amina. 'Tell me, when will she remarry, or won't she?'

'Honestly, I don't know.'

'Why not ask her, or advise her? It's very bad for a grown up girl like her to remain single,' said Talata with genuine concern.

'I think it's her affair,' Amina said with a shrug.

'How has Alhaji behaved with you of late?' Talata asked, changing the topic.

'I don't know. I've not seen him for some time.'

'I hear he's coming today.' She looked at Amina. 'It was a good thing you told your father. I hope it helps...when Alhaji is angry, God help us!'

'He's not been visiting me, so I'm not expecting him.'

'I think Jummai is a witch. She really hates you and has never bothered to hide it. She's so jealous. I'm sure she can't imagine herself in my position, but that's how I was brought up. To me, the more wives Alhaji has the less the housework and pressure on me,' Talata said with a shrug.

'*Assalama Allaikum,*' a female voice interrupted. Bilkisu stood by the kitchen door smiling radiantly.

'*Amin Allaikum Wa'asalam,*' Amina responded. 'How are you?'

'Very well,' Bilkisu said still smiling.

'You go and attend to your guests, I'll bring the food in soon,' Talata told Amina.

'I hope you've not forgotten about my party tonight,' Bilkisu told her comrades when they were back upstairs.

'Why are you organising a party?' Rebecca asked, her usually placid face alive with interest.

'Just for fun,' Bilkisu said sitting down. 'Actually it's our engagement party!'

'Amina, will you attend the party?' asked Fatima.

'Are you crazy?' Amina retorted, although she knew Fatima was only joking. 'If my husband divorces me, will you find me another one?'

'No, I don't have a spare one,' Fatima said, laughing. The other girls joined in. Hauwa brought plates of food and they started to eat in silence. Bilkisu ate a couple of forkfuls, then put down her plate, covered it and with a polite smile explained to Amina, 'I've just eaten, so I can't finish it. I hope you don't mind.'

'Don't worry, it's all right.'

'Of course any girl who has just left her fiancé's house should not be hungry,' Fatima commented.

'That's none of your business,' Bilkisu replied.

Amina was amused by their friendly relationship and envied the way they didn't get remotely annoyed at the other's jokes or comments. After the meal, Amina cleared the plates and Bilkisu resumed the discussion.

'A lot, if not all countries in Africa,' she said, 'have a long record of capitalist development after independence ...'

'What sort of independence?' Fatima interjected.

'I mean political independence. Independence of the flag and anthem.'

'That was a dangerous generalisation, because most countries don't have economic independence,' Fatima said forcefully.

'We have been trying to develop but instead we're going backwards. The ordinary African is hundreds of years behind. The masses—workers and peasants—live in abject poverty, millions have no food to eat, children are seriously undernourished, and the health care system is incredibly backward.'

'Honestly, when I think of Africa, I cry,' Fatima said in a solemn voice. 'All its countries are in serious economic crisis, while its leaders are among the richest people in the world. Just look at our beloved country ... in the grip of thieves and criminals. Corrupt leaders grip Liberia too; Sierra Leone is witnessing an orgy of violence; Congo has degenerated into savagery.'

'As you all know,' Bilkisu's calm voice sounded, 'Nigeria is a class society and the class formation process is still going on.'

Amina gathered the plates and went downstairs. She felt she had heard enough. When she went back to the room, they were still discussing different classes in Nigeria.

'Businessmen, traditional rulers, religious leaders, retired soldiers, police and naval officers, retired civil servants–these are the running dogs and errand boys of Western capitalist countries,' said Fatima. 'Including my former husband and my father.'

'Some people,' agreed Bilkisu, 'call it the "catastrophic" segment of the ruling class because of its dangerous and diabolical nature. Its members are the most cunning, unpatriotic, dubious and repressive types. Because of the power they hold and its sensitive nature in the economy, they daily and shamelessly embezzle public funds, loot the national wealth either directly and independently or by collaborating with other members of this class. They actively collaborate with the international capitalist countries to consolidate powerful and repressive regimes.' She smiled and added. 'Fortunately or unfortunately, my father belongs there too.'

They all laughed. 'Amina's husband belongs to this class too,' Fatima said. Amina flinched and looked down, just as there was a loud knock on the door and Alhaji Haruna strode in. He was frowning, but immediately on seeing the girls, his expression changed and he smiled. All the girls, Amina included, went on their knees and greeted him politely. He beamed at them. 'Please be my guests, sit down and make yourself at home. Bilkisu, how are you?'

'We are all fine.'

'I've just come from the airport where I saw your father off to the Holy Land to perform the lesser Hajj. From there, he'll go to London where he's expected to sign loan agreements and contracts on behalf of the state ... anyway, I can see you're all busy.'

'Yes,' Bilkisu replied.

Amina was too nervous to look at him, but Bilkisu continued: 'We've been discussing the role of Islam in the family.'

'Oh! That's great! I'm happy you're not only preaching the words of Allah but also educating my wife.'

'Alhaji,' Fatima interjected, 'we reached the conclusion that religion is the mainspring of life. We've agreed that religion gives heart to the heartless, conscience to those who wouldn't otherwise think so clearly and hope to the hopeless.'

'*Allahu Akbar! Allahu Akbar!* God is really great,' he said joyously. 'If Fatima can make such a statement, then nothing in this world is impossible. God is Great!' He looked at them with satisfaction. 'Do you have all you need?'

'Yes,' they chorused.

'Good, but if you have any problems in future, please don't hesitate to come to me. I can see that I'm disturbing you.'

'No, no, no,' Fatima responded. 'We've actually finished and were about to go.'

'May you all be rewarded by the Almighty Allah for your selfless services,' he prayed.

'Amen,' they responded.

As he was about to step out, Fatima asked him to sit down. 'I'd like to ask you something about religion,' she said playfully

Alhaji Haruna hesitated, then politely sat down.

'Don't you think that what is happening in our country today should make any true believer tremble or faint or both?' Fatima started calmly. 'I mean *any* believer! Don't we simply pay lip service to religion? Why is the Muslim population the most backward in this country, in Africa, in the entire world? Why?'

Alhaji answered cautiously, 'That is the wish of Almighty Allah.'

'That is the wish of our rulers,' Fatima said boldly, looking straight into his eyes. 'Our rulers have misruled us into this dead end. We refuse to help each other. We hate each other too much. For example, you've ordered the detention of so many young and intelligent people, fellow Muslims, simply because they have different views. Why don't you and your friends actively promote the teachings of the blessed religion?'

'Are you implying we're hypocrites?'

'Not at all! What I'm saying is that Islam is blessed with so many good injunctions, and if only Muslims carried out 25 percent of them, we wouldn't be in the situation we are today.'

'Instead of doing 25 percent, most do minus 25 percent,' Bilkisu added.

Alhaji looked puzzled, but responded: 'I believe in Almighty Allah, I pray five times a day, I fast during the month of Ramadan, I go on Hajj every year, I give alms to the poor; is that not what is written? What more do you want?'

Amina held her breath, but there was no stopping Fatima. 'Where is it written that you should detain people who have other views? Where is it written that you should divert public funds for private use?' She waited for an answer, but Alhaji was silent. 'From what I've seen of the West, it practises Islam without Muslims, while in Muslim countries, you have Muslims without Islam. In the West, there is accountability, faithful pursuit of knowledge, cleanliness, respect for human lives, property and dignity and so on. Look at our society—full of Muslims—what do you see? Aimlessness, corruption, greed, indolence, ignorance and repression.'

'But in the West they drink alcohol, they don't pray and cannot marry more than one wife!' Alhaji objected.

'But you still entrust your life and money to them. When you're sick, you go to them for medical attention. When you have money, you give it to them to keep for you.' Fatima shook her head in disgust. Gathering his dignity, Alhaji Haruna stood up and walked out, smiling. Fatima broke the tension by saying in a relaxed voice, 'This place is not safe for a meeting today. There's a class enemy around.' Even Amina joined in the prolonged laughter.

'Let's go to my father's house, as he's gone to London,' Bilkisu suggested.

'But isn't he going to Mecca first?' Amina asked.

'Alhaji got it wrong. He's going to London first to sign those questionable loans and deposit the loot in his account and those of his accomplices, and then he'll proceed to the Holy Land,' explained Bilkisu.

'Where Almighty Allah is supposed to forgive him for his sins, while the people of the state will be forced to repay these loans. Bastards!' Fatima contended.

'But he's your father, you can't reject him,' Rebecca pressed.

'I'm not rejecting him. I'm only facing the truth. I know what he does, what they all do. Anyway, I'm grown up and will soon get married,' Bilkisu replied with a broad smile.

'Mark you,' Fatima warned, 'you're only leaving one con man for another–going from a politician to a military man. Every soldier wants to rule, even though they're trained in the US or Britain, where the military performs an entirely different role. Once here, they just want to use their guns to terrorise people.'

Come on, it's time we left,' said Bilkisu, noticing Amina's discomfort. As she left, Fatima handed over a bag of books to Amina. She fell onto her bed in relief.

# 7

In an attempt to understand where Fatima got the confidence to challenge Alhaji, Amina started reading more. She registered with a vendor who supplied her with newspapers and magazines, and read almost every news item and article in her favourite Sunday paper. She was also attempting to read a book Fatima had given her: *The Wretched of the Earth* by Frantz Fanon, but struggled with some of the words and ideas. This particular Sunday, she had read the papers and tried other books but lacked concentration, so she lay back in bed, letting her thoughts wander.

Finally, she decided to go through her photographs. As she looked at them, she recalled earlier days, old friends, relatives, acquaintances and places. Some people who just recently seemed very close to her were now distant in her memory, as if they lived in another planet. One in particular sent her into deep thought. It was her on matriculation day in her matriculation gown, with a classmate, Muktar Khalid. Muktar was a close friend, not a lover, but they had had a short but memorable relationship. She first met him while on the preliminary course. One evening after prayers, he and Danbaki, Fatima's lover, visited them in their room. Danbaki informed them of his intention to contest the students' union elections. Fatima was appointed Danbaki's campaign adviser and he introduced Muktar as his chief campaign officer. Amina recalled how quiet and shy Muktar had been, and that she had wondered how such a gentle boy could be entrusted with a task usually associated with campus thugs and hooligans. She saw him daily during the campaign period, and Danbaki eventually won the presidency.

After the elections, Muktar had paid her irregular visits, always explaining that he was busy with political activism. He was also known to be a good sportsman. She remembered him as very intelligent, good natured and ambitious, and felt it terribly unjust that he had been expelled from the university for his part in one particular protest. He was too young to be robbed of his precious jewel in life—his studies, which he cherished highly. They should have just suspended him for a year. 'I should have done something to prevent it,' she thought. 'Maybe I should have discouraged him from his political adventures and advised him to concentrate only on his studies; but he wouldn't have listened. Although not stubborn, he was committed like Fatima. Well, as a man, he's still young. He's got everything ahead. He can still repair that dented part of his life. Who knows? It might even open up other opportunities for him.' Amina chuckled when she recalled a promise they jointly made just after the matriculation ceremony—to take a photograph together on graduation day. 'Poor us, neither of us graduated. I'd really love to see him again, to know more about him, encourage him, express my care and concern for him. If he loved me then, he never said anything, but l loved him. I dreamt almost daily of him–he was so handsome, well built, cultured; an ideal husband. He pretended not to know that I loved him, but he must have sensed it.' She stood up, almost in tears, and put all the photographs back in their box.

Suddenly she remembered the poster Fatima gave her and decided to hang it on the wall. She unfolded it, straightened it and chose a good place in her room.

## THE FAREWELL SERMON OF PROPHET MUHAMMAD

(*Sallallahu Allaihi Wasallam*)

O people, just as you regard this month, this day, this city as sacred,

so regard the life and property of every Muslim as a sacred trust.

Return the goods entrusted to you to their rightful owners.

Hurt no one so that no one may hurt you.

Do not take usury; this is forbidden to you.

Aid the poor and clothe them as you would clothe yourselves.

Remember! One day you will appear before Allah and answer for your deeds.

So, beware! Do not stray from the path of righteousness after I am gone.

O people! No prophet or Apostle will come after me and no new faith will be born

...It is true that you have certain rights with regard to your women, but they also have rights over you. Treat them well for they are your support.

Reflect on my words. I leave behind two things,

the Quran and my example, and if you follow these guides you will not fail.

Listen to me in earnest. Worship God; say your prayers, fast during the month of Ramadan, and give your wealth to charity.

All the believers are brothers; all have the same rights and same responsibilities.

No one is allowed to take from another what he does not allow him of his own free will.

None is higher than the other unless he is higher in virtue.

All those who listen to me shall pass on my words to others, and those to others again;

and may the last ones understand my words better than those who listen to me directly.

# Chapter 7

There was a knock at the door. '*Assallama Allaikum, Amarya*! Can I come in?' asked little Abdullahi.

'*Amin Allaikum Wa'asalam*,' she answered, letting him in.

'*Amarya*, when Fatima is coming again?' Abdullahi asked.

'Your wife should be here tomorrow or the next day, but if you really want to see her I can go to the university and find her.'

'No, it's not urgent. I just wanted to know how old she is and her daughter's age too.'

'Well, that's between the two of you. I wouldn't intervene in a family affair,' she teased him. 'You mean you don't know how old your wife is?'

'She's not and will never be my wife,' he stated firmly, but with a smile. '*Amarya*, I also have some questions for you.'

'I'll tell you my age even before you ask..'

'No, I'm not interested in that. I simply want to know why you sleep for longer hours these days. Are you sick?'

'I am healthy. Thanks for your concern. As for the physical changes and the amount I sleep—pose that question to Fatima.'

'No! Why can't you tell me?'

'Listen carefully! When a lady is expecting a baby, she needs more sleep.'

'Thank you,' he said and ran out.

Abdullahi was the closest child in the compound to Amina. He was endlessly in search of answers to various questions he couldn't ask his father or others in the compound. He turned to her as an educated person and as someone willing to answer. Recently he had asked her some questions to which she was yet to provide answers. 'Why does my father say that I must never trust a woman? Is it true that women, dogs and donkeys spoil prayers? Why are women not allowed to pray with men in mosques? Why are my sisters not sent to Arabic and Islamic schools?'

Alone again, Amina's thoughts turned to her pregnancy and her own mother. She was a strong, determined and hardworking woman. She was the first wife, and loved all the children, not only hers but all those in the family. She was very fond of Amina, watching her growth closely and carefully. She was interested in all she did, not criticising but correcting her if the need arose and giving her the encouragement only a mother can give a child. She never allowed Amina's father to beat any child in the family. She used to tell Amina: 'Be proud you are a girl and respect yourself, then others will respect you.'

Amina remembered how she had encouraged her in primary school, which she had been the first to attend in the family. Her two elder sisters had been only allowed to get married, but her mother spoke a lot about the importance of education and persuaded her father to let Amina go to school. 'When you're educated, you can be rich, you can help yourself and others but most important, you'll understand the world better,' she used to emphasise. One of the first things Amina did after starting primary school was to teach her mother how to write her own name. Oh! She was happy and excited. At first she wrote it in a crooked manner but later very straight and clear: M A R I A M U. When Amina completed primary school, her mother wanted her to further her education, and her father didn't object. But after secondary school, there was a war in the house. Amina's father had insisted she marry straight away, while her mother said she must go to university. She said her dream was to see her daughter an educated woman. When her father attempted to marry her off to a man without consulting her, she chose to leave the house rather than see Amina fall into the trap in which she and her other daughters had found themselves.

'It was a trying period,' reflected Amina. 'Father had already collected a dowry and fixed a date for my marriage but mother bluntly refused. I was actually planning to run away but I had nowhere to go and felt secure with mother on my side. Father returned the money but vowed not to pay my school fees or give me any money if I went to university. Being a full-time housewife, my mother had no source of income. She had to sell most of her valuables to support my first year in the university. My sisters contributed as well. I tried to show her all the love, affection and respect a daughter can show a cherished mother. I can still remember what she told me one evening: "Amina, you're a symbol of knowledge and light, you are like a tall tree that can see far and wide. You have good and healthy dreams, but can you realise them?" I said I could, although I didn't understand what she meant.

'Then came that terrible Monday, when Uncle Ali came to the university to tell me mother was dead. It took weeks to recover from the shock, and I still can't overcome the loss. I felt as if I was in a boat, which had capsized in the middle of a wide river. That was the moment father chose to make me submit to marriage. He simply passed me over to Alhaji Haruna. Imagine, I first knew Alhaji on my wedding day! But my pledge to pay back my mother will one day be accomplished. I wasn't rich enough in her lifetime to fulfil her wish, but if I have a daughter ...' and with that dream, she fell asleep.

When she woke up, the room was hot and dark. She opened the window and a cold wind blew in, raising the blinds. The sky was heavy with low dark clouds. Thunder and lightning frightened Amina away from the window. She switched on the light and saw some roast meat, five pieces of kola nut and fruit had been left for her. She presumed her husband had come in while she was asleep.

It began to rain, at first in single drops and later a torrent. It drummed on the roof and the wind whistled and blew into the room through the window. She locked it, and as she turned round, her husband entered. He seemed jovial and ready to be interested in her, picking up her books and looking at them.

'I see you're reading a lot of books,' Alhaji Haruna said. 'This is a good subject,' he pointed to one on polygamy in Islam.

'Yes, I've read it,' she said reluctantly.

'And this?' he said, holding up *How Europe Underdeveloped Africa*. 'Who is this Walter Rodney?' He struggled to pronounce the name.

'Fatima read the book and she knows,' Amina answered warily.

'*Petals of Blood, Devil on the Cross*; what are they about?'

'They're novels by a Kenyan author N'gugi wa Thiongo,' she explained to him.

'Does Fatima read all these?' Alhaji Haruna asked, examining more titles. 'She's a stubborn girl if she can deal with such a big book,' he said, fingering *Das Kapital* by Karl Marx. 'How long will it take you to read this?'

'I've tried to read it, but I couldn't understand it. I think it's about business, how to manage one's money.'

'Good. Read and understand it since you'll be going into business soon.'

'But you know I'm pregnant,' she said in surprise.

'Yes I know,' he said and picked up another book. 'This is about South Africa, I know this is Nelson Mandela. That's why I like our President. He hated the apartheid system, you know.'

Amina ventured to point out there were discrimination and inequalities in Nigeria too, but he had lost interest. He put the books down and left the room. While Amina was rearranging the books, Kulu walked in, wearing a silky blouse over two pieces of expensive multi-coloured cloth.

'You look beautiful in that,' Amina complimented her. 'Did you buy it in Kano?'

'No, it's from Lagos,' she replied boastfully.

The blouse looks expensive,' Amina said, touching it.

'I like sophisticated things,' Kulu said, offhandedly. 'I had a successful journey. I cleared my goods and resold them in Kano.'

'That's good.'

Kulu rattled on about her plans to open an orphanage, buy a new car and build a swimming pool and sauna. Amina in turn told her about the disagreement she had had with Alhaji. Kulu's reaction was swift and pointed.

'Amina, it's your fault. You're inexperienced; money buys everything, even love and happiness. I've got a medicine man in Dimbi village. He can give you beads, concoctions and perfumes, which will make Alhaji love you and you'll live peacefully. Let's go on Friday,' she urged.

When there was no response from Amina, Kulu looked shrewdly at her and moved on to Fatima, one of her favourite topics. 'She is dangerous. I regret ever befriending that idiot. She has beauty and wealth but doesn't want to use them. Instead she's in love with a bearded, rough and undisciplined boy called Danbaki—a boy with no ambition. They only know how to cause trouble on campus. Amina, I want to advise you sincerely; don't allow Fatima to brainwash you. I know what she is capable of doing. She's like a devil. Fatima can convince you with her poisonous tongue that milk is black, so be careful, my dear.'

As if out of boredom, Kulu picked up her handbag, brought out a wad of notes and started to count. Amina watched her count a full bundle, before she said, 'I like counting money, it's my hobby.'

They heard footsteps on the stairs, a single knock and a familiar voice; 'I'm beautiful, so I'll come straight in,' and Fatima entered, smiling. When she saw Kulu holding her money, she laughed. 'Oh God! I pity you, Kulu. You think I'm a thief, like you? Look at her clinging tightly to her money as if someone was about to rob her!'

'Please ... I don't want any trouble here,' Amina intervened.

'Is that your loot for today?' Fatima asked.

'It's my property,' Kulu spat.

'The source of property in our society is theft, which is your profession,' Fatima continued relentlessly.

'You're a liar! I worked for it. It's from my sweat.'

'Whose sweat? You smuggle goods, inflate contracts, cheat innocent people, steal openly and say it's your sweat, you hypocrite!'

'That has nothing to do with you.'

'It does ...!'

'What about you running after those boys?'

'Either you mind your language or I'll beat the hell out of you!' Fatima charged forward, seizing Kulu by her collar.

'Please, I don't want any trouble here!' Amina repeated her plea.

'You're jealous of my riches,' Kulu said, after she had been released.

As Fatima gulped water in an attempt to cool off, Kulu started to sing:

"Some people are jealous of me

Some people are jealous of me

Some people are jealous of me

Jealous, because of my money!"

Fatima choked. Massaging her chest, she managed to say, 'Listen carefully, Kulu, you know if I chose I could be richer than you and your husband, so why should I be jealous?'

Kulu stood up and walked to the door, Amina following her. Before she could leave, Fatima roughly pulled Kulu back and looked her straight in the eyes.

'Kulu, I know what you're doing here visiting Amina, and I'll take this opportunity to say what I think. I hate everything you do, but especially the way you go about cheating innocent people who put their trust in you. If I had my way, people like you would be shot.'

'You can't provoke me,' Kulu responded with a vicious smile. 'You can only chant slogans. I'd advise you to see a psychiatrist, because you're mad. You live in a world of illusion, talking about revolutions. There'll never be a revolution in this country. If I had *my* way, I'd deal with you and all those so-called socialists and campus radicals! You're a plague on society.'

Kulu wrenched herself out of Fatima's grasp and flung out of the room, leaving Fatima and Amina staring at each other.

'Why were you so abusive?' Amina asked in shock.

'I hate her,' Fatima said. Then she softened. 'I'm sorry if I offended you. She was lucky we met in this room. If we had met on neutral territory, the story would have been different!'

'What would you have done to her?' Amina asked nervously.

'I would've practised my karate chops on her ugly face. How's Flat Nose?' she asked, referring to Alhaji Haruna.

'He's fine. He visited me a little while ago and brought me some food. He saw the books.'

'What did he say?'

'Nothing really. He even advised me to read *Das Kapital*. He doesn't even know what the book is about.'

'That's good,' Fatima said, laughing loudly.

Amina unwrapped the spicy roast meat and they helped themselves and started eating. Within moments, Mairo walked in, greeted them, sat on the floor and, as expected, started to feed them with the latest news in the district. Though she was a quick talker, neither pausing nor arranging her sentences, what she said was always interesting. She first spoke of the cerebral spinal meningitis epidemic in the town. 'Over fifty people are believed to have died in just one week. My stepdaughter died this morning.'

'May Almighty Allah save us from such deadly diseases,' Amina prayed. 'And may her soul rest in peace.'

'Listen,' Fatima began, swallowing her meat, 'this "deadly disease" is actually curable. Most deaths occur due to deplorable hospital conditions.'

Mairo nodded agreement, and went on to the story of a woman who had died that day as a result of a dispute with her husband. 'She was a carpenter's wife. Yesterday, he gave her twenty naira to buy food. She said it wasn't enough because of increased prices. They argued for some minutes and she followed him outside to his shed. He ordered her back because she was in purdah, but to no avail. Angry, he hit her on the head with one of his tools. She died today in the house.' Amina sighed, but Fatima was ready with her analysis.

'All these are clear cases of misdirected anger. The most unfortunate thing is that women, irrespective of their class, profession and status, are always at the receiving end,' she said. 'A man is oppressed, but doesn't understand why, and because of this he's frustrated and annoyed. His annoyance increases daily, but he internalises it and when another person annoys him, he misdirects his anger to that person. That explains why you find most of these cases of violence among the poor, and the victims are predictably mainly the weaker sex.'

'Larai is back,' Mairo cut in.

'Who is Larai?' Amina asked.

'The wife of a peasant I told you was admitted to the hospital several months ago.'

'Oh! I remember. How's she feeling now?'

'Well, she's lucky she's alive, but she still drips,' Mairo said standing up. 'I've other places to go. Goodnight and may God be with you.'

Amina started loosening her plaited hair.

'What about Flat Nose? Isn't he coming later?' asked Fatima.

'No, he stays at the Legislators' Estate.'

'Tell me, who is this Larai and what happened to her?' Fatima inquired.

'She's one of these underage girls whose bladders are damaged because they give birth too young,' responded Amina.

Fatima seized her hands and said forcefully: 'Try and visit her. You may be able to help her. As my grandmother used to say, make people's dreams come true and Almighty Allah will make yours come true.'

'I'll try,' Amina promised, somewhat embarrassed. 'How's Danbaki?'

'Oh! My fiancé is fine.'

'Has he shaved his beard?'

'No. He looks handsome with it. Actually, I like it.'

'Have you discussed future plans yet?'

'Yes we have. Danbaki wants to marry me, but I'm rather reluctant to get married now. But I'm happy with him and I guess as time goes by I'll agree to his proposal.' Fatima paused, closed her eyes in deep thought and continued, 'This time around, I'll marry the man I love. I hope and pray we are blessed with children.'

'Have you seen Muktar of late?' Amina asked.

'Oh yes. He was on campus yesterday. He sends his warm greetings.'

'What was he doing on campus?'

'He visited Rebecca,' Fatima said with a smile. 'Okay, let me tell you the truth. He's now a journalist with a newspaper and was there to cover an event. Later, he dropped in on his newfound love,' Fatima explained. She did not notice the shadow that crossed her friend's face, and they continued talking, enjoying the freshness of the night air and the clear sky, swimming with stars. Then Amina offered her last prayers and they sat on the balcony ready to plait Amina's hair. In this intimate moment, Amina decided to ask something that had been preoccupying her.

'Fatima, tell me honestly, what do you gain from reading books?'

Fatima thought for some moments. 'From reading books you learn more about life and people. Books lighten your heart, brighten your vision, make you shed misconceptions and make you feel you're part of humanity. In short, books are my guides: they show me that I'm not alone in the struggle. Also, I get to know the world better, enhance my understanding of things and the ways the world turns and changes, so that if I cannot change the world the way I want, at least I know when to get out of the way before it changes or crushes me. But you have to read with a critical mind, because you don't find the necessary inspiration and knowledge in most of the books in our libraries. A lot of them are empty ...'

'Okay, that's enough,' Amina interrupted. 'Who won the debate between you and Bature?'

'I did,' Fatima said with a broad smile. 'What a shame you couldn't stay to the end, it was one of my best performances. Everything flowed, and the audience loved it. Seven out of nine judges voted for me.'

'And what about his promise?'

'Immediately after the debate, he congratulated me and asked for the list of political detainees. The next day, I gave it to him and he went straight to the State Governor and, somehow, within hours they were all released.'

'Amazing, isn't it? How many people were released?'

'Twelve prisoners of conscience.'

'What about the scholarship?

'That is probably more interesting. He's pledged to sponsor students but we haven't worked out the logistics yet. He's asked me to be in charge of a foundation for the scholarships. I'll submit my proposal next week but I still don't know what to call it. At the moment, it's called the Aisha Foundation. He has set aside a lot of money for me to buy books for the libraries and schools in the state. So we're in business!'

'So, you are willing to work with Bature.'

'If the people of the state will benefit, certainly.'

'I honestly didn't believe he would do anything.'

'I know I'm harsh on Bature, but it's a game we both enjoy. He's very principled, understanding and tolerant. If only we could learn from Bature!'

They sat silently for a moment, before Fatima said: 'I think it's important to analyse our past, to know what are traditionally ours, what are essentially Islamic laws and what are Arab customs introduced into our societies. Over the years, all these have been mixed up and unfortunately to the disadvantage of women in all aspects,' Fatima paused for a moment and continued, 'the stories Mairo told us were touching, but of course they're nothing new. Incidents of violence happen here daily but what I want you to note is that the killers either remain free or, even if arrested, will eventually be released by the courts. The laws are totally blind to women's rights.'

Fatima paused before she said gently: 'Amina, you cannot be a spectator. All this affects us, and it's our responsibility to do something to change the system and the status of women.'

'*Assalama Allaikum,*' someone said after knocking on the door.

'*Maraba da zuwa*! You're welcome,' Amina replied. A bearded old man with specks of grey in his hair, a relative of Alhaji Haruna, came in slowly.

'I just came to greet all of you. I've greeted the other wives. Although I'm old I still made it upstairs.'

'Thanks very much for coming. Please sit down.'

The old man sat down and looked at Fatima. 'I heard what you were saying,' he said, Please continue.' When Fatima smiled but remained silent, he laughed. 'I'm old and harmless,' he said, with a shrug. Amina looked at Fatima who smiled, and continued her exhortation:

'So, Amina, the people are waiting: from girls like Larai, to the half-naked beggars on the streets, to children yet unborn.

A whole generation expects us to do something positive because we are the privileged ones, the ones with education. Although it's difficult and involves a great deal of sacrifice, it's our task. Look at how our women live. Look at the children on the streets! Our rulers have betrayed and failed us, our elders have been confounded and are powerless.'

The old man coughed slightly to show he wanted to speak. 'I appreciate your courage', he said to Fatima. 'All you said is true but ... although you have very good ideas your hands are tied.' He stood up. 'You can see I'm old, very old, over eighty I believe. I can say that my generation was lucky to have had leaders who were not only pious, honest and listened to their subjects but also brought prosperity to the land. The present leaders are not God-fearing; they don't listen to their subjects, so prosperity has eluded us. My only regret in life is that I am leaving this world worse than I met it and there is nothing I can do. May Almighty Allah guide you to the righteous path. Have a peaceful night.' He left slowly. Amina volunteered to help him downstairs but he refused.

'Don't worry; I'm not in a hurry. I'll go down slowly.'

'You heard him?' Fatima said, 'The words of our elders are words of wisdom.'

'Okay, what do you think can be done?' Amina asked.

'A lot!' Fatima said seriously. 'Because of your position, you command respect. Form an organisation, as I advised you some time ago. But think hard about how best to do it. Ideas don't just fall into people's laps, they have to be developed in their brains. There's a saying that the biggest bird comes out of a small egg. If you don't do anything, the women here will come to visit you, praise and flatter you but respect you only because you're Alhaji's wife. There is one thing you have of your own–your character. Don't walk in Alhaji's shadow. Build your own character, use it to benefit those who have no power. Draw the women of your neighbourhood closer to you, organise them, educate them, make them feel they're human, then they'll respect you as a person. If you do that, this and the next generations of Bakaro will never forget you. But if you turn a blind eye to their sufferings or collaborate with their oppressors, then both this and the next generation of Bakaro will never forgive you.'

Amina listened, but she was used to Fatima and was still not convinced that there was anything meaningful she could contribute. 'Fatima's a dreamer,' she said to herself. 'What she advises has never been done before, and I wouldn't know where to start.' Aloud, she said:

'It's time to sleep.' She changed into her nightgown, gave Fatima who was already yawning on the sofa, where she slept whenever on a visit, a cover cloth, slipped into bed and switched off the lights.

# 8

When Amina woke up the next morning, she was still not convinced, and though Fatima wanted a commitment, she would agree only to help individual women if the need arose. Fatima left full of disappointment, but later in the day, Amina and Hauwa accompanied Mairo to visit Larai. As they walked at a leisurely pace, Amina looked around her at the streets and houses, noticing for the first time how dirty and smelly the alleyways in this part of town were. Everywhere were stagnant pools of offensive-smelling opaque water. The houses were rickety, built mainly of mud and thatched with grass, with very tiny windows. Everywhere she looked, she saw poverty. They arrived at the hut Larai lived in, which was squat, built of mud and surrounded by a low wall. Mairo went in first and Amina followed her, pushing aside an old brown cloth used as a curtain and entering the hot darkness inside. The place smelt stale and closed in. On the floor, a hollow-eyed girl lay groaning, apparently in pain. Next to her lay a baby, with a large head, brownish hair and large bulging eyes. Lean and haggard, mother and child looked equally helpless. Seeing Amina, Larai struggled to sit up, drew the weeping child closer and offered her breast, a loose, thin, empty flap of flesh. The baby grabbed it, sucked greedily, eyes partly closed and intermittently crying with dissatisfaction. Larai sobbed as she recounted her plight: her bladder had been damaged during the birth, and she was now incontinent and permanently in pain.

'How old are you?' Amina asked, in a shaky voice.

'I don't know. I think fifteen.'

'What happened after the operation?'

'I lived in the hospital premises with other girls whose bladders were damaged too.'

'What of your husband?'

'He married another girl while I was in hospital,' Larai whispered.

'What happened next? I mean in the hospital,' Amina inquired further.

'The hospital authorities sent us away. At first we lived in an unfinished building, but because of the rain, I had to come back here.'

'How did you survive there, I mean on the streets?'

'We depended on charity from passers-by.'

'How's your husband treating you now?'

'He gives us food sometimes, but it depends on his mood. He stays with his new wife, saying that I am smelly and dirty.'

'*Subahana Lillahi*!' Amina said, shaking her head.

Tears rolled down Larai's hollow cheeks. 'Oh! God, I beg you,' Larai pleaded, 'Please take my life. It's better to die than live like this. What have I done? God! What offence have I committed to deserve this punishment?'

'Stop it! Don't offer such prayers, don't cry, it's not your fault, you can't and shouldn't be blamed. You didn't choose your way of life. I'm sure if you had the opportunity, you wouldn't have chosen it,' Amina said sympathetically, holding Larai's hands. It was not her first encounter with suffering, but she had never seen it so close before, and for the first time it touched her. She thought of those months of pregnancy, labour, operation, childbirth ... pains ... agonies, days of neglect and anguish, nights of loneliness, saw how they had eaten deep into Larai's cheeks, her whole body, even her soul. But, thought Amina, at least she's managed to survive, though battered and haggard. There's still hope.' Amina's hands started to shake. It never ceased to amaze her how cruel and inhuman some people could be towards others. She consoled Larai, 'Don't worry, it's the will of God, have faith and trust in Him. He will help. Do you pray?'

'No. I didn't attend Koranic school, but I beg God to take our lives.'

'No! Never offer such prayers!' Amina gently scolded.

'But tell me, what's left for us but suffering?'

When she left, Amina gave Larai some money, promising to find a way to help her.

Amina arranged for a room in the house Alhaji had given her to be prepared quickly, and Larai moved in with her baby. Amina also took Larai to a private hospital where she was operated on. She was so grateful that she visited Amina regularly and helped with her errands, while Amina fed and clothed Larai and her baby. Amina herself moved to a room downstairs, in Alhaji's house, which had formerly been reserved for guests. Her explanation was simple: 'I'm pregnant and it's tedious climbing the stairs.'

Although she was expecting it, the early morning prayer call still disturbed her. She stayed in bed for a long time, thinking of many things: Fatima and her group and their meetings; Kulu and her business; Larai and her daughter. She wondered why Fatima and her friends were so committed to the cause of social change. What satisfaction did they get? They were not interested in personal gain, because they were already rich. What made them care about other women, the masses, class difference and the rest? What could they do to change anything? Although the movement was banned, new members were still joining and the old members continued to meet. Amina realised that she herself had begun to see the issues more clearly.

She thought about what Fatima had suggested: a women's association to organise, educate and help women. She tried to put the idea out of her mind; after all, it couldn't help women with individual problems, it could only deal with group issues. What effect would an association like that have? At the same time, she wondered what would have happened to Larai if she'd left her alone.

Bright lightning flashed, loud thunder followed. Moments later it began to rain and large drops drummed on the zinc roof. Amina looked at the enlarged framed photograph, which had been taken on matriculation day. There she was, standing in the middle in her gown. Fatima was to her left, also in a gown, and Rabi was on her right. Rabi had graduated, married and had then been to law school, after which she had started practising as a lawyer.

Amina thought again about starting a women's association. She tossed and turned on the bed, trying to convince herself that it was worth trying. She could see how much women were suffering, and for herself, it was hard to be idle and dependent. Amina decided to tell Fatima that she was ready to help, although only in an ancillary capacity.

That evening, Amina was performing ablution when Fatima walked in. She was sweating and panted as she explained, 'There's a shortage of petrol and the public transport system is paralysed. I walked from the university,' and she fell on the sofa, still gasping for breath.

'Allow me to say my prayers first,' Amina begged.

'Go ahead. Pray that God will send fuel from somewhere.'

After saying her prayers, Amina sat facing Fatima. 'What were you saying about fuel?' she asked.

'For three days now, there's been no regular supply of petrol in town,' Fatima said, and without waiting for Amina's response continued, 'Our corrupt and irresponsible leaders claim that there's a glut in the world market and a shortage of foreign exchange. But that doesn't explain why there's a fuel shortage, even though this is an oil-producing country.'

'The State House of Assembly promised to investigate the cause of the scarcity. Some members were blaming hoarders,' Amina offered.

Fatima turned on the fan, which whirred noisily. 'The hoarders are well known. Some of them are legislators who own petrol stations. This scarcity is artificially created to inflate ...' Fatima stopped abruptly. She must have remembered that Alhaji Haruna owned some petrol stations.

'I'm hungry,' she said with a yawn.

'Tiloti, I've only got boiled eggs, but more food will be ready soon,' Amina said standing up.

'Haven't you forgotten that name?' Tiloti was a nickname Fatima's elder brother had given her.

'No. Not yet,' Amina said smiling.

'Let's play a game,' Fatima suggested, picking up an egg and giving another to Amina. They knocked the eggs against each other and Fatima's egg cracked. She was not satisfied and suggested the other sides of the eggs should be used, no doubt hoping for a draw. They had another go and again her egg cracked. 'You've definitely won,' she conceded with a slight smile.

Mairo came later in the evening, armed as always with stories. 'A woman fought with her husband today and he declared three times that their marriage had ended. She's not from around here and has no place to stay, so she's going to sleep in the market because she has no money to go back to her village.'

Amina took a deep breath before she replied, knowing she would not be able to retract later. 'We shall do something soon,' she said. 'Fatima, I've thought further about your idea of setting up a women's association and I'm prepared to give it a try. But hold on,' she said, observing Fatima's excited reaction, 'you must understand, my role will have to be strictly limited to support. Okay?'

'Fine,' Fatima responded joyfully, clapping her hands. 'Wow! This *is* good news! One big step has been taken; more will follow. Thank you. This is a wonderful surprise.'

# 9

A few weeks later, Amina went to visit Mairo who was ill, accompanied by Larai and Hauwa. Along the street, they saw two boys beating a third one. Amina had already walked past, like many others, when suddenly she stopped and turned around. She told Hauwa and Larai to separate them, and when they did, the two bullies stood panting happily, while their victim cried, tears mingling with blood from his nosebleed. They were Koranic school pupils—*almajirai*—who went about begging for food. Dirty, rough and tattered clothes hung on their skinny bodies. Their trousers were so torn that their buttocks protruded, their legs thin as twigs and their hair matted. Armed with battered enamel bowls, they were among the small army of such boys who clustered around houses begging for left-overs.

'Why are you beating him?' Amina questioned one of the boys.

'Some days ago we went out begging for food and were given some in his bowl,' he replied pointing to the crying boy. 'He ran away immediately he'd got the food and ate it alone. Today we caught him and beat him up as punishment.'

Amina was startled. 'Please boys, I beg you in the name of God, never fight over food again. Rather, you should cooperate and help one another.' She ordered them to go in different directions. But when she heard the two swear to sort out the boy on another occasion, she called them back and gave them some coins to compensate for the food. They were satisfied and walked away happily together. As she walked along the streets, Amina looked at her surroundings with new eyes. She found herself facing a series of questions. Why did some people live in poverty and squalour, while others wanted for nothing? Why couldn't human beings cooperate and help each other? Why couldn't everyone have a decent home? Why were so many people hungry when there was enough food for everyone? What was stopping people from using their knowledge to provide everyone with the basic necessities of life? Why did our leaders pay little or no attention to these things?

As they approached, she took note of the house Mairo lived in. It was built of mud with a zinc roof, no better than all those around it. In a shed in front of the house, a group of *almajirai* with their wooden writing slates were reciting verses under the leadership of Mairo's husband. Suddenly Amina remembered how Fatima had once described the Koranic schools as the best form of perpetuating ignorance: "They recite the Koran like our northern cows: they chew but do not digest." An old blind man sat close to the entrance, holding a smooth walking stick and an empty bowl, preparing to go out begging. Before entering the house, Amina greeted him and dropped some coins into the bowl, and he thanked her.

Despite looking tired and weak, Mairo welcomed them warmly. In the room where she sat, six boys squatted in a circle around a bowl of pap. One after the other, they sipped from the bowl and passed it on. Amina shook her head sadly. As if for the first time, she observed the tell-tale signs of poverty: big protruding bellies, thin necks and legs, big heads, rough and dirty skin.

Most of the boys were beggars, while the girls were already engaged in street trading. What did the future hold for them? They provided a never-ending supply of labourers, water-carriers, wood-hewers, robbers, thugs, hooligans and addicts.

What if they could be taught to read and write? What if they could be trained for specialised vocations? Who gained from seeing them like this? Wasn't it the responsibility of either the rich or their representatives, the government, to provide them with the opportunities to live a better life? Amina could not help thinking how different their lives were from her own.

Just as Amina was taking these first mental steps towards doing something positive, that Thursday evening after prayers, she was seized with pains around her waist. In alarm, she called Talata, who smiled and reassured her that her baby was on the way. Amina was taken to the private clinic where she gave birth to a baby boy at dawn on Friday. A week later, the boy was named Abdulrasheed in the traditional naming ceremony.

The arrival of Abdulrasheed delayed Amina's participation in the formation of the women's association, but plans went ahead nonetheless. Bilkisu asked her father to help register it, and meanwhile, the movement of which Fatima was a member formed a new division called the Bakaro Support Group. The Muslim Students' Society agreed to provide as many teachers as were needed for Islamic and Arabic classes, and the Nurses and Midwives' Association also offered to help. But Amina was not ready yet. Bakaro waited patiently as Amina devoted herself to her baby boy.

She was lying in bed breast-feeding her son one day when Alhaji Haruna entered, sat on the sofa and demanded that she choose between the Bakaro Women's Association and the Legislators' Wives' Association.

'Bakaro first,' she stated firmly without any hesitation.

'Then your plan to work or go into business must be shelved, eh?'

'As it pleases you.'

He reflected for a while and left.

Amina had been expecting some further move from her husband since his furious reaction when he had first heard about it. Although he had calmed down when she told him that Bilkisu would be in charge, and the association aimed only to execute the ruling party's programmes—a party of which he was a staunch member—Bilkisu's warning was still fresh in her mind. 'In organising the women here, we'll come face to face with the dying feudal class and the emerging capitalists, who will be against it or try to sabotage it. We have to be determined. You give us the go ahead and you'll be surprised.' Amina had given them the go ahead and now she was waiting for the surprise. Then there had been the discussion with Fatima: 'Amina, fix a date for the launch. We are ready.'

'You'll have to wait. I'm still too weak,' Amina had argued.

'You've rested for a month and still need more time?' Fatima fired back. 'Think of the peasant women who work on the farms throughout their pregnancy and even give birth there. Most of them are back at work after a week.'

Kulu too had delivered her contribution. She had tried to persuade Amina against the association by pointing out the dangers of aligning herself with activist women. 'Just because these girls don't know how to enjoy the pleasures of life doesn't mean you should deny yourself. Look at you, you're young and pretty. It's not for you to carry the weight of women's problems. Can't you see how people are enjoying their lives?' she had tried to persuade her.

'Kulu, I just can't help it. I want to try and help. Anyway, it's just an experiment.'

'Everything in this world has been predestined. It is written that things will happen the way they are now unfolding. We are powerless before God Almighty,' Kulu had emphasised earnestly.

The idea of a women's association predictably raised a lot of dust in Bakaro. The ruling party in the state was initially against it but later gave in on one condition: the association had to be the women's wing of the party. The opposition party backed the association and argued that the women should be free to set it up. Religious organisations and other groups were divided. Some saw it as sacrilegious and against the teachings of Islam. Others made it clear that as long as it included religious programmes and wasn't in any way against religious teachings, then the women should be free to associate.

The nature of the community in Bakaro did not offer the best conditions for forming a broad-based women's organisation. It was a district in which people's identities were bound up in a complex network of religious, ethnic, political and family ties, in a country where injustice and discrimination had been carefully woven into the foundations of the social and economic setup. Furthermore, in a country with male unemployment and overall underdevelopment so high, sex discrimination was just the tip of the anthill of exploitation. Where poverty was the main issue, women's suffering and inequality remained hidden and forgotten, and to express with a desire for the emancipation of women was regarded as almost as a sin. In this context, the setting up of the Women's Association aroused a great deal of interest, and by the time all was set for it to take off, the people of Bakaro had high expectations.

The pre-launch meeting of the Bakaro Women's Association took place at the university. On arrival, Amina was introduced to members of the Bakaro Support Group. They were seven—four girls and three boys, led by Bilkisu. Amina had met all of the girls before. Bilkisu announced that the association had been officially registered with the appropriate state ministry. She read out the letter and passed it on to Amina in a file. Although she was to be the coordinator, Amina remained silent during the ensuing discussion. She didn't agree with everything that was proposed, but was excited because the association would put her in touch with other women and break her days of idleness. At last she saw an opportunity to explore her talents and abilities through closer contact with people and ideas, a chance to open her inner self to the world. Should something positive and permanent come out of it, her reputation would definitely be enhanced. Now, by the look of it, her days would pass more happily.

The meeting lasted about two hours, during which a date was fixed for the launch ceremony. Amina was to be there in person and read a speech. 'Good-bye and see you soon,' she said with a delighted smile before leaving. She couldn't stop smiling all the way back home.

# 10

'You are married now and your husband is your master. Obey him in all respects as marriage is a serious and sacred thing. You must believe that what your husband tells you is right and you do whatever he tells you to do. Respect for a husband is like respect for God Almighty, the Creator ...' said a firm, clear voice in her dream. She woke up, looked round the room, touched her baby and closed her eyes again. Usually she enjoyed early morning dreams, though she knew they were often linked to noises in the compound and its surroundings: cockcrow, birds' songs, motor car horns, prayer calls, shouts and cries. For about an hour she could sleep through such noises, until they graduated to irritating footsteps and at times knocks.

On this particular day she woke up earlier than usual and lay in bed, nervous but excited. It was Saturday, the day of the launching ceremony. After carrying out the usual morning chores, she sat in her room, not completely at ease with herself. After one o'clock, she washed quickly and dressed carefully. She put on simple clothes: a multicoloured blouse and wrapper, and applied a little make-up. As she was tying her head tie, Bilkisu entered and told her excitedly, 'We're on our way to the school. Here's the speech Fatima prepared for you.' She left a file on the bed. 'See you later.'

Amina's nervousness increased. Bilkisu left, and she sat breast feeding Abdulrasheed, wondering how she would be able to stand up and speak in front of people. When she was ready, she handed Abdulrasheed over to her sister Rakiya and went out.

As she alighted from the white Mercedes at the primary school, she saw Fatima and other members of the Bakaro Support Group busy making final arrangements. A lot of women had gathered. In front of the headmaster's office, a tent had been erected, covered with green tarpaulin that danced to the rhythm of the wind. This was for invited guests, for whom comfortable chairs were neatly arranged. Opposite the tent, in the field, benches and chairs were arranged in rows for the women. So far, half of the seats were occupied. Amina looked around. A Ministry of Information propaganda van was parked nearby with loudspeakers on it.

'Don't be nervous,' Bilkisu advised her. 'You'll soon get used to speaking before a crowd. Just be yourself, and if you want to prepare, I suggest you read your speech a couple of times to be sure you know it.'

Most of the invited guests were late. As Amina sat reading and rereading her speech, Muktar suddenly appeared from the crowd. She felt her heartbeat quicken, and her nervousness increased. She looked at him, his handsome features accentuated by the dark blue safari suit he wore. She thought he looked thinner than before, and wondered if anyone was looking after him. As he drew closer, she wanted to ask him hundreds of questions but she was too shy. She wondered if people around her had noticed any change in her demeanour. She looked up at him and his gaze sank into her so deeply that she almost collapsed there and then. She pulled herself together, lowering her eyes. He said something which she didn't hear, and forced a welcoming smile.

'How are you? How do you do?' she tried to keep her voice as even as possible.

'I'm fine, thank you, and you?'

'I'm fine,' she said.

'Don't worry, I'm taking care of myself. I hope to further my education in another university soon.'

'I pray that God will help you. Please take care. Why are you so thin?' she inquired, her voice still shaky.

'I've never been fat you know,' he remarked with a smile.

'Go and sit down. I'm sure this is not the last time we'll meet,' Amina said.

He turned and walked away.

Amina stole a glance at him. She wondered what thoughts were stirring behind his cool and unreadable, but undeniably handsome face. Bilkisu walked up to her. 'Amina,' she said, 'according to the programme, you'll speak after the national anthem and prayers. Just have confidence in yourself. Also, just to warn you, you'll hear your voice from the loudspeaker. Don't panic!'

When her husband, the guest of honour of the occasion and most invited guests had arrived, Bilkisu walked to the microphone, tested it and welcomed everyone. She signalled to an official of the Ministry of Information who played the national anthem. Everybody stood up. After the national anthem, a member of the Muslim Students' Society conducted opening prayers. Bilkisu then invited Mallama Aminatu Haruna, the founder and coordinator of the Bakaro Women's Association, to deliver her keynote address.

This was the moment Amina had feared. She stood up and walked carefully towards the microphone. As she reached it, she looked around and saw faces directed at her, eyes staring at her, and began to tremble. Her heart pounded, the papers in her hands started to shake. Forcing herself to speak in spite of her dry mouth, she was surprised how strange and unnatural her voice sounded.

'... Our main objective is to raise the economic, social and educational status of women in Bakaro... so that they can play an increasingly useful part in building a just and progressive society.

'... We believe and maintain that the participation of women in local, state and national life is vital for their emancipation ...' she raised her head, and felt all eyes fixed on her. The impact of all those people watching her was so strong that she felt as if they were examining her naked body. She went back to the speech. When she resumed, she realised she had jumped some paragraphs, but she read anything that was legible.

'... Given the historical legacy of the oppression, exploitation, subordination and alienation of women, we feel that the elimination of illiteracy among women is crucial. That is why our first step will be to launch an adult literacy campaign here among women. May I remind you of two very important Arabic sayings: "Wealth is brainpower not money" and "A country where the women are not educated is like a bird with only one wing." If we want to progress, we must educate women. If women are not educated the whole of society will remain in darkness.

'... We are making a strong appeal to the local, state and federal governments to pay special attention to the following areas: equality of women with men at work; full support and complete security for working women, single or married; encouragement of girls' education at all levels; discouragement of early and forced marriages; strict laws against domestic violence; full employment for all qualified women ...

There is a saying that:

"If you are planning for a year, plant corn

If you are planning for a decade, plant a tree

If you are planning for life, educate people."

We have decided to plan for the future of Bakaro. We want a better, happier and more prosperous Bakaro, so we have decided to educate women. If women's problems are not solved, local, state and national problems cannot be solved.

Thank you.'

# 11

The launch of the Bakaro Women's Association was much talked about. The opposition party welcomed its launch and described the association as a 'big step forward,' while the ruling party strongly disagreed with the demands made by Amina and the Support Group. Nor had Amina's speech gone down well with her husband. He quarrelled with her afterwards, questioning why she had 'attacked' the government, why she had allowed herself to be used. Partly out of fear, partly out of respect for him, she could not and did not defend herself. But his attack undermined her confidence and left her wondering why he had to interfere in her affairs. Why should she say what he and others wanted to hear?

Amina saw her sister off in the afternoon and went to the primary school where the first lesson of the Adult Literacy campaign programme was to commence. The first batch of women—over thirty—filled a classroom. They all sat stretching their legs under the desks, waiting eagerly. Like Amina herself, the women looked nervous but excited. Amina stood with five members of the Support Group facing the inquiring eyes of the women. There was a moment of uneasy silence in the room. A tall, slim student in a short-sleeved shirt and jeans stepped forward and introduced himself.

'I am Muazu Danlami, a political science student. We've agreed to take part in the Bakaro Educational Project until we are able to get permanent teachers. If we succeed we intend to move to other districts and maybe other towns. In this way, we believe that more women will gain from our knowledge. We shall be using the Al Hassan Adult Education model whereby an illiterate can be made literate in less than six months.

'As you're all aware, education is vital in any society. Prophet Muhammad (*Peace be upon Him*) was quoted as saying that "The search for knowledge is a sacred duty imposed upon every Muslim." For those women who for any reason cannot attend classes at the moment, we've plans to send our female members to teach them in their homes.'

After a pause, Muazu pointed to a clean-shaven, baby-faced student in a big white gown and turban, and said: 'This is Musa-Al-Ahmad. He and two others from the Muslim Students' Society will teach Arabic language and Islamic knowledge.' One after the other he introduced the other teachers. 'One subject on which we hope to spend more time is health education. Rebecca is in charge of the Bakaro Health Project. Two nurses, two midwives and two health inspectors have agreed to take part. They'll teach you how to keep yourselves clean and healthy, and how to keep your environment tidy. They'll pay particular attention to pregnant women and nursing mothers.' Rebecca whispered in his ear and he smiled and nodded. 'I'll be taking general studies, where I'll teach you about the lives of people of different ethnic groups, their beliefs and systems of governance. I'll also talk about the problems faced by our country, the continent and the world.'

He pinned a big world map on the board, and Amina went to the back of the classroom and leaned against the wall. Holding a long ruler, Muazu Danlami started: 'This is a map of the world. There are over one hundred and eighty countries, each with its own territory, population and government. There are many races, languages, tribes, nationalities.' He showed them the inhabited and uninhabited parts of the world. 'This is Africa, this is our country Nigeria, this is our town, where we are now, so you can see how we belong to the wider world.'

'Teacher, some people say the world is round,' a woman remarked.

'Yes, it is. This is just a map. You'll be taught geography, a subject that will explain all these things to you. You'll also be taught how rains fall and why there are different seasons and so on.'

'Teacher, where is Mecca?' asked a middle aged woman in the back row.

Muazu laughed and invited her to come up to the front and look at the map. He showed her Saudi Arabia, Mecca and Medina. She thanked him. 'My dream is to go there one day to perform the Holy Pilgrimage.'

'May your dream come true,' Muazu prayed.

After about an hour the introductory class ended.

Shortly afterwards, the other classes started. Although the Bakaro Women's Association had no permanent classrooms, teaching staff or state funds, the organisers were determined to get the project going. Some men refused to let their wives take part, while other women wanted to see how it went before joining. Amina's life also had started to change from idleness to activity. She thought mostly about ways of keeping the association functioning.

A few days after the inaugural lesson, Amina was sitting on the sofa with her son when Bilkisu and Fatima walked in. They apologised for their inability to attend the first lesson and said they had brought some teaching materials. One of the rooms of her home was used as the headquarters of the Women's Association. She had furnished it with a table and six chairs and arranged for a daily supply of newspapers and magazines.

Bilkisu spoke quietly to a young man who was sitting in her car. He brought out some cardboard boxes and a poster. He held the poster up for Amina to see. 'I'm Danladi, a fine-art student and Gloria's friend. I've painted this for your association and now present it to you.' Amina received it gently and looked closely at it. It was beautifully painted in three main colours—green, red and black—with images of women reading and working. Beneath these was the motto: WOMEN! READ, WORK AND ORGANISE YOUR LIVES! Amina showered thanks on him, and Bilkisu opened the cardboard boxes and showed her textbooks, exercise books, sticks of chalk and other items. 'They're all yours,' she said happily.

'We're very grateful,' Amina said, overwhelmed.

When Bilkisu left with Danladi, Amina looked at Fatima with concern.

'What's wrong with you? You look so tired.'

'I've got a bad headache.'

'I'll give you some tablets,' offered Amina.

'No, no, thanks. I need some rest. We had a parliamentary meeting which lasted until dawn and I had very little sleep,' Fatima yawned.

'You can sleep here for a while. I'll be in Talata's room.'

After a long afternoon nap, Fatima emerged looking fresher and stronger, and stayed to eat. The house became as lively as always when the ever-exciting Fatima was around. She played with the children and cracked jokes with the women.

'Amina, we need a favour,' Fatima said gently while getting ready to go. 'We're organising a small meeting on domestic violence, and we shall be inviting women from the town. We don't expect a large turnout but we don't want to meet on the campus, so we'd like to use one of the rooms at the association. But only if it doesn't disrupt things.'

'It's all right. When is it?'

'The 8th March, International Women's Day.'

'Fantastic! You're welcome,' Amina said with an amused smile.

'I've got another idea,' continued Fatima. 'We can organise a lecture for the association's members later in the evening. I can speak on problems facing African women.'

'I've no objection. I'll tell them.'

❖

On the 8th March, Fatima and several others, Amina included, assembled in a room at the Bakaro Women's Association headquarters. Fatima stood at the front next to a girl whose head was covered with a black veil, her head drooping. 'This is Saude, who's a victim of domestic violence. She's here to tell us first-hand of the horrors of our so-called humane and peaceful society,' Fatima said.

Saude was soft-spoken with a hesitant and nervous voice. She looked frightened and wept as she tried to find words. All she was able to whisper through tears was: 'Ever since I married him I have not known peace. He beats me regularly. He seeks any excuse, like the food is not delicious ... I didn't welcome him in a cordial manner, and so on. My husband beats me with anything he can lay his hands on, in the presence of my daughter. It's just as it was with my mother. The mother and the children live in fear,' she cried louder.

'Show us the injuries,' Fatima requested, 'don't hide them.' Saude was reluctant, so Bilkisu went to the girl and removed the veil gently, to reveal fresh wounds on her face, swollen lips and blackened eyes. Saude voluntarily showed the bruises on other parts of her body. 'A lot of women,' commented Bilkisu, 'hide such injuries because of shame and fear. The purdah system helps in covering up these brutalities, as most women can't even be seen outside to know how injured they are. Some live with the injuries unattended to because their husbands have refused to let them out!'

'Are you going back?' Amina asked Saude.

'Yes. I've nowhere else to go,' she replied.

'May Almighty Allah, the Merciful, the Benevolent, the Compassionate, give you the strength and courage to withstand the savage instincts of that so-called husband of yours,' Fatima prayed.

Bilkisu stood up. 'I assure you that your husband will never know you talked to us and whenever anything happens to you, please contact us or Amina here.' Saude bid them farewell and Bilkisu saw her out.

'She's just given us a typical picture of a brutalised woman. I count myself very lucky to have escaped that terror but now, I weep for our society that condones such barbarity,' Fatima said.

'The trouble is that most women are timid with very low self-esteem, so they're ready-made victims.' Bilkisu said as she returned.

'Because the army Major has never beaten you, eh?' Rebecca asked.

'Not yet and he promises never to.'

'Never trust any of those beasts in uniform,' Fatima chipped in.

'At least so far, he's still got a human heart.'

'Let Muktar try it, either we'll beat each other up or I'll beat the hell out of him,' Rebecca boasted, 'I only hope it never happens. He's too gentle and handsome to be beaten. He's so precious to me. He's made to be loved.'

A strong wave of jealousy swept through Amina. For the first time, it pained her to know that Rebecca was in love with Muktar, but she quickly consoled herself that he deserved to be happy with someone who loved him.

'The thing is, if a woman loves a man, she will accept even his beatings. What a contradiction!' Bilkisu said, laughing.

'I can't understand,' Fatima attempted to return to the topic in hand, 'why we women feel powerless against this evil in our society, why we even accept it.'

'Men who do this are cowards who can't face up to another man, so they punish us instead,' Bilkisu explained.

'Each and every one of us must share the blame and take responsibility for changing the situation,' Fatima asserted firmly. 'This girl is just one, but behind her only God Almighty knows how many thousands more are enduring torture and brutality. We've got a lot of work to do.'

In the evening a large gathering of women turned out to listen to Fatima. Amina, in the company of Hauwa, Larai and her son, walked again to the school. Though it was still very hot, they were gratified to see how many women had come out. Bilkisu, Fatima and Amina sat behind a table facing the sweating faces of the women, and Bilkisu stood up and welcomed them.

'Good evening. Today we're here to observe International Women's Day in Bakaro for the first time. On this day, women all over the world focus on their problems and attempt to find ways of solving them. This shows us we are not alone. To underline how much we have in common, Fatima is going to talk to us about the particular problems of women in Africa. I'm sure you know her very well and I hope you'll enjoy it.' Fatima stood up and adjusted her blouse and wrapper. She was a good orator, calm and confident. She smiled and started to speak:

'In the stories of men, we hear about how beautiful women are and how they comfort men, but not about how they are suffering. In some societies, women have won certain freedoms, while in others, women are like prisoners chained to domestic work. In Africa, we suffered under white colonial rule and we still suffer, despite the fact that most African countries have attained political independence. Most African traditional cultures are male-dominated, allowing women virtually no control over affairs affecting them. In our part of Nigeria, Islam, which is for the emancipation of women, is interpreted by religious leaders so as to oppress and subjugate women.

'In many African cultures, the woman is an object for pleasure and domestic labour, a commodity for sale, a baby-breeding machine. Most African women are slaves in the afternoon and queens at night.'

Fatima removed a handkerchief from her handbag, mopped her face and continued. 'Overcoming male domination in our society will be very difficult because it's been ingrained over time, sanctioned by the law and blessed by religion. But it is possible, if we stand up and fight. If we wait for men to give us our natural rights and freedoms we will never get them.

'I urge you all to support the Bakaro Women's Association. Try and attend all the classes and contribute where you can. Don't hide your problems, share them. Share your ideas, ask your questions. Amina and the other organisers are here to discuss things with you openly and honestly. Our people say: a person who asks questions never gets lost! Thank you!'

Sidikatu Lawal, a primary school teacher, now posed a simple question: What should they do to overcome male domination? Fatima consulted Bilkisu and stood up again.

'Our struggle as women must be linked with the wider struggle for change in the whole of society. But first we have to unite as women, to fight for the right to work and equal pay; against forced and early marriages; for the right to education at all levels; against domestic violence ... in short, there should be redistribution of economic, social and political opportunities, and this can be achieved only if this decadent, corrupt and male-dominated neo-colonial system is overthrown.'

# 12

One of the first projects for the Bakaro women was participation in a programme under the Bakaro Health Project: "Operation Keep Bakaro Clean." They came out on a Saturday morning and worked hard to clear the rubbish in their houses and on the streets. As they did so, they found that there was no provision for refuse disposal. Some students went to the Local Government Secretary, Alhaji Ibrahim, who refused to provide them with any help, saying the women should have made provision for the disposal of the rubbish beforehand. Amina was angry. She could not understand why a government official would openly refuse to help in something that was aimed primarily at improving the environment. In the evening, she narrated the incident to Fatima. 'I didn't expect him to behave the way he did. All we were trying to do was to keep the district clean.'

'One of the major problems in this country is that the higher the position you hold, the more irresponsible you are. A man employed to oversee the free flow of a river, deliberately obstructs it and may even be rewarded with a national award,' Fatima commented bitterly.

Abdulrasheed and Fatima fell asleep in her room, while Amina read. She was so absorbed, she did not even notice when Kulu walked in. They exchanged greetings in low voices, before Kulu pulled Amina outside.

'We're organising a small get-together in my house later in the afternoon. I'm sorry I couldn't tell you earlier, I was very busy.'

'I don't think I can attend,' Amina stated firmly.

'Oh? what are you doing?'

'Nothing,' Amina said and looked into Kulu's eyes, 'Will your husband be there?'

'Of course. Oh! I'm sorry. I forgot to tell you that he has accepted that what he did was wrong. He has promised to send a van and some workers tomorrow to dispose of the refuse.'

'Okay, I'll be there,' Amina assured her.

'Don't invite Fatima,' Kulu warned in a whisper. 'It's no place for her, she can't reap where she didn't sow.'

Behind her smile, Amina knew she was drawing further and further away from Kulu and her like, and closer to Fatima and the ordinary women she was meeting every day.

Kulu led a *Jindadi* lifestyle—one of ostentation and conspicuous consumption—exemplified by the clothes she wore and the fleet of cars she had on display at the entrance of her house. She welcomed Amina at the front door of her ten-bedroom mansion. There were only a few guests so far, and she explained: 'The purpose of this party is just to entertain some of our close friends and business partners. Very soon, my hotel will open and I'll want them to patronise it.'

'I see,' responded Amina non-committally.

'Secondly, when the hotel eventually takes off, I'd like you to be one of its managers. I didn't want to tell you earlier because Fatima was there. The devil in her is so powerful that I'm afraid she could even persuade you to reject such a lucrative offer.'

'Are you sure that you want me to manage it?' Amina asked with astonishment.

'I'm sure. I can see your husband is wasting you and your time.'

'But I don't have any experience.'

'Don't worry, I've employed an Indian, Mr Kumar, who'll manage it at first. You'll be his assistant for a year or two, so as to get on-the-job experience, after which you'll take over the full management.'

They were still discussing this issue when a big-bosomed, bejewelled woman interrupted. As she drew Kulu aside, Amina took in her big reddish eyes and loud manner. She appeared to be tipsy, her make-up was very conspicuous and together with her short permed hair, made her look like a clown.

'That woman,' Kulu said when she was gone, 'is a businesswoman, Mrs Joy, who owns several hotels. I pity the prostitutes she rents her rooms to.'

Amina was shocked. 'What do you mean?'

'Her charges are too high. I intend to charge very low rates.'

'Isn't the hotel for ordinary customers?'

'It's for both. There are two blocks, one for regular accommodation and another one for prostitutes. You see, Amina, the presence of the prostitutes will surely attract many people into staying in the hotel. I hope that one block will help the other!'

'But, isn't that bad from a religious point of view?'

'Perhaps, but just pray regularly to God and He'll forgive you. After all, most of these rich Muslims either have shares in leading breweries or are alcoholics themselves. Didn't you know that most of the men who patronise prostitutes are Muslims? According to Islam, usury is an offence, but show me a rich man who doesn't practise it. You see, you have to be pragmatic.'

Asabe, the President of the Legislators' Wives' Association, approached and greeted Kulu cordially. She treated Amina to a cold stare, acting as if she had never met her before. Amina smiled and walked away. Standing alone, she saw Alhaji Ibrahim on the other side of the spacious room and their eyes met. He smiled and nodded his head but she quickly turned away.

A distinguished looking middle-aged woman came over to Amina, smiling. 'Good evening, my name is Mrs Ladi Abdullahi, I'm a Magistrate.'

'I'm Amina Haruna, the coordinator of the Bakaro Women's Association.'

'My husband speaks a lot about you, ' Mrs Ladi said, with honest enthusiasm.

'Who's your husband?' Amina curiously asked.

'He's a lecturer at the university and is very interested in your association.'

'I don't think I've ever met him,' Amina replied.

'He knows Fatima and Bilkisu very well. He thinks that your organisation is a model for many things to come. He's thinking of writing a book on you.'

Kulu's arrival prevented further discussion, and Mrs Abdullahi walked away as a tall young man in a black suit and bow tie, with a trimmed moustache, bowed slightly, greeted Kulu and left after a short discussion. 'He's one of the youngest millionaires in the town,' whispered Kulu. 'He has so many houses and cars and is still single. He's a businessman and a clever one.'

'What do you mean?'

'He imports and hoards essential commodities. He re-bags rice and salt.'

'I don't understand what you mean by "re-bags".'

'He reduces the quantity of rice from its original bags and fills new ones,' Kulu explained.

'Is that why you say he's clever?'

'No, not only that. He is very good at inflating contracts, bribery, falsification of documents and so on. He owns a factory that has closed down, but he regularly applies for and receives import licences under the name of the factory. Instead of importing machinery or raw materials, he imports fake items, luxurious cars and so on. He's making it now in the oil sector. He connives with foreign firms and shipping companies that lift the crude oil illegally and they in turn give him his percentage. He puts his money in Liechtenstein and Luxembourg. He thinks the banks there are more discreet. I've been told by reliable sources that he and Lucas Danfulani will be managing the mineral resources of the state.'

'That's interesting,' murmured Amina, trying to take it all in.

'That's a job I'd really like to do but Bature and my husband don't get along very well.'

A stout man in a neat kaftan and red cap approached next and greeted them. Amina recognised him as a business associate of her husband.

'You know that man, don't you?' Kulu asked, as he walked away.

'Yes, but not that well.'

'I'll tell you how he got rich. When he was a storekeeper in a ministry, he sold all the items under his care and set the building ablaze.'

Amina could not control her expression. 'What?' she asked loudly, her mouth dropping open in disbelief.

'It's true. When he was an accountant, he embezzled state funds and resigned. A week later, all documents relating to the case were burnt in a mysterious fire in his former office.'

'I don't believe it.'

'It happened. My husband told me everything. What's more, he's not the only man in this "fire" business. Now he's one of the richest businessmen and intends to contest for a parliamentary seat soon.'

A young woman whispered something to Kulu who left to declare the party open. Amina felt increasingly uncomfortable and pleaded to leave, but Kulu begged her to stay. She stood in a corner watching the guests chatting excitedly, feeling detached. Amina's eyes met those of Rabi, her former roommate at the university, who was chatting to some guests. Rabi avoided eye contact. Just when Amina felt like walking up to her, Rabi walked away calmly. The mingling of cigarette smoke and too many perfumes was becoming overwhelming, and she suddenly felt nauseous. Then she observed Alhaji Ibrahim standing close to her, chatting with some of his female guests, and moved away, only to be beckoned by Kulu again.

'This is Ms Ngozi, the new chief pharmacist in the General Hospital,' Kulu introduced a fleshy older woman.

'How's the Bakaro Health Project?' she asked haughtily, looking Amina up and down.

'So far, fine,' Amina replied cautiously.

'I must say I admire your courage in organising the women.'

Amina did not know how to take this, and after a brief discussion with Kulu, the woman walked away.

'I want to be close to her,' Kulu whispered. 'I want to establish a clinic in the town in the near future.'

'You mean you'll divert drugs from the hospital to the clinic?'

'No, not directly. I'll pay for them of course,' Kulu explained. 'But I was told she charges a lot of money.'

'Why not import drugs and medical equipment directly?'

'The taxes levied on private clinics are very high, so they have to rely on state hospitals.'

'Why can't you pay the taxes and pass the extra charges on to the patients?'

'It's much easier to get the medical supplies from the state hospital. You don't have to worry about all the paperwork and so on.'

Amina had had enough and begged to leave. This time, Kulu agreed. On the lawn outside, they met an old man in a flowing white gown, wearing a bright turban and holding a long set of prayer beads. He apologised to Kulu for being late.

'And who is he?' Amina asked, immediately after he had passed.

'He's the District Head of Dimbi village. He's known as the "powerful debtor." A couple of years ago, he borrowed money from a bank to the tune of millions. He was so indebted that the bank was at his mercy. He simply refused to pay it back and the bank went bankrupt.'

As she left, Amina thanked Kulu but made it clear that she would not want to do the hotel job, bade her farewell and headed towards the car.

Fatima was bathing Abdulrasheed in a big plastic basin in her room when Amina arrived. Abdulrasheed was full of smiles, but as Fatima lifted him out of the water he started to cry. Amina took him and dried him, before handing him back to Fatima to be dressed. She told Fatima about the party, but Fatima was not surprised. 'What you've seen and heard is just the tip of an anthill. I've seen more than that and heard worse.' She removed a safety pin from her mouth, pinned Abdulrasheed's nappy carefully and asked, 'If it were a competition, and you were a judge, who would you give the prize to?' She handed over Abdulrasheed to Amina.

'Kulu of course!'

'Why?'

'Because she's honest about it,' Amina said, starting to breast feed her child.

'Did you have the pleasure of meeting Alhaji AB Dansaki?'

'No.'

'He was the Commissioner for Education for about ten years. Some years ago, Bature bought him a house in London. He was not impressed by it and thought it was too small. He liked the area very much and guess what he did?'

'I can't.'

'He bought the whole street! All the money that was supposed to go into educating children here was used to buy a whole street in London. That's not the end of the story. The estate agents eventually duped him. He did not read the small print in the contract that said that the houses would revert to the owners if he did not live there for three years. He went there after three years and was ejected by the police.' Fatima shook her head. 'What about Kulu's husband? Do you know how he made his money? For over ten years he and Bature were selling arms and ammunitions all over Africa. They deliberately encouraged warfare and conflict so that they could sell arms to both sides. Eventually they fell out and he's lying low now as the Local Government Secretary. I can spend all night telling you about these so-called rulers of ours! I don't want to spoil my mood.'

'What about your husband? I mean, how did he get rich?' Amina asked.

'That's a long and interesting story, but I'll keep it short. He began as a diplomat who served with my father in London. From there he was moved to head the Airport Authority, but complained there wasn't a lot of money in it and managed to get himself moved to the Ports Authority, and from there to the Railway Corporation. He was Chief Executive there for a decade, and it was there he made his millions. During that time, the government launched an ambitious programme to connect eighty percent of the country by a modern railway network. Money was pumped into the project, but look around today, you'll see not a single track was ever laid. Even the existing ones are not maintained. He got money from the government and from foreign banks to supposedly finance the project but nothing came of it. Almost all went straight into his account and those of his accomplices.'

'What does he spend his money on?'

'He's obsessed with fast cars. He's got whole garages full of cars in Abuja, Maiduguri, New York and London, including a few Ferraris. He's got a couple of yachts somewhere in Europe, and also collects paintings. He's a compulsive gambler and dabbles in the stock exchange. One night, I reminded him that when he dies, he'll only be buried with a white cloth. He got so angry that he beat me up!'

Abdulrasheed was now asleep. 'Fatima, you know, I now remember what you used to say before about this class of thieves, liars, swindlers and the like in our society. You argued that the source of property lies in theft and robbery. Today I understand exactly what you mean,' Amina remarked.

Fatima picked up her bag. 'The Holy Bible said something ...'

'Don't tell me you've read the Bible ...' Amina interrupted.

'No! Not all of it. I've read some interesting parts, one of which I like which says something like this: "For unto every one that hath shall be given, and he shall have in abundance; but from him that hath not shall be taken away even that which he hath." 'Does that justify capitalist exploitation?' she asked.

After a few moments of deep thought, Fatima suddenly became excited. I forgot to inform you that I've been invited to speak at the Jibril Bala Mohammed Memorial Lecture. The topic is *Knowledge and Society*, and it's going to be broadcast live on two television channels and state radio. The Deputy Governor, six Commissioners including the State Commissioner for Education, the Chief Judge, the Vice Chancellor and seven heads of departments, and of course hundreds of students on the campus will be present. This is the best opportunity I've been presented with so far and I'll make sure I use it. I've refused to give the organisers my speech in advance. Would you like to hear the gist of it?'

'Of course.'

Fatima brought out some sheets of paper from her bag, stood up, went to fetch a bottle of water from the fridge and filled a glass. She drank a little bit, cleared her throat and adjusted her red beret before starting to read:

'Anyone with a basic interest in international affairs will know that some Western countries have an enormous influence on our daily lives. Within the last few decades, the rate at which they have interfered in our internal affairs has been increasing and it is reaching a dangerous level. Undoubtedly, this is because of their economic, political and military powers. What is the main source of their power? Where does this enormous strength come from? The main reason they are powerful is their ability to produce and manage knowledge.

'We have more than seven months of rainfall each year yet we still don't know how to collect, treat and manage the water supply properly. We have more than ten hours of sunlight a day, yet we still can't use the energy from the sun. We have some of the most useful plants, roots and flowers, yet we cannot make our own medicines. We have idle land and idle hands, yet we cannot feed ourselves. Why can't we build roads? Why can't we make clothes? Why can't we organise ourselves in a way that will make our people prosperous? So many whys! But then we also have so many universities and research institutions!

'Our universities are not designed to produce knowledge; they are places where ignorance is systematically produced and recycled. To produce knowledge we must first of all learn to tell the truth. Science cannot flourish where people are superstitious and fatalistic!

'We must depend upon our universities and institutions of higher education to give us answers to our pressing needs. But to do that, our politicians must have the humility to accept new ideas. Meanwhile, most of our rulers can't even read or write in any language.

'To understand the system that produces the likes of Bature, we must study Western history, Western medicine, Western philosophy, Western literature, Western psychology and Western economic systems.

'There is a Hausa saying: *"Hanjin jimina, akwai nachi, akwai na zubarwa"* which means "from the intestine of an ostrich, there are things you eat and things you throw away." We must learn to tolerate other people's views even if we don't agree with them. Let us learn to appreciate people's contributions and reward them accordingly. We must create a situation that brings the best out of people.

'Everyone in society must change their attitude towards knowledge. We must learn to be hungry for *all* knowledge, not just religious knowledge. We must learn to reason, to reflect, to invent and to innovate. We mustn't attribute our failure to educate ourselves, to expand our economies, to stimulate our cultures to our colonial past.

'We must use knowledge to combat the dreadful poverty around us, because poverty anywhere is a threat to prosperity everywhere. Why is this so when neither our religions nor our cultures tolerate corruption, ignorance, indolence and arrogance?

'As long as we depend on the knowledge created and perfected by others, we shall remain subservient to those who use knowledge wisely. This brings me back to my good friend Bature. As long as we depend on Bature to explore, exploit, process and market our resources, we will always be his slaves. Bature has the power to twist and turn each and every one of us because of the knowledge he possesses.

'We must learn from Bature. He greatly admires achievement and creativity. Having said that, please, ladies and gentlemen, never trust Bature. He has a hidden agenda. Bature has no permanent friend and no permanent enemy, only permanent interests.

'Every society that has flowered has done so on the basis of how it produces, appreciates and uses knowledge. My ancestors the Arabs were once superior to all other people on earth simply because they produced knowledge. They were so ahead in astronomy that they discovered and named the stars. Today very few Arabs can read a very simple map!

'Jibril Bala Mohammed was an intellectual, an activist and a teacher. He fought for the creation of a knowledge-based society. He once told me that his mission in life was to search for truth and knowledge. Let us continue Bala's journey.

'Ignorance leads to slavery, knowledge leads to freedom. Knowledge is power.

'Thank you very much for listening!'

# 13

Over the past weeks, Amina had been turning an idea over and over in her head: if you give people food, they will eat it. If you give them the means, they will feed themselves. She thought of a piece of land she owned, which was lying idle. The women could be taught how to produce food, they could farm the land and share the produce. She thought that other women might have undeveloped land too, women who would welcome the idea of a cooperative farm movement. 'If women could cooperate … if they could form a movement under which resources were pooled … poor people could work independently and benefit from their labour ... cooperation was the key.

'Good day, madam,' a voice interrupted her thoughts, and Fatima and Bilkisu walked in.

'This is for you,' Bilkisu said, giving Abdulrasheed a bag half-full of toys and children's clothes, 'I went to Kano and bought them especially for you.' She bent down to where he was lying and shook one of the toys. Abdulrasheed gurgled with pleasure and grabbed it from her.

'Danbaki sends his greetings,' Fatima said proudly. 'I was with him last night.'

'How's he?'

'Oh! Fine,' Fatima said and gulped some water.

'How are Muktar and Rebecca?'

'They're still friends but ...' Bilkisu said after a deep breath.

'But what?' Amina inquired.

'They have a problem. She loves him but he doesn't seem to love her as much as she loves him,' Bilkisu said. 'It's a bit difficult to explain.'

'Rebecca has been cold with me, thinking I was having an affair with Muktar because he visits me regularly,' Fatima pointed out. 'But of late he has been visiting her more often. She's just too jealous and insecure. To be honest, Muktar has not shown any serious sign of commitment yet and that is worrying, especially for Rebecca.'

'Where's Rabi now?' Amina asked.

'She's fine and has a daughter called Jamila.'

'I saw her at Kulu's party but she avoided me. I really want to make up and move on.'

'Yes, you're right,' Fatima agreed shaking her head, 'Life is too short to have petty quarrels. I'll try and arrange a meeting but from what I know of Rabi, she'll be reluctant to meet you.'

'How time flies,' reflected Amina.

Amina told them about her idea of the cooperative movement.

'That's a lofty idea, but I'm ...' Bilkisu left the sentence uncompleted.

'I welcome the idea but I'm pessimistic about its success,' Fatima stated.

'Why?' Amina demanded.

'You see, the rich in the district and the state will not sit and watch you organise such a movement. They'll do anything to sabotage it. They're so insecure and short-sighted that they'll see it as a threat to their wealth and power.'

'Fatima, I think you misunderstood me,' Amina said seriously. 'I'm not saying I'll organise all the peasants, jobless youth and labourers, just a few women. I see no reason why the two classes can't harmoniously cooperate in the interest of our community. We have to learn to share space and responsibilities.'

Bilkisu laughed. 'Our rulers aren't willing to share anything.'

'Okay. We'll do our best,' Fatima assured Amina. 'We'll discuss it at the Support Group meeting. For my part, I'll contact the Ministry of Agriculture and discuss it with the trade union. I'll also arrange a meeting for you with a cooperative expert on the campus, who'll be delighted to explain the problems and prospects of the cooperative movement.'

'I'll talk to my father, get some money from him and we'll give this idea a try,' Bilkisu said and requested some cotton pads before going to the toilet. Fatima left too and within minutes came back with Abdullahi.

'Now tell Amina what you just said outside,' Fatima ordered.

Abdullahi bowed his head and covered his eyes with his right hand. 'Go ahead, we're listening,' Amina prompted.

'I've agreed to marry Fatima,' he said in faint voice.

The women laughed. Fatima released him and he ran out. Moments later Abdullahi came back. 'I have a question to ask,' he said, 'I want to know where you come from.'

Fatima pulled him towards her and told him: 'My great-grandfather came from somewhere in Arabia. He's an Arab. I don't know exactly when he came here or what he traded in, but I was told he settled near the lake with a group of friends. My grandfather was also a trader and a religious leader. He was a learned man who had a very big library and travelled a lot. My father, who is still alive, studied in the famous university in Cairo and worked as a diplomat. I followed him to many countries in the world.

My great-grandmother was also an Arab. She was the only daughter of one of those who settled by the lake. Her father was the head of the community, and she had ten children. My grandmother was half Arab and half Shua. She came from a very religious family too, and had nine children. My mother is Shua. My father married her before he went to Cairo but they had children only when he came back. She had five but one died. My three elder brothers, who are living and working in Europe, are all married with children. I have one daughter and I'm still studying.' Fatima brought out some photographs from her bag and showed them to a very curious Abdullahi. 'This is my grandfather in front of his Koranic school with his pupils. Here he is in front of his huge library. He used to say, "A house without books is like a room without windows." This is my grandmother by the lake. This is my father in the White House with a former President of the USA, here he is in London with a former Prime Minister, here he is with me in Tokyo, while presenting his credentials as the new ambassador and here we are in Saudi Arabia. I'm Shua-Arab! My tribe can be found by Lake Chad although they could be anywhere now.'

'Where are your parents now?'

'They are in Maiduguri.'

'And your daughter?'

'She's with them.'

'What about your other friends?' Abdullahi asked Amina.

'Rebecca is from Zuru. Her father is a senior police officer. Gloria is from Zangon Kataf. Her father is a farmer. Bilkisu is from Azare. Her father is the Deputy Governor of the state.'

'When are you going to tell me more stories?' Abdullahi asked.

'Very soon, I'll tell you the story of Ali Baba and the Forty Thieves. Did you like the story of Baba Abdullah in The Arabian Nights?'

'Yes, I enjoyed it.'

'Did you understand the meaning of the story?'

'No.'

'Then ask you father to explain it to you,' Fatima said with a smile.

'I will. Thank you very much,' he said and ran out.

'Some time ago I had a conversation with Abdullahi,' Fatima reflected. 'Then I was just amused, but later realised its implication. We spoke about life and people generally. He told me there are good and bad people in this world. The rich are good, the poor are bad. He argued that the rich are good because they feed the poor, they perform the holy pilgrimage, pray regularly, don't steal, wear good clothes and send their children to school to learn manners! According to him, the poor are bad because they always beg from the rich, or try to steal from them and don't do what the rich do. And that was how I was brought up too.'

Amina was reading the newspaper at the women's headquarters when a white Volkswagen Beetle drove up and parked. She walked out and met Fatima and an elderly man who had just alighted from the car. Fatima smiled as they approached Amina. 'I'd like to introduce you to Mallama Amina Haruna,' she said, as if presenting the president of a country to a visiting leader. With that same air Amina welcomed her guest. 'Professor Idi Abdullahi, a lecturer in the university and a specialist in cooperative movements,' the professor introduced himself and humbly greeted her. He was tall, fat and simply dressed in a white short sleeved shirt and black trousers.

Amina led them inside, opened the window more widely and sat down. Still standing, the professor started to speak in a pleasant voice: 'I'm impressed by your idea of a cooperative movement. Fatima has already briefed me on the activities of the Women's Association. Actually, I've been following your activities with keen interest. A cooperative movement can be a social and economic force in society, but in our country today, the cooperative movement is regrettably very weak or non-existent. In principle it can be effective in transforming a society. What I mean is, peasants, and other jobless people can be organised to work on farms and other productive ventures and social services in equal partnership.'

'Businesses can be run as cooperatives too,' Fatima chipped in.

'You are right, but that's more complicated,' he replied, warming to his theme and speaking fast without bothering to explain some of the difficult words, ideas and terminology he was using. Fatima was jotting down notes. Amina thought the two of them understood each other well.

'I must emphasise that the role of the cooperative movement largely depends on the policies of the government. In some countries it has been used effectively to accelerate national development. In our country, it's not a secret that agriculture has been badly neglected for many years. If we want to solve our agricultural problems, cooperatives will be one of the best means. They can stop rural-urban migration and so many other social, political and economic problems.'

Amina lost interest as she found a lot of what he was saying irrelevant. She just wanted him to tell her straight whether it would work or not. Professor Abdullahi was paying no attention to whether or not she understood him.

'Abdul Nasser, the former President of Egypt, pointed out that the weakness of the co-operative concept is the existence of an exploitative class in the countryside, which will always work to prevent drastic and fundamental change. I have to warn you, your cooperative movement might encounter problems like this,' he said, looking directly at Fatima. 'A cooperative movement can solve many problems. Marginalised peasants and the lumpen proletariat can be organised, or they can organise themselves into cooperatives. This will not only draw them away from political banditry and hooliganism but will help them economically, and as the cooperatives grow, their members too will mature and ...'

'Our cooperative movement plans to involve only women,' Amina cut in.

'In that case,' he said after an apology, 'your major problem will be in the area of mobilisation. Where will you get the land on which to start?'

'I have some,' Amina answered.

'Where will you get the seedlings, farm implements, machinery and other equipment?'

'I've met members of the workers union in the Ministry of Agriculture and they've promised us equipment and technical assistance,' replied Fatima.

'I see ...' he said, impressed.

'What do you mean?' Amina questioned Fatima.

'That is, they'll cultivate the land free of charge, supply us with the necessary seedlings, technicians, drivers ... at least for a year. As from next year, we have agreed either to hire the equipment or buy everything at subsidised rates,' Fatima explained.

'Have you developed a plan for how your cooperative will organise itself?'

'I'm working on that right now,' answered Amina.

'Then what are you waiting for?' he asked loudly.

'Expert advice and then registration,' Fatima calmly replied.

'Well, I'll be happy to assist you with the former,' he assured them, picking up his bag. He bade them farewell and left.

As soon as his car had glided away, Amina laughed. 'There's nothing like expert advice. He confused rather than educated me. It was lucky you were around. I would have sent him back! Are all experts like him?'

'He's comparatively good. At least he appreciated your efforts, agreed to see us and made some useful statements. Most of these lecturers know virtually nothing, they just learn books by heart and recite them at lectures like parrots.

Outside work, some drown their intelligence in alcohol and chase girls up and down like dogs; the only difference is that dogs have seasons and they don't,' commented Fatima.

Amina laughed and moments later they returned to the topic of the cooperative. 'I think I've spotted an opportunity here.'

'Great. There are so many opportunities in this country. I'm listening.'

'All women can cook.'

'Right.'

'At the moment they are hugely underemployed.'

'Also correct.'

'We can tap into this resource.'

'How?' asked Fatima, who was now excited and curious.

'Some women just cook for themselves. What I've got in mind is a business enterprise that will create jobs that will eventually give women dignity.'

'I don't understand.'

'What I intend to do is get a group of women to collect ingredients for say bread, yoghurt, *fura,* (balls of cooked flour), *masa,* (a small round cake of flour) and other food. They can prepare the food at home and give the cooperative the finished product. They'll be paid for these services, of course. Then we get another group to pack and sell the food and they'll be paid for doing that.' Amina paused for a while, unsure of what to say. 'I've been thinking of how we should continue when you and your friends are no longer around. Soon you'll complete your studies and go, but I'll still be here. I'm thinking of ways we can build on what we have achieved so far. I want to involve the women in business. My fear is that if we don't make our own money, we'll end up as a charity, spending all our time begging for money.'

'Yes, I agree with you.'

'I want this cooperative to be independent. I want a business-oriented cooperative which will provide services and goods for profit. If we don't make money, the cooperative can't run. This is what I'll be working towards over the next few years. If we succeed with one food, I'll try another. If we succeed in one district, I'll try again in another. Take schools for example; I intend to open a kiosk in every school in the town by the end of next year to provide healthy food for our pupils. All profits can be reinvested in the whole project.

There are also many women who have a good knowledge of local traditional medicines and how roots, leaves, flowers and tree bark can be used. I want to harness their potential and get them to produce medicines jointly and sell them to the co-operative. They will be paid of course … Larai is talking to them at the moment. These women will earn money that their families desperately need. I've not thought about how to get the money to start but I'll find it.'

'Please Amina, whatever the temptation; do not accept any money from the state, Bature or any other members of the ruling class. Their wealth is ill gotten and bad money corrupts good ideas. Their money will hinder your development.'

'But you once told me that it was permissible to turn *haram* into *halal*.'

'Yes I did,' Fatima said with a smile. 'However, I suggest you borrow the money from a bank. This will mean strict financial discipline is required. We have to prove to ourselves and to others that we are capable of running a business. And please don't forget to involve girls like Larai in all the negotiations and deals. You must think of the next generation.'

'Of course! Larai and I discussed this a few days ago and she's very excited. She's already talking to women in the district about it and wants to do a trial project here. Larai and a secondary schoolteacher called Binta are also compiling books of poems and short stories written by women in the district. They are organising a week-long storytelling festival. This is entirely their idea. She wants to talk to Muktar about the possibility of publishing the poems and stories.'

'That's great.'

'Do you know Hadija?'

'No. Who is she?'

'She's a post-graduate student in nutrition from Bakaro. She was here a few days ago with a lot of ideas on how to improve our diet using only local produce. She wants to try them out with us here. She'll be working with Mairo.'

There was not a single cloud in the sky as the two women started walking back to the house. When Amina raised her head, a reflection from one of the zinc-roofed houses shone so fiercely that she had to close her eyes for a few seconds. It was the hottest time of year, very few people were on the streets and those who were had taken refuge under the trees. Sharing the shade, waiting for the sun to set, were goats and sheep, and a few cocks and hens standing motionless, their beaks hanging open and their eyelids drawn down.

'The heat is becoming unbearable again,' Amina said, as they walked quietly and slowly. They met Rebecca near the compound. She was wearing a light blue short-sleeved shirt with its collar raised, a denim skirt and leather sandals. She smiled and greeted Amina. 'I've just come from the Ministry of Health. Some health officials have agreed to carry out a vaccination campaign next Saturday morning, but it's not free.'

'How much will it cost us?'

'Not that much. Anyway, we've already paid for it.'

'That's very kind of you. Where did you get the money?'

'It isn't that much, it was subsidised.'

'What is the vaccination against? Fatima asked.

'But you were there at the meeting,' Rebecca said. 'You took part in the discussion and now you're asking.'

'I'm sorry,' Fatima apologised.

'Against what?' Amina inquired.

'Cerebrospinal meningitis.'

'That's timely,' Amina reflected in a low voice.

Amina did not know what to do about the strained relationship between Fatima and Rebecca. She wanted to reconcile them. As she approached Rebecca she heard her say, 'Goodbye, I'll see you on Saturday morning.'

'Goodbye and thank you,' Amina replied.

# 14

Amina now lived a regimented life like a soldier preparing for battle. She woke up in the morning, bathed herself and her son, cleaned her room and walked to the headquarters where she either listened to the radio, read books and newspapers or held meetings. In the evenings, she walked to the school and observed the classes. It was demanding yet she was determined to maintain her "can do" spirit. She knew this tense programme would relax as soon as more teachers and more women actively took part. She was also convinced that it was part of the price she had to pay for the success of the Bakaro Women's Association.

As she became more involved, she found herself dealing with many aspects of the women's lives. One Thursday evening, she had just arrived home, tired from school, when Larai walked in crying. Her daughter had been hospitalised about a week before with an undiagnosed illness. Weeping, Larai managed to say: 'My daughter is dead. She died a little while ago in the hospital.' Amina tried to console her and to help with the practical arrangements.

On Saturday morning, as Amina stepped out of the house, she could see a crowd of women and children in front of her house. It was a sight she loved. She was greeted warmly as she made her way to where Rebecca and five medical officers were waiting. Rebecca suggested that Amina should address the crowd. Reluctantly, Amina spoke briefly about the need to combat meningitis, not just in Bakaro but also throughout the state. She also thanked the Support Group for their tremendous help and assistance. A Medical Officer spoke extensively on the best measures to be taken at home to avoid the spread of the disease. While he was speaking, Bilkisu drove her car slowly towards the crowd and parked nearby. Fatima and Muktar emerged from the car. Amina's heart leapt. She did not listen to the speech, instead she stole glances at Muktar in his white kaftan. She noticed he had grown a beard.

Amina had never liked needles but now she had to have her vaccination and courageously too, without showing signs of fear or pain. Just as she was about to be vaccinated, Muktar approached and urged the officials to wait for him. He adjusted his camera and told them to go ahead. He clicked the camera several times. After Amina had been vaccinated, the women formed a queue and one after the other had their vaccinations. She joined the students and Muktar stepped towards her. They stood silently for a few moments, without moving. He looked at the crowd while she bowed her head. When she raised it she asked, 'How's life with you?'

'I'm fine and working as you can see.'

'Is Rebecca taking good care of you?'

'Aaah! Well, you see, she's just a friend. Yes. She's doing her best,' he managed to answer. 'How's your husband?'

'He's fine. He lives in the Legislators' Estate.'

'How are you coping with the women? Difficult?'

'Of course not.'

'That's good. I'd like to interview you for our newspaper ... now.'

'No, not now and maybe never.'

'Why?'

'I can't cope with it.'

There was a moment of silence. Amina looked up at him shyly.

'Muktar, why don't you shave off your beard? It doesn't suit you.'

'I will, as soon as I get home,' a surprised Muktar promised.

'And tell Danbaki to get rid of his too!'

'Ha ha. I'll tell him you said so, but I know he won't.'

'Why not?'

'He loves his beard more than Fatima.'

They laughed and joined the others.

'This loan is unacceptable. Nigeria is not for sale,' she heard Muktar say as the discussion continued. 'We must apply pressure on them, we must not allow them sell us into modern slavery.'

Fatima walked up to Amina and explained what was going on. 'The Federal Government, under these wayward and aimless rulers of ours, wants to borrow more money from the International Monetary Fund and we are opposed to it ...'

Mairo interrupted and pointed to a group of boys. 'Some women are not allowing men and boys to be vaccinated.'

'Get everybody vaccinated. Boys and men too,' Amina ordered.

By noon the campaign was over. While Muktar strode towards Bilkisu's car, Rebecca walked over smiling. Amina expressed her gratitude for the organisation of the vaccinations and Rebecca reassured her that the students would do all they could to see Amina succeed. 'We've just arranged to pay another visit next Saturday to vaccinate those who've not yet been done,' Rebecca said running towards the car.

'Muazu Danlami has filled in the Cooperative Movement forms while Professor Idi Abdullahi signed the guarantor form. That means your Cooperative Movement has been officially registered,' Fatima confirmed. 'Muazu spoke to some agricultural students who've agreed to offer assistance.'

'Thanks. I didn't know students could be so helpful.'

'Some can be. The main problem is they lack positive initiatives and those with ideas have no way of realising them. As soon as something is started they can be mobilised.'

'How are things between you and Rebecca?'

'Fine! Muktar was at the university last night and we settled the whole matter. I think she simply overreacted. She feels insecure, and doesn't want anybody close to Muktar. She's so madly in love with him that she's lost her grip on reality. It's been so serious of late that even when someone just mentions the name Muktar she trembles. Everything stops for her—she can't concentrate, she can't do anything!'

'And Gloria?'

'Hmm! Gloria is having some problems with Danladi. She wants to marry him but his parents are laying down the law–they want her to change her faith, because she's a Christian.'

'Is she prepared to do that?'

'She loves him so much that she'd do anything for him but her parents are against her converting, although they're not against her marrying a Muslim.'

'The whole thing is so complicated.'

'Yes! I think his parents are being unrealistic. They forget that there is no requirement to convert in Islam.'

'How about Rebecca and Muktar.'

'Yes! Another case of a mixed religious relationship. His parents are not against the relationship, actually they like her very much. But her parents are against the idea of her marrying a Muslim. His parents are so understanding that they have tried not to let the religious differences affect their relationship with her. Rebecca and his mother are extremely close and get on well. Rebecca's in real trouble now because her parents have thrown her out as she insisted on continuing her relationship with Muktar. Muktar on the other hand is not ready for marriage yet. I know that Muktar doesn't love her. I think the main problem is that Rebecca is not a match for Muktar.'

'What about Bilkisu?'

'Lucky girl! Her fiancé has just been promoted and they are getting married soon.'

'How about you and Danbaki?'

'We love each other, and his parents, whom I met recently are not against our relationship. My parents can't decide for me any longer. I'm liberated!' Fatima boasted. 'We've been talking about marriage too. We may actually tie the knot as early as next month.'

'Hey, that's good news. Where are you going to get married?

'At my parents' house in Maiduguri. Then we'll go to Lokoja to meet his relatives.'

'I'm really looking forward to it and I wish you a happy married life.'

'Thank you very much.'

Alhaji Haruna's voice rang out. He entered with Rasheed who had the marks of dried tears on his cheeks. 'I haven't been vaccinated yet,' he jokingly commented.

'There'll be another campaign next week,' Fatima said.

'I'm very healthy.'

'Rich people get diseases too, you know.'

'What are they?'

'I'm sure you know.'

# 15

The sun had disappeared from the horizon when Amina set out on foot with Hauwa to visit Kulu, whom she had heard was sick. It was the prayer hour and the streets were deserted, with only an occasional light flickering here and there. They walked at a leisurely pace through the narrow streets, which gradually opened on to broader ones. The close-packed houses gave way to imposing houses in large walled grounds tended as carefully as parks. Amina tried to imagine the splendour and magnificence of their interiors. Even the air smelt of riches and elegance.

Kulu lived with her husband in one of these houses, an imposing duplex building, with a wrought-iron fence covered in creepers. As Amina approached the gate, the quiet was disrupted by two fierce-looking Alsatian dogs, which raced towards it barking noisily. A floodlight blinded Amina and Hauwa, who were forced to cover their eyes. As the dogs continued to bark and hurl themselves against the gate, Kulu's voice came through a loudspeaker attached to it: 'Please wait, I'm on my way.'

Minutes later, they heard the sound of keys jingling in the dark, a door creaked and to their relief Kulu appeared. Wearing a long blue silk nightgown, she walked slowly towards them, holding a torch. She opened the gate and invited them in but Amina asked her to chain the dogs up first.

'Why, are you afraid?' Kulu asked.

'I can trust human beings but not beasts.'

'Do you think I'd expose you to danger in my house?'

'We'll come tomorrow afternoon then, when the guards are on duty. Goodnight,' Amina said calmly, not willing to share the path with the dogs.

Kulu reluctantly chained the dogs up. They had stopped barking and were now wagging their tails. As soon as her guests had stepped inside, Kulu re-locked the gate, explaining, 'There are too many thieves in this area. If you're not careful, before you can blink, someone will sneak in.' The dogs barked occasionally as people walked past. Suddenly Hauwa shouted and ran forward without her wrapper. One of the dogs had leapt forward and pulled it off her waist. Kulu removed it from the dog's wide mouth and threw it to Hauwa saying, 'He was only playing with you.' They walked silently on a well-lit cemented pavement with flowers on the edges. As they approached the second gate, Kulu asked, 'Why didn't you come by car?'

'I felt like walking. Why?'

'I would've opened the gates electronically and the car could have parked here,' Kulu explained.

'Sorry, I didn't know,' Amina apologised.

After the second gate, which as before she locked immediately, Kulu opened a sliding door and locked it after they had stepped into the room. They removed their sandals and sat on a settee.

The living room was spacious, airy and well decorated with expensive furniture and paintings. Ten single chairs, five on each side, faced each other. Opposite them were a generously-sized armchair, a small glass table and a heavy free-standing gold ashtray. The air was chill from the two air conditioners, while the floor was covered with colourful carpets. Hanging on the walls were enlarged photographs of past and present Heads of State and a large painting of Alhaji Ibrahim in a polo outfit on horseback, holding a gold cup. A medium-sized framed photograph of a group of students wearing white kaftans and white caps also hung there, with "Bakaro Old Boys Association" boldly printed below it.

Kulu pressed a remote button to call the housemaid.

'How're you feeling now?' Amina asked.

'Better. A few days ago my health really deteriorated. That's why I've been praying hard recently.' She pointed to an open copy of the Holy Koran on a video recorder. 'I pray to God to give me a long life to enjoy the wealth He has given me.'

'What did your doctor say?'

'He said nothing, only advised me to have a long rest.' She whispered to Amina, 'I'm afraid I have hypertension. May God forgive me since He's the only one who knows everything.'

'How's your husband?' Amina asked.

'Fine but very busy. Local government elections are coming up soon and he must campaign hard for the ruling party. He intends to contest for a senatorial seat in the next general election.'

The door opposite them opened to admit Alhaji Ibrahim accompanied by an old man. Alhaji Ibrahim was slim and of average height, wearing an immaculate white gown and a red cap. As he sank into a comfortable chair, the old man sat on the floor beside him. Alhaji Ibrahim placed his prayer beads on the glass table and lit a cigarette while the old man chewed a piece of kola nut.

Amina did not want to be the first to greet Alhaji Ibrahim. In a recent radio interview, he had openly accused her of anti-government activities and vowed to sabotage the women's association.

There was silence in the room. The only sound was the gentle chiming of a clock on the wall. 'You're welcome,' he said finally after puffing on his cigarette.

'We came to greet your sick wife,' Amina said.

'She's not really sick. All the same, thanks for coming … Ah ... erm ... how's your association?' he asked.

'It's fine.'

'I'd like to see you when you have time in my office. We've some bags of rice for voluntary organisations. Come and collect your share.' He crushed his cigarette butt in the ashtray. 'After collecting the rice, I'll want you to fix a date for me to address the women. I'd prefer to speak to them while presenting the bags ...'

'Why?' Amina asked in surprise.

'I'd like to address them on their civic rights and duties, on the advantages of Western democracy, and educate them on how to vote in the coming local government elections.'

'Can a woman contest for the elections?' Amina questioned.

'According to the constitution women can, but in practice, it has never happened here. And it's not likely that it'll happen here, during this and forthcoming elections. Anyway, the ruling party has no vacant seats.' He smiled. 'Women will have to wait their turn!' He nodded several times.

The telephone rang, and Alhaji Ibrahim answered it in a mechanical and unnatural voice.

'God Almighty is Great! *Allahu Akbar*!' he said loudly after a lengthy discussion. 'The Emir's car has finally arrived.'

'Who was that on the phone?' Kulu asked.

'The Secretary to the State Government.'

'What model is the Emir's car?'

'A specially designed limousine from General Motors in America.'

'How many cars has he got?' Kulu asked further.

'Ten,' he said and coughed slightly.

Alhaji Ibrahim became excited and talked more freely. 'Amina, I'd like you to see my own car which arrived a week ago. I threw it in when I went to place an order for the Emir's official car. It's a Mercedes convertible and very comfortable, but regrettably, our roads are too bad. However, it's an extra car and since I'll hardly use it, I think it'll last for a few years. I'm not like my wife who changes cars like her underwear. Ah! Women are never satisfied. Do you know that if Kulu bought a car and a brassiere today, she'd change the car before the bra?' He laughed loudly, lit another cigarette and asked, 'Amina, couldn't you tell your husband to buy you a car instead of being driven around?'

'She came on foot,' Kulu said to her husband.

He laughed incredulously, and suggested that Amina register at the Golf Club and exercise there.

'I'm too busy with the women,' she replied.

'Amina,' he said solemnly, 'I've been following your activities closely and my advice, in all sincerity, is that you should have a rethink. I'm honestly not impressed with what you're doing with the women, but since you're not my wife I can't control or dictate to you.'

'Alhaji, thanks for your advice but I know what I'm doing and I suggest you leave me alone,' she replied.

'I can't leave you alone, partly because your activities affect my position as the Local Government Secretary and partly because I'm a Muslim.' He paused. This statement made Amina uneasy, especially when the old man smiled and nodded. Alhaji Ibrahim continued, 'Our religion, Islam, means total submission. We all have to be submissive to the will of Almighty Allah. The Women's Association is not well received by our religious leaders. Although I've done my best to explain to them that we're in a democratic country, your activity is still regarded as errant behaviour.

'Look Amina, you're married to a very wealthy man. Why not settle down and enjoy what he has to offer? Bothering yourself about poor women will lead you nowhere. There's nothing you can do to change their lives. That's how it has always been, and that's how it will remain. In our society we live the life presented to us by Almighty Allah! You should not take the initiative or attempt to make changes. Only Almighty Allah has the power to make changes. He knows what is best for us. The only thing,' he emphasised, 'you can do, is to pray for Allah's help and guidance.'

The old man sitting by Alhaji Ibrahim's side nodded approvingly, and Kulu got up and invited the women to move into her room. She slotted in a videotape, switched on the air conditioner and said, 'I presume you've not been here since the interior decorators changed the furniture.'

'Where are all these things from?'

'The window blinds are from France, the carpets from Morocco, the water-bed from America, the paintings from Italy and all the electronic gadgets from Japan.'

Kulu left Amina and Hauwa in the room, and soon after, a teenage housemaid entered with a tray containing two covered plates, glasses, a mug of water and spoons. She placed it on a small table and greeted Amina. As she stood up to go, Amina stopped her. 'What happened to you here?' she asked pointing to a fresh wound on her neck. The girl was afraid to answer, but Amina assured her that Kulu would not know about their conversation. Eventually she spoke, her eyes darting towards the door every few seconds.

'Yesterday, I mistakenly ate the meat reserved for the dogs, and Kulu beat me,' she mumbled and dashed away.

Amina and Hauwa looked at each other in silence. They turned to the food and were eating when Kulu returned.

'Have you decided to go into business?' Kulu asked Amina.

'No, not yet. I enjoy my work with the women.'

'Don't waste your time. Time is money, as the Americans say. Forget about these women and go into business while it's still lucrative. Have you forgotten the saying, "Make hay while the sun shines"?'

'The Women's Association is still a baby and I want to see it grow healthy and strong.'

'You'll gain nothing from it. You're wasting your time, money and talent on people who'll never understand nor improve themselves.'

'No, it will be self-sustaining and profitable,' Amina said, though she herself was not really sure of it.

'How?'

Amina was silent for a moment, searching for an answer that would satisfy Kulu. 'Our husbands will want the women to vote for the ruling party in all elections. I think you and my husband want to build a textile factory, so the women can simply be converted into paid workers.'

'That's excellent. I didn't know you could be so sharp and enterprising!' a delighted Kulu said.

'How's your daughter?' Amina changed the topic of conversation.

'Fine. She's very intelligent.'

'Do you plan to have any more children?'

'Yes I do, but not now because I'm busy. I cannot combine pregnancy with business. I almost went bankrupt while carrying my daughter five years ago.'

Kulu started whistling a tune, shaking her head and buttocks. 'Gone were the days when girls were girls. Now they're toys and handbags. When I was at the university I danced. Even now I still dance in the club.' She danced slowly in the middle of the room.

'Tell me, does my husband also dance at the club?' asked Amina.

'My dear, you won't hear that from me. Someone else might tell you. He spends more time in the polo section of the club. Your husband is a good polo player but his horses are weak and tired.'

'There are horses in the nearby villages.'

'Poor and ignorant Amina,' Kulu said with a laugh. 'The horses for polo are imported from various overseas countries, mainly Argentina. It costs thousands of dollars to purchase and transport them. They're a special breed and need special food, must be kept in special stables with air conditioners and they need a veterinary specialist to take care of them.'

'Polo is a dangerous and expensive game and all this money they use to buy, transport and maintain horses could be used to provide schools and other amenities, or to feed and clothe hungry people,' Amina couldn't help saying.

'You've started talking politics. I'm not a politician,' Kulu said and eyed Amina in annoyance.

Soon afterwards, they left.

In the compound, Larai informed Amina that Fatima had visited in her absence as she was travelling to her home town the next day on an urgent visit. Abdulrasheed was asleep. Amina changed her clothes and lay by his side. In the dark room, different thoughts came to her. She thought about Kulu and her husband's luxurious lifestyle.

They buy different types of expensive cars, horses for thousands of dollars, take money from the state treasury when there are no drugs in the hospitals. They have expensive houses while schools are few. Kulu's husband even invited us to collect some rice. Oh! poor rich country! Why should a country like ours with all its human and natural resources be dependent on foreign rice with people reduced to mere beggars, queuing up for it? How could the Secretary of the Local Government use the money allocated to his area to buy a car for himself? How could an Emir of a town in a backward country compete with millionaires all over the world, just by owning a fleet of the most expensive cars? Soon they'll have to buy him a private jet!

How can a man like him be thought to have any virtues when he does nothing while his subjects die daily of hunger and common diseases? Yes! Something must be wrong somewhere.

# 16

Distant thunder heralded the beginning of the rainy season. Over the past months it had been excessively hot, but the rain was likely to fall very soon. Clouds hung heavy in the dry, static air. It would be the first major rain of the year. Rain was needed by the people: to cool the air and houses; to fill the wells and rivers; in short, rain was needed to give new life to the dry district. Rain meant a lot to the people. It was part of their life cycle.

The rainy season had no exact starting time. This particular year, as in the recent past, the rain was late, so the people offered special prayers to Almighty Allah. Last year, at the request of the Emir and religious leaders, the people held these prayers outside the town. The belief was that after such prayers, rain would fall immediately, but it did not fall. Two days later, a religious group suggested burial grounds should be inspected and open graves covered. There was a belief that open graves scare clouds away. It was dutifully done, but still no rain fell. On the fifth day, extreme religious groups organised a demonstration in the town, aimed mainly against prostitutes and drunkards. They went into beer parlours and hotels, beating up those inside and destroying alcoholic drinks. Prostitutes were severely beaten in their rooms. These extreme religious groups claimed that immorality, indecency and obscenity delayed the rain. Still no rain fell. The rain came exactly two weeks after the special prayers.

# Chapter 16

Amina looked at the dark clouds gathered idly in the sky and prayed. The heat and lack of rain were not the main problems worrying her. Her son was ill. She stood at the window looking out, wondering when Alhaji Haruna would come home. She had not seen him for days and now badly needed him to take her son to the clinic. She had no driver and she could not go to the Legislators' Estate without his invitation.

It was a Friday, and it dragged on slowly. Amina's apprehension and uneasiness increased when a driver told her that Alhaji Haruna had promised to call in the evening, and wanted to talk to her. The condition of Abdulrasheed deteriorated as the minutes ticked by. He had vomited up the tablets she given to him. As evening approached, thick clouds enveloped the whole district. Her son was now shaking violently. She begged a driver to take them to the Legislators' Estate but the driver claimed his car had a flat tyre. Disappointed and confused, she sat in her room trying to decide what to do. She did not want to risk going out to get a taxi to take her to the Legislators' Estate. All her hopes were now pinned on Alhaji's arrival. A strong wind was blowing, raising thick dust, closing the window noisily right in front of her. She could hear the movement of the air outside.

'How's he feeling now?' Laraba, the second wife asked.

'Still bad, if not worse,' Amina replied.

'Have you given him some medicine?'

'Yes, but he threw it up. I've been waiting for Alhaji to come so that we can go to the clinic.'

'And it's about to rain, so he might not come. He always says he's busy.'

'Oh God, please send Alhaji now,' Amina prayed.

Laraba advised her to give her son a particular tablet.

'Where's Hauwa?' Amina asked.

'I've sent her to my sister.'

'Who can I send to buy the tablets?'

'There are some boys outside.'

Amina called Ladan, a woodcutter. 'Please go to the chemist and get these tablets,' she gave him money and an empty packet. In the room, she covered her son with a blanket. Bright lightning flashed and a devastating thunder shook the whole district. Amina was frightened and recited some verses of the Holy Koran.

'Amarya, I'm back,' Ladan shouted from the gate.

'Bring it here,' she said, trying to hold her son who was vomiting again. Ladan gave her the tablets. As he turned to go Amina pleaded, 'Please hold him for me while I give him the tablets.' He took the crying child. She poured water in a cup, removed a tablet and ordered Ladan to sit down and hold her son firmly. She dropped the tablet in a teaspoon half-filled with warm water and waited for it to dissolve. Abdulrasheed jerked when she poured the bitter liquid into his mouth and cried. Between thunderclaps she heard Alhaji's voice calling Jummai. Ladan was confused and afraid. Amina assured him she would explain things to her husband.

'What's going on?' Alhaji's voice shook the room. 'What's going on in my house?'

Amina continued giving the medicine to her son. Abdulrasheed had reluctantly swallowed the bitter liquid and was trying to vomit it up. She gave him warm water, which he drank quickly. She stood up. 'Abdulrasheed is ill and I'm giving him some medicine.'

'What's this boy doing here, soiling my bed?' Alhaji Haruna angrily shouted pointing to Ladan.

'He bought the tablets for me and I asked him to hold my son while I gave him the medicine. I can't do both. Rasheed was crying and jerking,' she explained and took Abdulrasheed from Ladan. Ladan quickly stood up and tried to go but Alhaji Haruna stopped him.

'Why did you enter a married woman's room without her husband's permission?' he asked Ladan.

'She said I should help her and I did,' he said fearfully.

## Chapter 16

'You're a liar!' Alhaji roared.

'It's true,' Amina said, trying to comfort Abdulrasheed.

'God Almighty is my witness. Honestly I was only trying to help ...' A slap on his cheek silenced Ladan. He staggered backwards.

'*Wallahi Tallahi*, I was only helping her,' he managed to say.

'Keep quiet,' Alhaji said cruelly, his eyes gleaming. 'You people use God's name to cover up your dirty dealings.' He turned to Amina and said scornfully, 'I've heard of your flirtatious dealings, now I've caught you red handed.'

'Alhaji, *Wallahi Tallahi* ...' Ladan pleaded but a powerful blow caught him on his chest. He lost balance and fell, groaning and begging. When Alhaji kicked him severely several times, Amina knew his anger would turn on her next. She tried to order her heart to stop its wild beating and rest quietly under her trembling breast as she carefully put her son to bed.

'Alhaji, please understand, Hauwa wasn't around, Rasheed is seriously sick, I was confused, all I needed was help, so I asked him to help me. In the name of Allah and the Holy Prophet ...'

'Shut up,' he thundered. His lips twitched with fury: 'I can't understand this.' He slapped her. She saw Ladan run out though the door as she started to cry. Alhaji Haruna slapped her again. She dodged the third slap. His muscles were taut. He used the other hand to slap her. She covered her face and wept. A blow caught her in the stomach. She bent down, staggered backwards. Two blows landed on her head within seconds. He was using both hands. She fell on the floor, hitting her head on the cupboard. The rain started to fall, drumming the roof, with occasional lightning and thunder.

'You'll learn to respect your husband, the owner of the house, and our traditional values. Above all, you'll learn to respect Almighty Allah! I'm coming back soon.'

'We're totally innocent,' she sobbed, but he had gone.

She touched her head where it ached. She was aware of Abdulrasheed crying, then Talata, Laraba and Hauwa were in the room, clustering around Amina and helping her to stand up.

The rainfall increased, thunderclaps following one another continuously. Alhaji Haruna came back dripping with rain. When he saw the other women, he ordered them out of the room angrily.

'You think I paid your dowry so that you can invite men into my room to soil it?' He charged forward. 'What do you want that I've not given you? Why do you disgrace me openly? Why did you humiliate me? This is a question of honour!'

'I'm innocent and faithful ...' Amina pleaded.

'That's not true ...'

'Alhaji, your son is sick. Look ... didn't your driver tell you?'

'Keep quiet! How can I be sure he's my child?'

'Oh! My God, Alhaji, don't say that! He's yours! Please help us. Please help. He's dying!' Amina desperately pleaded.

'This is your last chance. Next time I suspect you of immoral behaviour, I'll throw you out onto the streets!'

Amina could not believe what was going on. She looked at him in horror, still crying uncontrollably.

'I'll teach you to be obedient to your husband,' he said, advancing towards her like a strong wrestler on a weaker one. 'See this whip,' he proudly showed her, 'It's specially made for unfaithful and dishonest wives.' He raised it and brought it down on her back. As Amina felt the searing pain, she screamed, pleading with him, but more lashes came with increased speed. She tried to run in an attempt to dodge the whip but could not even see where the door was. She hit the cupboard, and the tip caught her close to the left eye. She closed both eyes in terror, hit the mirror and fell. She struggled to stand up, but Alhaji Haruna caught her by the neck and the last thing Amina felt was her face being smashed against the wall.

When she came to, the room was in darkness and the door open. She could hear the violence of the rain and wind outside. Amina attempted to stand, wanting to close the door and cover her child, but her legs gave way and she slumped down again. She lay praying, 'God, please send someone to help me.' Swallowing her tears, she crawled painfully to the bed but could not climb on to it. She heard Abdulrasheed's faint cry, but could not reach him. Mother and child wept in the darkness. She crawled painfully towards the door shouting for help, but the torrential rain smothered her voice.

Amina awoke lying on the floor to the sound of Laraba shouting, 'Oh my God, he's dead! Rasheed is dead!' Amina watched in a daze as the other women in the compound trooped in. Laraba was holding the child, shouting and crying for help. Larai helped Amina to rise, and with her right eye she saw Abdulrasheed take his last breath. She slumped onto the bed sobbing in despair, as Talata carried his body out of the room.

When she awoke later, after the tablet someone had given her, Amina could not believe what had happened. She hoped it was a nightmare, but at the same time wondered bitterly where she had gone wrong, what she could have done to avert such a disaster. When the women came to console her, she covered her head and told them to go, saying, 'I'll be all right soon.' She could not understand why Alhaji had overreacted and refused to understand her situation. She prayed, 'God, free me from this life of uncertainty, worries and troubles. Take me away through merciful or merciless death. How long do I have to live, spiritless and cowed? God, why don't You send reason and understanding into people's heads, care and love into their hearts?'

There was a thick blood clot near her left eye, her lips were swollen and her eyes red, and sores all over her body. Too weak to get up, she lay in bed sobbing gently. Her head ached. She placed her head on her hands and wept without wiping the tears away. She cried because her mother and son were dead; cried because her husband had beaten her mercilessly and called her degrading names. She cried because she understood how vulnerable and insecure she was in this house. She lay mourning and moaning all night, knowing she was faithful and innocent.

For a fortnight, Amina was deep in grief and humiliation. Memories of the dreadful night were sharp and fresh. She was wild but weak. She remembered his arrogance and how he had misdirected his strength and anger on her and their son. He had succeeded in making her loyal, obedient and faithful, though. For the first time since that fateful night she smiled, albeit wryly. She looked at her late son's photograph and for the first time she did not cry. He had lived a short life, just over six months, and died in a tragic way. She recalled her prayers as Alhaji was beating her, when she had wanted to die. Rasheed had died and life continued.

Her swollen red eyes shone with tears as she walked to the window. The clouds hung low and a cold wind was blowing. Though the physical pain was becoming more bearable, the tears rolled down as she wondered how she could make herself understand his death. Why was life temporary? Why were we afraid of death? What did people gain by being wicked? Were wickedness and heartlessness part of human nature? Who was responsible for people hating, maltreating, and killing each other? God or Man?

She wiped away her tears and thought of the future. She decided not to seek a divorce, but to stay where she was. If she divorced, who would marry her? Her father had already given her away, so where would she go? She would stay where she was, and throw her whole energy into her work with the women.

As Fatima entered with a broad smile, Amina turned her swollen eyes and battered face. The astonishment on Fatima's face almost made her laugh.

'Rasheed is dead,' she said, in answer to her stunned expression.

'WHAAAT!'

'Sit down and I'll tell you ... it's a long sad story.'

Amina narrated the whole incident. Fatima was aghast. She could not believe it, even when Amina showed her scars. Her usual control gave way, and all she could blurt was 'This is barbaric and criminal!' before she started to cry.

'Don't worry,' said Amina, struggling with her own tears. 'I've now recovered physically. It's one of those things that is destined to happen. But Fatima, I'm tired of life, and ashamed of myself; ashamed of the way I'm being treated. I've tried to understand what happened, but it's impossible. Even the scars remind me of my humiliation, of how I've been despised, and brutalised. I think I'm a stranger here, in this world; I think everybody hates me, everything is against me, I distrust everybody, I mean everybody ...' she stopped and cried louder.

When she heard Amina talk like this, Fatima wiped her tears away and Amina's too. She tried to strengthen her friend and reassure her. 'It's natural to feel hatred when you're unhappy, suffering or under stress. But don't let resignation set in.'

They heard Alhaji's voice outside and they exchanged glances.

He entered, smiling, and holding a bag. Fatima stood up: 'I have to go.'

'I'm not sending you away,' Alhaji said smiling.

'I didn't say that. I've other engagements.'

'I met your father at the party conference in Lagos.'

'I know he was there.'

'Soon you'll be a lawyer.'

'Not until I've finished at law school,' Fatima said. She turned to Alhaji and looked him straight in the eye. 'I'm terribly disappointed by what you did to Amina. She is your wife, not your slave. She is a human being like you. What you did is probably the most disgraceful and humiliating thing you have ever done to her. You have a problem! Whenever a man thinks that beating his own wife is right, then that man is not brave but brutal and stupid. A wife is supposed to be loved not beaten ...'

Alhaji Haruna interrupted her 'Don't insult me in my own house.'

'I'm on my way out! I just feel I should tell you how uncivilised you are ...'

'Go away and leave me in peace,' he shouted.

Fatima left, saying to Amina: 'I'll visit you soon, Amina. Please don't think and cry too much. And accept my sincere condolences. May Almighty Allah accept Rasheed's soul.'

The sight of Alhaji Haruna horrified Amina. A sort of hatred had grown towards her husband, even though it was not her nature to hate and she tried to push negative thoughts about him aside. She tried to convince herself that what had happened was the result of destiny, to accept it as fate. At the same time, she still hoped that as time passed she'd be able to change him for the better. She could not explain to herself why she had this ambivalent attitude towards him.

Over the last few days his attitude had changed. He paid her short visits but they did not discuss their altercation in detail. He spoke mainly about his business and avoided any subject that would cause friction. Amina tried as much as possible to keep an open mind towards him, and would sit there and listen to whatever he had to say. They continued this game, waiting patiently for something to bridge the gap between them.

It was midnight and Amina was asleep. Alhaji Haruna entered, quietly closing the door behind him. If he slept with her, it would be the first time since their quarrel. Amina woke up, frightened by his image in the darkness. 'How are you feeling now?' he asked sitting on the bed.

'Fine,' she said, barely above a whisper.

Although Alhaji continued to speak, Amina hardly heard him because she was reliving events in her mind. She saw him from the corner of her eye as he lay by her side. He wasn't making any sense, he uttered only half sentences and detached words. As his body touched hers, she started to cry.

The activities of the Bakaro Women's Association went on as planned. The cooperative movement was launched in Amina's absence, with three other women also donating their unused land. The Support Group launched "Operation Consolidation," and bought classroom furniture, books and other teaching materials.

Amina was satisfied with the progress so far, but thought it would be a good idea to organise another "Keep Bakaro Clean" project, as she had noticed that the streets were getting dirtier. This time, she thought the men should be involved. The children too could be directed to hoe or mow bushy areas; and they could fill the ponds and pot-holes with sand and stones. The women would sweep their houses, compounds and the streets.

# 17

The morning sunlight burst through the window and touched Amina's sleepy face. She yawned and stretched her body. It was very early in the morning and only a few people were out and about. Bakaro itself was just waking up as Amina walked to the window and opened it wider. The wind blew in, cold and refreshing. She went into the compound, washed and had her breakfast.

Later, as she walked towards the women's headquarters, she saw that a crowd of men, women and children was responding to the call for another Operation Keep Bakaro Clean, and was excited. Gloria greeted Amina in front of the crowd with a broad smile. 'Everything is set,' said Gloria, 'Rebecca's gone to find the sanitary inspectors.'

'What's happened to you?' Amina whispered drawing Gloria closer. 'You've lost a lot of weight.'

'It's a long story,' Gloria replied. 'I'll tell you one day.'

Amina saw some students behind a table with a map of Bakaro. They were discussing where to dig secondary drainage systems and how to link them with the river. The group leader introduced himself as Nathaniel, a student in the Town Planning Faculty, and explained briefly what they were trying to do.

'Difficult task?' Amina asked.

'Of course, but interesting.'

'Who'll do the digging?' Amina asked.

'The men there,' he said pointing to a group of men with diggers, shovels and wheelbarrows.

'We're intellectuals,' a voice interjected.

They all laughed. 'I know you're intellectuals,' Amina said.

'You see, Madam,' Nathaniel started, 'we want to link these gutters together here and divert the water there.' He pointed on the map. 'But we're having some problems.'

'What are they?'

'Lack of materials. According to what we've been taught, the only option here is to dig an underground drainage system.'

'Why not let the water flow here and divert it there?' she said, running her finger on the map.

'The owner of the land refused.'

'Okay, think of the best way and good luck,' she said and walked towards Fatima who had just arrived.

'I'm impressed with the turnout,' Fatima said. 'It's a statement of solidarity with you, that you're not alone. The people believe in you and trust you, and they have demonstrated it by coming out to do whatever you tell them to. As for us, you can always count on our support! We shall always stand by you!'

'I'm pretty shocked by the turnout,' Amina admitted, 'and flattered by what you've said. Thank you very much!'

'How's Flat Nose?' Fatima asked.

'Fine. He's going to Saudi Arabia soon.'

'Has he apologised for what he did to you?' Fatima inquired.

'Well ... How should I put it? He accepted he overreacted without any justification but did not say he was sorry,' Amina managed to say, tears instantly springing to he eyes. She wiped them away.

'God!' Fatima murmured, shaking her head sadly. 'They're all the same.'

They looked at each other. Amina sighed and shook her head gently. 'Don't worry. I'll be all right. It's now in the past ... history.'

'Yes! Just take heart, don't give up.'

'Why did you launch Operation Consolidation?'

'When this thing happened to you, we felt that although Rasheed is dead, the women's association should not die.'

By evening, the cleaning exercise was over and Amina was exhausted, though all she had done was supervise the work. The men and students had dug the drainage system all day until evening. By then, the sky was finely veiled with layers of cloud, and after evening prayers, rain started to fall in heavy drops. Later a thunderstorm raged. Wind banged at the window and torrents of water shook the room. The downpour continued for hours and later reduced to showers, which fell until daybreak.

In the morning, Amina did not have time for her breakfast and hurried out. The sun was shining brightly and the morning was warm. She inspected almost all of Bakaro. Most people she met greeted her with respect and admiration. People stopped whatever they were doing to thank her, men and women showered praises on her. The roads were free from the usual puddles and potholes, streams were flowing through the gutters. Bakaro was unbelievably clean, and she allowed herself to feel proud.

Alhaji Haruna went to Saudi Arabia. Amina stayed at home and passed her days in absolute solitude. She occasionally sat outside her room but was disturbed at the sight of babies and children, and mostly she would sit alone, thinking. When it was dark, she would lie in bed and cry passionately. She found solace only in reading. Other people's experiences touched her heart deeply, reminding her that her problems were not unique and gradually relieving of her own sorrow and agony.

She visited the co-operative farm one day in the company of Larai. As they walked in between the ridges, she touched a corn stalk taller than herself. The women clearly had green fingers. Even without fertilizer, they would have a good harvest. It would be an historic and memorable day, and she prayed that God would spare her life to witness it.

They met Rebecca as they approached the compound. 'We've a surprise package for you and the women,' Rebecca announced.

'What is it?' Amina was eager to know.

'We're organising the Bakaro Health Day on Saturday.'

'That's good. What role am I to play?'

'Mobilise the women as usual. You have to work actively this time. Fatima insisted you must be involved.'

'That's fine.'

'Ah! Also, you should know that Muktar was involved in a minor accident.'

'Where's he now?'

'He's at home recovering.'

'Please give him my best wishes.'

'I'll do that,' Rebecca promised and hurried away.

On Saturday Amina, together with officials from the Ministry of Health, doctors, nurses, sanitary inspectors and Rebecca visited almost all of the houses in Bakaro. They attended to sick people and offered free medical advice. On Sunday, Amina woke up very weak and tired. She was still in bed at noon when Bilkisu and Fatima visited her. She sat up and sneezed six times. The girls laughed. 'How's Rebecca?' Amina quickly asked.

'She was still sleeping when we left,' Bilkisu answered.

'It was a great success,' Amina said in a barely audible voice. 'But it was difficult. I'm weak and tired. I walked and talked all day,' she coughed slightly twice and sneezed again.

'You'll soon break the world record in sneezing,' Bilkisu joked.

'...and your name will appear in the Guinness Book of Records,' Fatima added.

'But,' Amina exclaimed. 'It was a real experience.'

'What's wrong with your finger?' Fatima asked.

'I cut it when I was helping an old woman cut her toe nails, which she couldn't reach. It's not that deep. Don't worry. I felt so sorry for the woman. She lives alone in a hut.'

Amina went out, had her bath and changed her clothes. Later she told them how some of the women had reacted to their injections. She had barely finished her breakfast when Fatima said, 'Soon, there'll be a women's conference on the campus. We want to present a paper on the Bakaro Women's Association on your behalf. We have compiled some materials on other projects and we'd like to ask you some questions about the health project. Rebecca will be there on the day to explain the project.'

'I've no objection,' an excited Amina said.

'What lessons have you learnt from yesterday's campaign?' Fatima fired the first question.

Amina gathered herself, aware that she no longer dreaded being forced to speak in this way. 'I'll tell you the aims first,' she said after a pause. 'We visited these houses in an attempt to improve cleanliness and give immediate medical help free of charge. We visited over ninety percent of the houses and attended to men, women and children ...we were in the poorest parts where as many as one in four babies die before their first year. The doctors attribute this to factors like maternal ignorance and poor health. Drinking water is obtained from the river or wells and the water is not boiled before use. That explains why cholera and worm infections are very common.

'Most women live miserable lives and that's why they look older than they really are. I also discovered that poor housing seriously damages health, and the young ones are the most affected in these overcrowded conditions. Yesterday, we treated or heard of so many cases of children burnt by fire, boiling liquids and so on. A young doctor also said that because some families live in one room and cook there, they suffer from respiratory diseases due to poor ventilation.'

'What were the main problems you encountered?'

'The campaign started at a slower pace, because some men harassed our male doctors and medical officers and some allowed only female doctors and nurses to examine or treat their wives. As you know, there are very few female doctors. Most, I mean those on national service, are not from this state. They had difficulty in speaking to the women because of the language barrier. That explains why I've nearly lost my voice.'

'What can you say about the state of people's health?' Bilkisu pressed further.

'Basic health education is vital. A lot of preventable diseases exist but are unfortunately left untreated and therefore some minor ailments turn into serious ones. We've resolved to add more teaching hours to health education. Another disheartening thing is that simple, curable diseases like diarrhoea and dysentery become fatal, especially among children. According to medical experts, most of the women's health problems are related to stress.

'From yesterday's experience, I can say that a health care delivery system could reach the mass of people cheaply and directly but some people might lose more than their voices,' she concluded with a laugh.

'Ah! I've forgotten a point,' Amina continued. 'We've agreed to advise the government to set up a sanitary court to be made up mainly of women who would go round on a weekly basis. The local government has promised us refuse bins. We've also made tentative arrangements to re-open the district dispensary which closed down about six years ago. Two nurses have agreed to treat cases in the evenings on a shift basis. As a permanent measure we intend to use some rooms in my house as a community clinic. We'll then try to have our own doctors and nurses.'

Amina sipped her cold coffee. Fatima brought a small tape recorder and replayed the last part of Amina's interview, to confirm the quality of the recording.

Amina was surprised. 'Have you been recording the interview?' she asked.

'Yes. How was Rebecca's performance?' Fatima asked.

'Excellent. Wonderful. She worked really hard.'

'She can be good but she lacks initiative,' Fatima said.

'No, I don't agree with you,' Amina asserted. 'She performed well and you must appreciate and defend her for a job well done.'

'Rebecca was trying to explain how you ate lunch yesterday. What happened?' Bilkisu asked.

'A peasant woman fed us. The woman told me that her husband had been sick for many months and that they'd been to almost every traditional healer but he'd not recovered, and so she had resolved to pray to God. Not only that, they had no money to go to a private clinic. She said that on the eve of our campaign, she prayed hard to God to send them a helper who would treat her husband free of charge. When I told her that he'd receive treatment free of charge, she almost collapsed.

Her husband was thoroughly checked. The doctors prescribed him some drugs and I gave her some money. One doctor promised to visit him as often as possible until he recovered. I'll pay for the medicine required. After midday, she invited us for lunch. The food was not very good but I ate just to please her. It was too peppery for Rebecca.'

'Is the woman an active member of the association?' Fatima asked.

'No, she said her husband barred her from joining.'

The discussion shifted to other areas and Bilkisu disclosed that a lecturer friend from a neighbouring university was visiting her soon for about a week.

'Who's that?' Fatima inquired.

'You know her very well. Hajara from the Literature Department. She's the coordinator of the Women's Organisation at her university.'

'Then we shall continue our unfinished fight,' Fatima said. 'Last year, I was at their conference where we seriously disagreed. She could be helpful, by lecturing the women.'

Later in the evening, Kulu came and consoled Amina. She had not been in the country when Amina had lost her son.

'Why didn't your husband take you to Saudi Arabia?' Kulu asked.

'I rejected the offer. *In Sha Allah*, I'll perform Hajj when I'm in a better state of mind.'

'Amina, you're silly. It would have given you the opportunity to buy many valuable things. In case you don't know, Almighty Allah has blessed the Saudis with great wealth, and jewellery is very cheap there. You can buy and resell here and make a fantastic profit.'

'But he promised to buy me some things.'

'What if he forgets? You know men. He has plenty of money; he's swimming in it. Why not help him spend it?' Amina did not respond. 'I'll be going to Saudi Arabia soon and this time, I'll take you with me. I'm taking some other women as well. We'll work out how much jewellery you'll carry for me and your share of the profit.'

Amina was no longer surprised at her forthright reactions and ability to stand up to Kulu. 'I think we should get something straight,' she said equably. 'I'll go to the Holy Land when I satisfy the strict religious tests and for religious purposes only. I am not going there on business or as a carrier of goods for you! If and when I go to Saudi Arabia, it will be to perform the pilgrimage only.'

Amina remembered the medicine man in Dimbi village that they had visited to get some beads in order to win Alhaji Haruna. 'Let me test the efficacy of this man,' she said to herself, looking round to make sure her gold watch was not visible.

'I've lost my watch,' Amina told Kulu.

'Let's visit the medicine man,' Kulu promptly suggested. 'Not only because of the watch but to give you new medicine so you can gain control of Alhaji Haruna when he comes back.'

'Is this your new car?' Amina asked outside the compound.

'Yes, brand new,' Kulu said proudly.

'It's very comfortable,' Amina said sitting in it.

'That's why I like it,' Kulu replied, putting on her seat belt.

She started the engine and zoomed off.

'Where's the Mercedes Benz?' asked Amina.

'I've parked it for good.'

'Why do you like changing cars all the time?'

'It's my hobby.'

The drive continued in silence. The car crossed a wooden bridge and slid on muddy ground to the man's house. He was short and slender with sunken eyes. He welcomed them cordially.

'Your friend Kulu trusts me,' he told Amina. 'She's been my client for over five years. I know why you're here: you've had a bitter disagreement with your husband and have lost an expensive item. You're an honest and careful woman but there are people who want to make you unhappy.'

Kulu confirmed his assumptions. Amina was afraid initially, but in the process of performing his miracles he said it was true the watch was stolen.'Tell me,' asked the man, 'apart from Alhaji, does any other man enter your room?'

'No.'

'But wait,' he said and muttered inaudible words as he twisted his chain of multicoloured cowries. 'Yes! Now it's clear! It's a woman, the third wife. She's jealous because Alhaji visits you regularly.'

As he talked, Amina felt like laughing. She remained silent, marvelling at all the lies as he continued, 'Who else has admired your watch?'

'A seamstress called Stella.'

'Then she's the one.'

'But she's never entered my room,' Amina countered.

'Then it's the third wife. Go back and tell her that I, Alhaji Hadi, have told you that she stole your watch. I'm known all over the North for my accuracy.' He turned to Kulu, 'I've seen that your husband still chases those schoolgirls. Add this substance,' he said handing her something wrapped in paper, 'to his food twice and he'll forget them and love you.'

Kulu opened her bag and gave him some naira notes.

'See you soon and please drive carefully,' he advised as they left.

'I want to inform my retailers that my goods have arrived,' Kulu said, driving towards the central market.

She parked in front of the market and got out. Left to herself, Amina laughed. She recalled Fatima describing fortune-tellers who sold charmed beads, perfumes and magical concoctions while offering fake advice as charlatans. She wondered why people consulted them when they played on fear, superstitition and ignorance.

Kulu got back in the car. A beggar with a stick walked up to Amina, who wanted to give him some money but Kulu drove away.

'Our Queen, let me tell you something,' Kulu broke the silence as she drove through the narrow streets towards Bakaro. 'Soon you'll be in business in our textile factory. Try as much as possible to make a profit. As far as I can see, you get nothing from these women. You're too young and too beautiful to carry their burdens on your shoulders. Look how people are enjoying themselves. You must never deny yourself the pleasures of life. You see, you have to be somebody. You must take your proper place in society.

'Do you know that some customs officials duped me in Kano? I always bribe them whenever I go to clear my goods but recently they demanded a higher bribe and I refused. When I went for my goods they ripped me off, and even their boss defended them. I didn't expect those dirty boys to treat me like this. I know when you're in business you'll try to show some human feelings. Don't! If any feeling comes, hide it the way you'd hide your gold watch from thieves. Either you're the robber or the robbed—simple. As I advised you earlier, strive for money. If you have to be ruthless, do it and offer prayers to God. He'll forgive you.

'You're married to a very rich man. Do you know how Alhaji got the land you've now given to the women? He chased the peasants away. There are thousands of young and beautiful women who are not as fortunate as you. You're lucky to have a ready-made wealthy man. What if he divorces you, what will you do? What will you have to show for it apart from your worn-out clothes? You must think of your future!

'If my husband says it's all over, fine. I can survive on my own. I've got a solid foundation. A rich woman can live alone and be happy; she'll be respected and worshipped. The battle ahead will be fierce. The new civilian government is breeding millionaires overnight. There are too many vultures for the meat. The earlier you grab yours, the better!'

Amina remained silent, and Kulu parked in front of the compound. A group of praise-singers sang a new song, but Amina ignored them. 'Parasites!' she said to herself, as she entered the compound. She thought that people would remain backward, dependent and poor as long as able-bodied men like them did nothing but loiter around telling lies.' Amarya, who was the lady fighting with Fatima yesterday?' Abdullahi asked Amina later in the day.

'They were not fighting; they were discussing something.'

'They spoke loudly.'

'But you know your wife likes talking. Who do you like then among my friends?'

'Gloria, but please don't tell her.'

'Why do you like her?'

'She's quiet, she hardly talks.'

'Okay, I'll tell her to wait for you.

'No.'

'When you grow up, I'll look for a very beautiful, well behaved girl for you.'

'Who doesn't talk too much.'

'Agreed!'

Abdullahi left with his new bicycle. Amina got ready and went to the headquarters where Hajara was to speak. The women had gathered already but the students had not arrived yet. Some of the women talked in groups, and one group, headed by Larai, danced.

'I have a short song,' Larai said, standing in the centre of the crowd. 'It's called "Poor Peasant."' She sang and some girls joined in the chorus.

"The peasant starves

No one feeds her

The peasant drowns

No one saves her

The peasant suffers

No one cares

The peasant cries

No one looks

The peasant groans

No one helps

The peasant dies

No one mourns

Oh! Poor peasant!"

The students finally arrived. They all settled down and without introduction Hajara started her speech on "Culture and Society." She was a short, slender woman with a tribal mark on her left cheek. She spoke slowly, unlike during her argument with Fatima.

'Many years ago, our poems, songs and music reflected the daily lives and experiences of the people who composed them. Although there are still musicians who don't sing praise songs, they're not promoted and supported and are dying quietly ... the system of greed and hero-worship has changed everything but our skin colour.

'How can our traditional rulers be "custodians of culture?" What's traditional apart from their imported regalia? They are liars! They want us to see the future through the eyes of the past. They ride in limousines, play polo and golf, seize the land of the people, tax the people heavily, sell the best land to foreigners, and follow no traditions. Yet they are called traditional rulers. I'm sure they don't even know anything about their histories and traditions. Illiterates!

'It's also wrong to call them leaders. People are said to be leaders if they have vision. These ones are blind. Although they enjoy the results of modern science and technology, they deliberately promote a culture of ignorance. They watch with unbelievable joy and satisfaction as their own people decay and slide into darkness and obscurity.

'My dear women, don't let them fool you! In other parts of the world traditional leaders encourage and support development in their societies, they try to satisfy the needs of their subjects, they encourage people to modernise their societies, they help their people by building schools and other educational institutions. Our so-called traditional rulers do the opposite. They refuse to let education flourish, trying desperately to hold us down with primitive laws and customs.

'WOMEN are the true custodians of culture, not these cheats who claim to be traditional rulers. We give birth to babies, bring them up and transmit knowledge and morals.

In this way, we ensure the continuance of our society and traditions. Thank you!' Hajara concluded.

Bilkisu thanked her for speaking. Fatima too was visibly anxious to speak, and Bilkisu tried but failed to stop her. Fatima stood up: 'There is a saying that, "You get whatever you deserve." We get these types of crooked rulers because we're very good at accepting and celebrating these terribly backward ideas and cultures. We're not sincerely and genuinely interested in creating and promoting healthy changes. If we were we should have been able to think positively and act accordingly. There is power in knowledge. All societies that developed had to think, work and produce something. We cannot develop when our life is organised around sleeping and praying only, when we're always waiting for miracles to happen. If we want to develop we must look critically at our decadent cultures. I'm not saying everything is bad! A culture that promotes idleness, ignorance and indolence is not a culture of the future. A culture that is blind, deaf and dumb to the wishes and aspirations of its people is not a popular culture. We must make our culture receptive to changes, or else we're doomed!'

Although Bilkisu had tried to avoid a debate between Fatima and Hajara, both continued to argue until they left.

# 18

Weeks later, Alhaji Haruna entered Amina's room one afternoon with a broad smile. 'I'm tired. The proceedings in the Assembly were hectic. We discussed the supplementary budget.' Amina did not answer. 'I'd like to build a new warehouse.'

'Why another warehouse?'

'I want to import rice, vegetable oil, salt and fertilizer. They're very profitable.'

'You can establish farms and employ more people to grow rice, or you can establish a fertilizer factory.'

'It might be ten years before I made a profit, maybe more. Everybody imports. If one grows local rice it won't sell,' he complained. 'I heard you spoke at the university.'

'Yes, I did.'

'Was it a religious meeting?'

'No. The Bakaro Students' Union invited me to speak about our association.'

'How do the students get the money they waste on the association?'

'Each student from Bakaro contributes a certain amount to our association, and the Students' Union also gives us materials.'

'Did you mention my name and my contributions?'

'No, because everybody knows them already.'

'You could have reminded them, to make me popular and improve my future political prospects. You know I'm planning to contest for a senatorial seat in the next elections.'

'The lecture was on the women of Bakaro.'

Alhaji Haruna was anxious to leave. 'My business partner has arrived from the United States,' he announced. 'He's in Kulu's hotel. I must see him today.'

Several groups of women were sitting on the veranda in the headquarters when Amina joined them. She noticed pots of different sizes and shapes lying in the sun. Some women were knitting underneath a tree while others were plaiting hair. She went into one of the rooms that served as the co-operative shop, where Larai was explaining to a group of school children how she ran the shop.

'We buy products from the women, pay them and sell the items. The profit made is put in the bank so that we can buy more products. In the near future, we'll buy goods directly from producers and sell them cheaply.'

Amina smiled with satisfaction. Every minute she felt more certain that she was living an active and upright life. She was impressed with the activities and initiatives of the women. She went into the office and concentrated on reading for about an hour. Eventually she was disturbed by Alhaji Haruna and a white man, who came into the office. 'This is Mr Tom Whitehead, my partner from the US,' said Alhaji Haruna. The man stretched out his hand and shook Amina's. Tall and lanky with short, well-trimmed hair, he wore a dark suit with a bow tie and was carrying a black briefcase. After introducing Amina, Alhaji added, 'I hope she'll manage the textile factory and supply the female labour. I'll supply the land, local materials and funds, while you supply the foreign capital, equipment and specialists.' Alhaji Haruna took his leave and went to speak to the women.

'Can I sit down?' Mr Whitehead asked.

'Please do,' Amina said and sat down too.

'I'm impressed with your efforts in organising the women.'

'It's just an experiment.'

'I like having business dealings with Nigerians. Your husband is very cooperative. I have business concerns in many African countries.'

'What sort of businesses?'

'I deal in anything. I've just come from Ghana where I bought some state hotels. Also, I'm working on a space programme for the Accra government. I supply natural water to the President of Kenya and arms to almost all African countries. Zaire, Sierra Leone and Liberia are the top three countries. I export diamonds and other mineral resources to Europe and America. Depending on where I am, the business is different. I also arrange for loans from Western financial institutions and sometimes arrange for aid. So, you see I'm an all-rounder.'

'That's interesting.'

'Yeah! Equally interesting is the book you're reading.'

'Yes. It's educational; an eye-opener!' she replied.

'Mrs Haruna, Europe didn't underdevelop Africa as the title of this book seems to imply. Rather Europe developed and is developing Africa. Europeans brought civilization and Christianity, they built, for you folks, roads, harbours, bridges, railways and so on which you never had before.' As he continued to buttress his position, Amina felt the urge to reply. When he paused she said in a shaky voice:

'It is clear that Europe underdeveloped Africa. Western European countries robbed and exploited Africa from the beginning. Slavery has never been a good thing for those affected!'

Mr Whitehead jerked back in surprise and blinked. She continued, 'The colonialists built this infrastructure you mentioned with our labour, not for humanitarian purposes, but for their own economic gain. Were the hospitals and schools built for the African people? Compare what they put in with what they took out. I insist they exploited, robbed and underdeveloped us. One day, African history will be objectively written. This book,' she said holding Walter Rodney's, *How Europe Underdeveloped Africa,* 'is just a beginning.'

His mouth was now partly open. 'Listen!' Amina continued to speak confidently. 'During the colonial era, the Europeans ruled and exploited us directly. Now in the era of neo-colonialism, people like you—agents of multinational corporations—travel around Africa with very little capital, outdated machinery and so-called expertise. You "invest" and make fantastic profits through dubious means. You connive with greedy, unintelligent and unpatriotic Africans to cheat and plunder our resources. Your bosses remain in the European or American cities and direct unpatriotic African leaders and fraudulent businessmen and violent and ruthless soldiers who run up and down like dogs protecting your interests. For this filthy job, they receive crumbs of the ill-gotten profits you accrue from the sweat and blood of African people.'

Mr Whitehead looked as if he had been bitten by a snake. 'Madam,' he countered in a pained voice, 'our investments are to help you develop your economy.'

'You can't expect me to agree. The fact that my husband connives with you doesn't mean I will. Your tricks have been uncovered, you rob us in daylight and claim you're helping us. If you swindlers were and are still interested in our development, why don't you import tools? Why do you always import finished goods? Why don't you teach us how to make the equipment? Why are you interested in taking our natural resources away? Why don't you process these resources here? Why don't you encourage local industries to grow? Why are you not interested in building and funding research institutes here? Why are you always supporting unpatriotic African leaders just because they help you to steal our resources? Why do you import arms when you know that they'll be used to kill innocent people? Why do you export diamonds from areas affected by wars like Liberia? In other words, why do you promote wars and conflicts in Africa? Why do you support corrupt, oppressive and bloody regimes all over Africa?

'You arrange loans that you know cannot be repaid. Loans with interest so high that most African countries spend half their budgets just paying the interest ...'

'Your esteemed leaders signed these loans. They are not forced ...,' Mr Whitehead interjected.

'Of course they are not. You get greedy and illiterate men–either in civilian clothes or in uniforms—to rule a country and tell them to sign papers; they'll sign anything. Our rulers could do business with the devil and sell their mothers and you'd be happy to serve as an intermediary!

'I've no business with you,' he said, looking perplexed.

'Yes, I know! I did not invite you. You can't come here and make such statements and expect no reply. There is a difference between my husband and me!'

Alhaji Haruna entered.

'I can see you like reading books, and you believe in whatever is written,' said Mr Whitehead opening his brief-case. He brought out a book entitled *USA and AFRICA: Partners in Progress*. 'Have a nice read,' he said handing it to her.

'Thank you and goodbye,' she replied, receiving the book.

When Mr Whitehead and Alhaji Haruna left, Amina smiled with satisfaction. She was jubilant at winning her first intellectual battle. Her inferiority complex had disappeared, and she knew from now on she could hold her own in an argument.

Alhaji Haruna came back later that evening looking demoralised.

'How was your business meeting?' asked Amina, unable to suppress her gleefulness.

'He's no longer interested,' Alhaji Haruna sadly. 'He said there's too much insecurity in some African countries.'

'Yes,' an excited Amina cut in, 'political instability discourages foreign investment.'

'But our country is fertile ground for foreign investments. There's no war going on. Our President has always begged for foreign investments and assured investors that they'll be protected.'

'Did your partner give any other reason?'

'No! He was afraid of the future of this particular company.'

Amina took a deep breath. Since her husband had beaten her and her son had died, she had hardened towards Alhaji and was no longer afraid of him. She decided to speak boldly. 'Alhaji, let me be honest with you. We do not need foreign investment, what we urgently need is a clear understanding of how to use the money and resources we have. I know you have lots of money stacked on shelves in your "safe rooms" in the Legislators' Estate and in Abuja. I know it has become a pastime for you and your friends just to sit and admire this money—just for the fun of it! That is exactly what not to do with money. For money to have any meaning and usefulness, it must circulate. The moment you keep it in one place, it becomes useless.

'My suggestion is this: invest this money. Set up factories; use the money to buy equipment, land and labour. In the process, it becomes useful. People will work and earn a living and they'll forever be grateful for the jobs. They'll have dignity,' Amina paused hoping for a response, but her husband appeared baffled by her argument. 'Why don't you invite Nigerian experts, sit down with them and think of how to use your money so that people can benefit?' she asked.

'Why?' asked Alhaji, genuinely disturbed. 'I don't have any education as such. Moreover, all Nigerians are crooks. Anyway, I have Bature to do the thinking for me.'

'Bature will always do what serves his interests not yours.'

'I trust Bature wholeheartedly!'

Amina was becoming frustrated but she continued calmly. 'What I have in mind is something like this: You set up two or three factories, farms and transport companies here in Bakaro to start with. Maybe you could add a food-processing plant. You train people to work in all these areas. With the money they earn, they buy the goods and services you provide. You can set up a good school for their children and they will pay for the education of your future workers. You can build an estate for all your workers and they'll pay the rent. In short, everybody will win. The state revenue will increase because they have to pay taxes; the school will get money to pay teachers; the workers will have money to buy goods and services and will be very happy; your wealth will increase.

In this way you will be setting an example for others. As they say, demand will then create its own supply. Other people will provide services that you cannot. You and other industrialists will then make the government provide infrastructure like good roads, electricity, water, telephones and so on. All this will eventually broaden the economy. Eventually, we'll have a very healthy economic situation where everybody is happy and prosperous.'

'Listen Amina, how did you get these ideas?'

'I read some in books, but mainly I thought about things for myself and opened my eyes.'

'So many things in books don't work. Your ideas will never work here.'

'Give it a try. If you don't trust Nigerians at least trust your wife with your money. I'll take care of the business. I'll write a proposal and give it to you soon.'

'I don't need your advice.'

'What's the problem?'

'Bature will not agree. He prefers me to send my money abroad for safekeeping.'

'So that your money does exactly what I've explained to you now, but not in your country; in Europe.'

'I believe in and trust Bature.'

# 19

Months passed. The rainy season gave way to the dry. In late September, the Women's Association organised a "Social-Educational Week." Amina spoke at gatherings both on campus and at the association's headquarters. Posters and pamphlets on education, health and religion were distributed to the women. The Support Group met, reviewed the activities of the association and discussed future plans.

'What do we do with our harvest?' Amina asked Fatima as they settled in her room.

'Share it according to the work each member has put in,' Fatima suggested.

'That's unrealistic! We should be fair to all.'

'Sell the grain and deposit the money in the bank,' proposed Fatima.

'No. They wouldn't feel the impact of their work,' Amina argued.

'Okay, share everything among them according to the size of their families.'

'We did mixed farming,' Amina explained, 'Vegetables have been harvested and sold at subsidised rates. Fresh corn was harvested on one farm and sold as well, only to members of course.'

'Your practical experience makes you understand the women better than me. Do what you think is best,' Fatima finally gave up.

'We've sewn a blouse and wrapper for each member,' Amina hinted.

'For you too?'

'Of course, I'm one of the women.'

'How time flies! Soon it'll be a year since we started this association ...'

'Then it seemed impossible.'

'...like a dream.'

'Alhaji Ibrahim will soon marry a new wife,' Mairo relayed the latest news.

'Who? What?' Amina turned in amazement.

'Yes! Kulu's husband. His first wife told me. He was reported to have made a secondary school girl pregnant and the father of the girl, a State Commissioner, insists he marry her.'

'What about Kulu?'

'I don't know what she thinks yet.'

'That's interesting.'

'Tell me, what's happening this evening?' Mairo asked.

'Today's our harvest day. There'll be a dinner party and we'll all cook and eat together. We'll sing, dance and watch films. To start with, there'll be a group photograph, so remind the women to wear their new dresses.'

'I'll do that.'

The moment Amina had waited for had come at last: the women were to share the fruits of their labour together. She dressed in the co-operative attire and walked to the headquarters. Her heart lifted as she saw the smiling women, all wearing the same attire. They posed for a group photograph, Amina in the middle of the front row with two rows of women standing behind her and others squatting in front. As the photographer clicked his camera, Bilkisu's car pulled up. Fatima, Rebecca, Bilkisu, Muazu, and Muktar jumped out and some of the women cheered. The students quickly squatted in front of Amina, but Muktar refused to join the photo.

After the second photograph had been taken, the women got down to cooking. Pots, dyed and woven clothes and materials, knitted sweaters and other handicrafts made by the women were on sale at subsidised prices.

'I'd like you to take some more photographs of the women and the students as they cook, talk and dance so that we can have a whole album of the ceremony,' Amina told the photographer.

'Let me take one portrait of you,' he requested.

She obliged and stood still. As he adjusted the lense, bending forward and backwards, she moved her head slightly towards the right. Her eyes met Muktar's and as she smiled the camera clicked.

Many men joined them for dinner, including the district musicians. After dinner, they started to play their drums, flutes and trumpets, and some women started to dance, while others watched and cracked jokes. Larai was at her best, singing and dancing. Amina watched with great satisfaction on her face and in her heart. When a familiar song rent the air, Amina looked at Fatima and their joyful eyes met. She pulled Fatima into the crowd, removed her sandals and walked to the centre. The women left a dancing space for them and they both danced amidst great applause.

As it grew darker, more people joined the women's festival and the celebration continued. The women loved the darkness. Amina fixed the reel of a film and waited for silence. It was still noisy when she switched on the projector. She did not concentrate on the film but looked at the sky and saw the full moon appear through scattered clouds. They cleared, and brilliant moonlight bathed the vast, open expanse of the flat Savannah. Insects and night birds joined in with their songs. Fireflies flicked in the lingering moisture.

Amina silently reviewed the major events in her life, starting from her childhood, in primary school; how she was forcefully enrolled and then refused to go; how she had to be chased out of the house to the school; how her mother gave her the necessary encouragement; her old and forgotten schoolmates; her secondary school life; her mother and sisters; her short spell at university; how she met Fatima on the first day of registration, and they had agreed to share a room; her marriage, her dead son; the Women's Association; the literacy and health campaigns; the cooperative movement; and today, the harvest. She could not say whether out of joy, relief or sadness, but she felt tears wet her face.

One afternoon, Amina was sleeping when Alhaji Haruna rushed in. He shut the door noisily behind him, locked it and stood panting. Amina opened her eyes and watched him as he sank into the sofa. He looked frightened and in distress.

'Do you have any food?' he asked.

'No, I can prepare ...'

'Don't worry, I'm not even hungry.' He stared at her for a moment, lowered his head and began tapping the floor with his foot.

'What's wrong?' Amina asked several times but he gave no reply.

She wondered what it could be. Had somebody been badmouthing her again? Or had his business partner told him about their discussion? Maybe he'd been duped. Everybody in the family was fine as far as she knew, he was still a member of the House of Assembly, and was even acting for the Speaker.

'Oh, God!' he broke his silence. 'Why now?' He stared straight at Amina. 'Why can't people be Godfearing? Why can't people be satisfied with what God has given them? Why do some people want to see our downfall? Why are people against us? Why?'

# Chapter 19

'What has happened?' Amina asked again.

'I'll tell you,' he said sitting by her side, 'but you must keep it secret. Let our secrets be secret.'

'Agreed.'

He was breathing heavily and sweating profusely. He shook his head sadly and whispered, 'We've received news that some young army officers want to overthrow the civilian government.' He wiped sweat off his forehead. Heavy feet walked menacingly into the compound and Alhaji's big red eyes flashed towards the door. The footsteps passed. 'They plan to take over on Independence Day during the military parade,' he said nervously.

'Why are you afraid?' Amina asked calmly.

'Why wouldn't I be? I'm now the Acting Speaker. The Speaker travelled to London for a medical checkup and his Deputy's gone on honeymoon to Dubai.'

'Don't worry, have faith in God,' comforted Amina and advised him to remove his gown. He was too agitated and ignored her.

'Why are they against democracy after so many years of military dictatorship? What do they want? Why can't they remain in the barracks they've built for themselves? Why must the military interfere in politics?' he asked Amina.

'I don't think anybody will stage a coup now, it's the wrong time.'

'Are you saying they'll take over later?' he asked looking straight into her eyes.

'Three years of civilian rule is too short for ...'

'Keep quiet, Amina. You don't know anything about politics.' He started pacing up and down. 'It's the Southerners. They're disappointed they didn't win the presidential post. That's why they're against our President and want to wreck democracy.'

'The coup might be organised by Northerners.'

'No, the President is a Northerner,' he countered.

'But not all Northerners like him. Actually most Northerners have not benefited from his government and are against him.'

'What do you mean?' he demanded.

'I, for example, don't like the way he governs. If I have the opportunity I'll support any group that will overthrow him and the system.'

'Are you crazy? Look! Our President is the most God-fearing! He's not only a man of religion, but also a man of responsibility and honour. We should count ourselves lucky to have such a leader ...'

Loud steps came closer and there was a knock on the door. Alhaji went wild. He ran to the window, but there were bars. He looked around in panic. 'Please don't open the door!' he pleaded several times in an unusually subdued voice. He opened the wide wardrobe and hid inside. 'I'm not around,' he said. Amina closed it and opened the door.

'Sorry *Amarya,* I was told he was here,' said his official driver.

'Who's looking for him?' she asked.

'Some people are waiting for him in his office.'

'Okay, he's not here, but I'll pass on the message,' she said and closed the door.

Alhaji emerged from his hideout sweating and panting. Amina succeeded in suppressing a tremor of laughter that was about to burst in her. 'I just don't want to be on the parade ground,' he said switching on the fan. 'I don't mind losing my post but l don't want to lose my life.'

'You might still be requested to be there.'

'Yes. I'll fall ill today ... governing people in this country is very difficult. I don't blame those rich men who take all their money abroad and live there peacefully. Even hypertension can kill a leader here.' He removed his big gown and Amina noticed that his chest was unusually bulky. As if answering her unasked question he said, smiling, 'I'm wearing a bulletproof vest.'

'A bulletproof vest?' she asked in disbelief.

'Sssh! Yes, we're wearing them to get used to it,' he explained. 'God said you help yourself before He helps you.'

'What if they bomb you there or throw grenades or fire shells from their tanks?'

'No, surely they can't! I'll agree to a bloodless coup, and we'll continue with our business ... oh! why must they organise a ...'

A loud knock on the door silenced him. A male voice shouted, 'Alhaji, you're wanted urgently!' He dashed back to his haven within seconds.

'Who's there?' Amina asked.

'Madam, we've little time, please release him. Tell him it's time to go. We must go together.'

Alhaji identified the voice, came out and asked, 'Where to?'

'The airport. The Speaker is arriving soon.'

Alhaji dressed quickly and dashed out.

Amina laughed loudly and fell on her bed. She laughed until tears rolled out. 'A group of soldiers will take over again, new rulers will emerge, old ones will be accused of wrong-doings but be set free. Some of them will be co-opted into the new administration. Hopes of the poor, already dashed by the former administration, will be raised. Promises will be rolled out. In the end nothing will change. Those in power will continue to loot the treasury without shame. What a country this is, where an illiterate soldier, with no formal education, can terrorise his way into the leadership. Otherwise, nothing positive will happen, apart from changing the portraits of the rulers in our office. It's like a fairy tale!'

Fatima arrived soon after, and Amina wasted no time in telling her everything.

'When will they strike?' Fatima asked.

'In two days time. Independence Day.'

'Well, in our country today the power is on the streets and anybody can pick it up at any time.'

Independence Day came and went; no coup took place. Meanwhile, the activities of the Women's Association continued, new subjects were introduced and more students registered as teachers. More women now took part in weaving, knitting, sewing, dying and other handicrafts. On campus, the Students' Union elections were held. The new leaders were from Fatima's movement and they pledged continued support to the association. More students were appointed to the Support Group. Bilkisu handed over the leadership to the new vice-president, Laila.

When the adult literacy campaign was a year old, the adult education unit in the university conducted examinations and held a prize-giving day, when certificates were given to all of the women. The director of the unit, the guest of honour at the occasion, praised their efforts and announced that his unit would soon take over the literacy campaign. Amina would be the paid coordinator and was to set up similar campaigns in other districts of the town.

Amina fell ill. She was rushed to a clinic and later transferred to the hospital where she spent about a week. As soon as she had fully recovered, she went to the headquarters. The women were delighted to see her.

'What was the cause of your sickness?' Larai asked in the office.

'I had a miscarriage,' Amina answered after a sigh.

'I am sorry, how terrible,' Larai said sympathetically.

'It's all right, I've fully recovered. But I'll have to wait for some time before I can try again for children.'

Larai walked out with a bowed head. Amina was going through a journal when a car drew up with a screech of brakes.

'Can I come in?' a man asked moments later.

'Yes!' she answered.

## Chapter 19

'Good day, madam,' said an elderly man in a blue safari suit. 'I am Dr Idris Dandodo, a lecturer at the University and a consultant to the United Nations.' He handed her a letter. 'The UN has asked me to write a report on your association.'

Amina read the letter and offered him a seat. 'Madam, I'd like to interview you and take some photographs. I've already interviewed thirty women and some teachers. I attended some of the classes and I visited the farms. I've also spoken to some members of the community. Bilkisu, Fatima and Gloria were very helpful.'

'It's all right with me. Tell me, Dr Idris, how did the United Nations know about us?'

'Nothing is hidden under the skies,' he said with a smile, pointing upwards. 'What you have done so far is incredible.'

Amina was perplexed. As he prepared for the interview, she wondered how the UN had found out about the association. She was excited to have seen her name and that of the association boldly written in the letter. He recorded Amina's views on the main aspects of her work.

On being asked about the literacy campaign, Amina explained, 'Education has never been a priority here and most men still regard women's education as unnecessary. Conservative groups who are allergic to change are still launching hate campaigns against us. We're doing our best to educate the average woman in Bakaro, who would not usually have had any basic education. The Al Hassan Adult Education model has really worked. Education is as essential as air and water. Our rulers have deliberately condemned us to ignorance, but after this first year, I can say that the shell of ignorance among the women in Bakaro had been cracked.'

Next Amina told him about the cooperative movement. 'There are plans to broaden our activities and involve jobless young men and peasants. It's a disaster that peasants have been left with only hoes to scratch the soil. This country needs cooperative movements badly to feed itself. The government imports fertilizers and rice which are too expensive to buy;

land is still in the hands of a very few rich men. In short, instead of pursuing a genuine long-term agricultural policy, those in charge only think of the money they can make in the shortest possible time!

'Another big issue is health. We're doing our best in Bakaro to eradicate simple diseases and give people basic health education. No drugs are available in our hospitals and the state has no policy on health education. Our hospitals are like mortuaries where people go to die. Hopefully we'll have a fully staffed and well-equipped clinic in the district in two years.

'In terms of the future, we intend to set up new movements in different parts of the town and then throughout the state. We also intend to go into food preparation and packaging. We have so many women who are unemployed or underemployed, we might eventually move away from agriculture and concentrate on food. We'll be setting up a library primarily for women and children and a weekly newspaper to provide a forum for information and debate. A woman in the district has come up with a novel idea of harvesting, preserving and managing water. Muazu Danlami and other students are carrying out the experiment and if it succeeds, we'll implement it. As you know, water is one of our biggest problems here.

'I have to say that I'm very satisfied that most of our plans have prospered. I'm eternally indebted to my friend Fatima for her advice, help and assistance, and to other members of the group.

'Although we can't change things overnight, we have paved the way for a better future.'

One afternoon, Amina, Fatima, Gloria and Laila, all dressed in their best clothes, attended Bilkisu's wedding ceremony. 'You look different without your beret,' Amina told Fatima as they walked towards Alhaji Umar Usman's house. There were hundreds of people in and around the house. They went into the compound and joined the other women.

'Congratulations,' Amina said with a smile as she entered the room where Bilkisu was seated.

'Thanks very much for coming,' said Bilkisu in a joyous mood.

'You have so many people to attend to. Let's talk later.'

'Thanks for your understanding,' Bilkisu responded.

'I'm very happy for her,' said Laila, as they walked towards the shady part of the courtyard. 'I've never seen her so happy.'

Later, the bridegroom, Lt Colonel Abubakar Usman, emerged into the courtyard. As he walked towards the women, Amina raised her head to get a clear picture of his face. He wore dark glasses and was expressionless. He walked straight to Amina. 'It's a pleasure to meet you at last. Thanks very much for coming,' he said in a hoarse voice.

'Congratulations and I hope your marriage lasts for a long time and that Almighty Allah blesses it with children.'

'Thanks! I've heard a lot about you. One of my friends described you as a silent revolutionary.'

'Really?' Amina asked, shocked.

Lt Colonel Abubakar Usman thanked the other women for coming and left.

Later, in her room, Amina spoke to Fatima about their plans for the association. After a moment of silence Fatima, in an emotional voice said, 'Amina thank you very much for agreeing to form the association. A lot of people, myself especially, have learnt many things. It's been a source of inspiration.'

'I should thank you for giving me the idea and for the support you and the others have given it. My involvement has made me very happy. I swell with joy when I see the practical and positive results of our work and I feel so appreciated. I feel I've gained knowledge and experience and understand life better, and above all, I've rediscovered myself.'

'I forgot to tell you,' said Fatima, 'Dr Idris Dandodo has submitted his report. We expect the United Nations to accept it and award you a Certificate of Honour.'

Amina smiled shyly. 'I've been wanting to tell you something but I don't know how to put it,' Amina started speaking looking a bit puzzled. Fatima looked at her as if saying, 'Go ahead.'

'Over the past months I've been experiencing some strange but somewhat positive changes. So many things you've said in the past are beginning to have a new meaning to me. Also I look at the world around me and I begin to understand and appreciate things differently. In short my attitude to life is changing. I presume you must have gone through or are going through this process ...'

Fatima looked baffled and unsure of what to say, 'Hmm, I think I understand what you are trying to suggest.'

'My attitude towards life is changing: I'm questioning my priorities, I'm seeing the world through new eyes ...'

'This is what some people call the emergence of the second person–the more sensible and mature person!' Fatima suggested

'I think it was the death of my son that changed me.' Amina continued, 'I have undoubtedly learnt a lot from you and your friends and Alhaji's behaviour completely changed the way I look at married life, but Rasheed's death completely altered the way I see things.'

'I can only imagine how traumatic it must have been for you,' Fatima said with a sympathetic smile.

'You see,' Amina continued trying to explain her thoughts, 'I feel that there are so many conflicts I need to resolve within myself. On another level, I feel I have reached a crossroad and sooner or later I've to decide the path to take.'

Fatima let out a deep sight. 'We are always at crossroads. The most important thing is to take the right path and I hope and pray Almighty Allah guides you in choosing your path.'

The two women looked at each other and smiled.

'How are the classes going?' Fatima asked.

'All activities have been suspended for a month because of fasting.'

'That's no excuse.'

'You must be realistic. A lot of women are overworked. Secondly, the political and religious atmosphere is tense. There have been bloody clashes that claimed over ten lives last week. Hauwa narrowly escaped death yesterday when two religious groups clashed. The lives of our women shouldn't be put in danger.' Amina then changed the topic. 'Why do you think Lt Colonel Abubakar Usman called me a "silent revolutionary"?'

'I don't know. He calls me the most dangerous woman on earth. On the one hand, we should not be bothered at all. Most of these army officers don't know what they are talking about anyway. On the other hand we should be concerned.'

'Why?'

'Lt Col Usman comes from a feudal class that is neurotic about changes in society. He's known in the army as the Prince of Darkness because of the vicious way he dealt with alleged opponents of the former military regime some years ago. Actually, it is believed that he was one of a group of coup plotters but betrayed his comrades and ambushed them at dawn, making sure that none of them survived. He has a reputation for being extremely ruthless, and he only operates in the dark. He got his nickname because of what he did while serving as an Acting Military Administrator for the state.

'What did he do?'

'The first thing he did was to close down the university on the pretext that the students were planning to demonstrate. Some lecturers protested, arguing that his intelligence report was false. He arrested them and made sure they were not paid while in detention. He said their families should suffer too. Then he closed down some secondary schools saying there was not enough money. He starved the Ministry of Education of funds so most teachers were not paid for almost a year.' Fatima paused. 'I've seen many anti-intellectuals in our society, but he's among the top ten.'

Amina introduced a new topic. 'Recently a girl who looked disturbed approached me for help. She claimed she was raped some months ago and was pregnant. She was hawking food when a boy stole her purse and ran into a building. She tried to retrieve her money but he overpowered her and raped her. I traced the boy, the son of a police officer, and took the case to the local court. We wanted the boy to accept responsibility and take care of the girl but to our great dismay and disappointment, the judge said the girl was at fault: that she wore tempting clothes, walked sexily to entice the boy, and that she didn't scream while being raped. He didn't allow her to state her case, but the boy was allowed to defend himself. He freed the boy saying there were no witnesses. I objected loudly and he threatened to have me caned. He ordered the girl to be flogged with six lashes of the cane for seductive dressing. I couldn't believe my ears.'

'You've seen what they call justice?'

'She was about six months pregnant and I feared a miscarriage.'

'Where is she now?'

'She lives with Larai in my house. Her father sent her away saying she was carrying a bastard and was a disgrace to the family.'

'Poor you! You were trying to chase justice but were caught by injustice.'

'I was overwhelmed by guilt. It was as if I'd taken the girl there to be disgraced, humiliated and punished. I still find it hard to look into her eyes. But what other option did I have?' Amina asked, struggling with her thoughts.

'Amina,' Fatima consoled, 'you're not to blame! You did what any conscientious person would do. You'll face more frustration because you are a woman fighting for and on behalf of women. '

Amina looked at Fatima, and decided to articulate something she had been thinking about for a while. 'Fatima, let's produce a document on how to improve the conditions of the poor in the state. I can write on how best to form and organise cooperative movements; you can write on how to change the educational system; Rebecca can write about health education. We can then produce a document—The Bakaro Manifesto—to educate people on how to change the system for the better. We could send copies of the manifesto to government officials, rulers, judges and the press.'

'That's a very good idea,' Fatima responded with her usual warmth, 'we're too busy now with final examinations are coming up. But let me talk to the others.'

# 20

After the holy month of Ramadan, the activities of the Bakaro Women's Association resumed in full force. Amina and the students agreed to work on her idea for a manifesto, with Amina writing on cooperative movements. This was the first opportunity she had had to put her thoughts into writing and it excited her. She did a lot of background reading and as she developed her own thoughts, she wrote them down. One evening, she was going through her notes when Alhaji Haruna walked in and observed, 'You've been busy recently.'

'Yes, we're trying to put together our suggestions on how to develop the state.'

'What do you mean?' Alhaji asked. He was no longer surprised at Amina's enlarged understanding, and secretly had begun to respect her opinions.

'It'll take a long time to explain. We'll send copies to the House of Assembly,' she assured him. He was satisfied, especially as he had a more pressing matter on his mind.

'I'll soon be honoured with a traditional title,' Alhaji disclosed.

'So, we'll have a new wife in the compound?' Amina speculated.

'No. No! If God wants ... I've no plans but what if I do?'

'We'll live together if I'm still your wife,' Amina reacted with a shrug.

'Of course you'll still be my wife ...' Alhaji reassured her.

'Traditional ruler in charge of where or what?' she asked.

'The eastern part of Bakaro.'

'But no one lives there.'

'There'll be people there in the future!' he said shortly, and left.

Later Fatima, Bilkisu and Laila visited Amina, bringing their own contributions to the manifesto. 'This is what we've written on political, health, education and social reforms. It's still a rough outline. Read it, and then we can go through it in detail together,' Bilkisu said as she handed Amina the file.

'I wrote the chapter on how the reforms should be carried out,' said Laila, with a certain air of pride.

'We don't have much time. Why don't you read out your main points,' Fatima suggested.

Amina found her notes and started to read the highlights. She called on the state government to form cooperative movements in all districts, especially involving women; to establish cooperative banks and grant generous loans to peasants, small-scale farmers and industrialists; to enact a law making peasants automatic owners of the land they worked; to combat desert encroachment, and hand over all regained land to the landless to cultivate; to sell fertilizer and seeds directly to peasants or cooperative movements at subsidised prices; to oversee the sale and distribution of harvested crops to discourage hoarding; to return all lands illegally acquired from peasants. She looked up to explain, 'Sorry, it's still a bit disjointed at the moment. I'll structure my ideas and think of more points. I've only looked at agricultural cooperatives so far.'

'They'll never agree with any of our suggestions. They'll throw them in the dustbin, I can bet my life on that,' Fatima said.

'Why?'

'You're telling them to commit suicide. I predict your husband will be among the first to reject these proposals.'

'You know what sort of man he is,' explained Bilkisu.

'I'm not calling for a revolution, just reforms,' said Amina. She refused to allow herself to be discouraged when the manifesto was taking shape so positively. She had put all her new thinking and passionate conviction into it, and the solutions seemed so obvious.

Two weeks later the *The Bakaro Manifesto: Strategies for Reform* was released by the Support Group. Copies were sent to the State Governor, Commissioners, Legislators, Local Government Secretaries, the Emir, State Judges, the press and top civil servants. A symposium was organised at the university, where Amina was invited to defend her part of the manifesto. The debate over the document was intense and lively, moving out of the lecture halls on to the streets. It was not well received in some quarters but the mere fact that it was debated pleased Amina. She discovered that the people of Bakaro were not as politically ignorant as she had earlier thought, and came to understand and identify different strands of opinion.

She realised that people wanted changes but did not know how to go about getting them. The idea of women being equal to men raised eyebrows in all quarters, and even women came out strongly in defence of the male-dominated society. Amina found it hard to understand the reasons for such a general consensus. It worried her.

'We've received your document,' Alhaji Haruna told her one evening.

'What do you think?' Amina flashed a smile.

'Nothing so far,' Alhaji Haruna said sitting down. 'Actually I'm sponsoring a bill on women in the House of Assembly. It's on the traditional role of women in society. The Assembly lawyers are still drafting it.'

'You once said you could not think; who told you what to put in the bill?'

'I discussed the matter with many people.'

'Will women be invited to the debate?' Amina asked.

'What debate? Absolutely not! Only the legislators will deliberate on it!'

'We need to have a say in the policies that affect us,' Amina tried to explain to him. 'You can't pass a law on women without at least one woman there to speak on the issue. Please, democracy means listening to the people you're governing, not excluding them in your deliberations!' Not, Amina thought, that many women had been consulted in the past about anything.

'Listen Amina! I cannot stand your nagging! Goodnight!' Alhaji Haruna said and departed.

Amina sprang up quickly when Fatima walked in, days later, looking resolute. 'What's wrong?' Amina asked anxiously.

'Many things are wrong: the Students' Union has been banned and two of our leaders suspended from university for a year: the president, Peter Akin, and the vice-president, Laila. Do you remember the lady who was on trial for adultery in Funtua?

'Of course I do.'

'She's been sentenced to death by stoning.'

'You must be joking.'

'The bill on women sponsored by your honourable husband is totally against women. We've very little information. The speaker, we were told, ordered members not to release the contents to any woman until it was passed into law.'

'How did you get that information?'

'A legislator from the opposition told us. Because he protested, his copy of the bill was confiscated in the House!'

As Fatima started to read parts of the bill aloud, Amina became more and more angry.

"-All Muslim women and girls must wear veils on the streets.

-Only a certain percentage of girls will be allowed into schools.

-Street trading by women has been banned.

-All women's organisations must be re-registered.

-All re-registered women's organisations will be under the strict control and supervision of state officials and religious leaders.

-Women engaged in domestic industries will be taxed.

-Single women will no longer be allowed to work in the state civil service.

-Single women living in government housing estates will be evicted.

-Single women will be tried for adultery if they are pregnant.

-Maternity leave for married women has been cancelled.

-Women workers will no longer qualify for protection against dismissal.

-Vigilante groups shall be set up in every part of the state to monitor the way women dress.

-Courts shall be empowered to penalise women for dressing immodestly.

-Women will no longer have the right to own land.

-Single mothers will be tried for having illegitimate children."

Amina was listening in disbelief. 'My God! How can they be so unrealistic? We've been attacked from behind. This is serious. We can't stand back and let this happen!'

'How soon can you mobilise the women to fight this?' Fatima asked.

'Tomorrow,' Amina replied without any hesitation. 'We've very little time.'

'That's right. I'll speak to them.' Fatima smiled. 'This is the most trying moment for us. We must be firm and steadfast. See you tomorrow and get prepared for the battle of a lifetime!'

The following evening, Fatima, Bilkisu, Laila and Amina walked quietly towards over a hundred women who were waiting. Fatima mounted the veranda and started to speak about the bill which was before the State House of Assembly.

'This is a mischievous attempt to undermine us and impose an obsolete way of life on us. The natural right of a mother, which Almighty Allah gave her, has now been stolen: the right of custody to children. According to the bill, custody rights now belong to men. Women in this part of the country have always been barred from receiving modern education. Now they have been totally condemned to ignorance and illiteracy.'

Veins on Fatima's neck were bulging as she sweated without wiping off the drops. 'These so-called legislators are hypocrites! They say that a single mother will now be tried for having an illegitimate child ...Who slept with her? Can a woman make herself pregnant? Why should the woman be punished and the man go free? This government will do nothing for us. We must stand and fight for ourselves! We must not submit!'

To Fatima, the idea of pleading or begging did not even arise. She believed the law, the system and its operators must be answered not verbally with pleas, but with punches in a clear fight. 'Deal with them ruthlessly, strangle them, hit them as hard and as fast as possible. That's the only way. No one but us can get rid of these problems, and to get rid of these problems we've to get rid of these rulers!'

Amina looked at Fatima and smiled, admiring her courage and outspokenness. The meeting ended, and the women walked back to their homes, each with her own thoughts and judgement. Amina wondered if they understood the seriousness of the situation, but there was no way she could measure their mood. As they walked back, Fatima turned a stern face towards her saying, 'I have to go back to the university now. We've an urgent meeting tonight, and I'll be travelling to the Federal Capital for the hearing of a case at the Supreme Court of Justice. Too many battles on too many fronts.' She paused. 'Amina, the tasks ahead of you and me are difficult. The challenge has been thrown at us. Let's pick it up and throw it back to them.'

Amina understood what Fatima was saying, but felt time was needed. 'Fatima, let's wait a bit and allow the women to process what we've told them,' she suggested.

Fatima, however, was adamant. 'Listen, in any fight, the side that withdraws accepts outright defeat. They attacked us, and if we let them go unchallenged, they'll continue to attack and will eventually inflict terrible damage on women in particular and on our generation in general. This group of spoilt children will never engage in any dialogue.'

On her own, as she thought over the meeting and Fatima's fierce proposal, Amina decided what was needed was a strong coherent leadership. Mere verbal protest was not enough. At the same time, the state was powerful and had all the means of winning, but Amina knew she could not afford to think about that. To be ready for the big fight, what she needed was a strategy.

The next morning, Amina resolved to meet the legislators as a first step, to see if she could persuade them not to pass the bill into law. She asked Larai and Hauwa to go with her. Amina was full of determination and assured herself throughout the journey to the House of Assembly that these men would listen and understand. On arrival at the House of Assembly, they were met by Alhaji Isa, the House Chairman on Social Welfare, Youth and Culture. He was short and stocky, with an aggressive posture.

'Yes! What can I do for you?' he fired.

'We came to persuade you to give us a chance to speak before you pass the bill on women into law,' Amina replied politely.

'You should speak to your husbands who can lobby on your behalf,' he contended.

'But the law is against women's interests and we want to make our voices heard,' she countered.

'But women have no interests,' he laughed contemptuously. Amina was not perturbed.

'We want the bill withdrawn ...' she stated firmly.

'Your husband sponsored it,' he said pointing at her. 'You should have told him your feelings in bed. For your information, it has already been passed into law with only one member opposed. It is a timely law that will restore order and decency in the state. The State Governor should by now have appended his signature ...'

'You mean I wouldn't be allowed to speak to the members?'

'*La Illaha Illalahu!*' the man exclaimed and laughed scornfully. 'What sort of world are you living in! Are you dreaming? Are you crazy? Who do you think you are? You want to speak to the honourable members? Don't you have any respect for the elders?'

'Listen!' Amina interrupted, 'you cannot pass a law on women without their say.'

The man was startled. 'This is pure madness! This is unbelievable! Amina, you're a madwoman!' He shook his head, looking straight into her eyes. 'A woman talking to a man, an honourable member of the Assembly, as if they're equal. You think because you are educated you can dictate to a man? I've four women in my house—four good wives: well behaved, obedient and respectful women, unlike you.'

Amina held her ground. 'I didn't come here to talk about your wives. Time is running out!' she pointed out.

'We've very little time too. We're now trying to pass a bill into law prohibiting the manufacture, sale, distribution and consumption of alcohol in the state. We shall discuss naming a street after our good friend Bature. Then we shall take a month's recess.'

Amina was baffled. She explained desperately: 'Listen, these are not the priorities now! The people need food, water, electricity, shelter and other material things that would improve their lives. Please! You should pass laws that will give people the incentive to work, that will educate them, that will make them enterprising and innovative ...'

'Stop!' he shouted. He called the security guards and ordered them to march the women out of the Assembly premises.

Amina and her companions headed towards Government House, where the state governor lived. Despite this reception, she still believed she could stop the law being implemented, that perseverance would yield her positive results.

At Government House, Amina was informed that the governor had signed the bill.

'Can I see the Chief Judge?' Amina asked.

'No, you cannot,' said an official.

Amina left Government House, disappointed but still undefeated. They headed towards the Emir's Palace. She was discovering that the leaders lived in another world, a strange fantasy world. They lived behind barriers and were immune to the needs of the people.

In deference to her husband's status, Amina was received by the Emir. He listened courteously to her short plea, before he said, 'Please go back to your homes and live peacefully. Your husband is the master of the house. Respect for a husband is like respect for God.'

Amina went back home confused. She invited some women waiting for her outside into her room, turned on to the local radio and they all listened to the news. 'Today, some disgruntled women from Bakaro, led by a Western-educated woman, marched through the main streets of the town and rudely interrupted the proceedings of the

Honourable House of Assembly. The women were said to have demonstrated against a democratically enacted law, and demanded so-called rights and freedoms. The leader, according to eyewitnesses, was said to have abused and manhandled an honourable member of the State Assembly.

The honourable speaker of the Assembly, Alhaji Bako, disclosed that a committee had been set up to investigate the cause of this embarrassing situation. He stated that the law had been enacted in good faith in order to prevent immorality and inappropriate behaviour in women, stressing that the contents of the law were in accord with our traditional and religious laws and customs.

The honourable speaker advised women not to be misled but to stay in their homes peacefully. He advised any woman who was not satisfied to seek redress in court and pointed out that the demonstration illustrated the dangers of educating women. In another development, the state governor has banned the Bakaro Women's Association and disbanded the Bakaro Women's Co-operative Movement. Their bank account has been frozen and all assets seized. Women's meetings, processions and demonstrations are banned. The concerted efforts of our team of correspondents to contact the women's leader, Mrs Amina Haruna, proved abortive.'

She switched off the radio and thought for a while. The women looked at her expectantly. She raised her head and smiled at them. 'There comes a moment in someone's life when they've only two options: live or die; submit or fight. We've reached that moment. Prepare yourselves to meet soon and decide what to do next.'

On Friday, Amina called a meeting in the afternoon when all the men had gone to the central mosque for prayers. The turnout was poor but she addressed those present, and a decision was reached that she should seek ways to repeal the laws. The women reaffirmed their loyalty to her leadership.

'We're used to suffering,' Larai noted. 'A woman on her knees shouldn't be afraid of falling. If you go forward you'll die, if you go backwards you'll die. So choose to go forward!'

The *Eid-il-Kabir* sallah celebrations were to take place in a few days' time. As all the men would be heading to the outskirts of the town to pray, Amina thought the women could effectively use that day for their own purposes.

'What do you think you're doing? Who's the owner of the house, you or me?' Alhaji Haruna's questions shook the room. 'Why did you embarrass me in my absence? I am to blame for allowing you too much freedom. In the interest of peace and stability, forget about the Women's Association.' He walked closer, looking disturbed, and Amina was afraid, expecting him to be violent. But Alhaji Haruna was visibly confused. He did not know how to persuade his own wife to leave the women. He pleaded, she resisted and he made promises which she rejected. 'Do you know you're jeopardising my business and parliamentary seat? Do you know that I was almost removed in absentia as the majority leader in the Assembly? Do you know I may not get the title I was promised because of your misbehaviour?'

'These are your problems, not mine!' Amina said with a shrug.

'I sponsored the bill in good faith,' he tried to explain.

'Alhaji,' Amina said drawing closer to him. 'Do you know that many people in this state suffer greatly, mostly women, and that these laws will increase their hardship?'

'But there's nothing I can do,' Alhaji defended himself.

'So you want to increase their hardship?'

'Honestly, I know people are suffering but I don't know who or what is responsible and I don't know how to ease their suffering.'

'We wrote and suggested ways to do it.'

'Your suggestions were unrealistic. You know nothing of affairs of state.'

'I'm a citizen and have the right to be heard. I've had the experience of working with a lot of people, and have many ideas on how to remedy poverty. Why are you leaders so insensitive to the people?' Amina asked, staring at him boldy.

Alhaji Haruna looked puzzled. He had grown accustomed to his wife speaking to him in a direct manner, but was struggling to reassert his authority. 'Tell me,' he asked angrily, 'which political party or who is causing your troubles?'

'These problems are caused by you, people like you and the class you belong to.'

In the face of her determination, he resorted to begging. 'Please stop this dangerous adventure.'

'I will not abandon it halfway. I must see it to the end. If you think that aligning myself with poor women is adventurous, then I'm ready to walk on this adventurous path.'

'Then you have to leave this house,' Alhaji Haruna played his last card.'I'm prepared to, but after the *Eid* celebrations,' Amina responded calmly. Alhaji was shocked, but tried not to show it.

'Yes, I agree,' he said, and nodded. But his wife had one more surprise in store for him.

'I'm pregnant,' she revealed as he walked out. He stopped and looked at her, trying to grasp the importance of her statement. Defeated, he bowed his head and walked away. Amina was triumphant. What sort of woman did he think she was? Very soon, he'd know why she was called after Queen Amina, a warrior heroine who fought for her people.

As she lay in bed, she conceived a plan which she was convinced would work. First, she must meet Mairo. She called Hauwa and Larai and asked them to accompany her to Mairo's house. As part of the plan, she dressed carefully, putting on high-heeled shoes that made her three inches taller than her normal height.

'It's all clear,' Larai told her. The three darted through the dark deserted streets and smelly alleyways. Mairo did not at first recognise Amina as she was heavily veiled. Amina briefed her on the plan and her responsibilities. As they were finalising plans, Mairo's husband approached the door. Mairo dashed out and told him someone was waiting for him near Alhaji Haruna's mosque.

'Don't receive any visitors, especially that evil woman called Amina,' he warned.

'She's a good woman,' Mairo retorted.

'Rubbish! She's a troublemaker. It's not for human beings to change God's plan. It's Alhaji's fault. He shouldn't have married her. Educated women are always troublesome and dangerous. That's why I strongly support the law discouraging the education of girls. Educating women is a waste of time and money. Look at Amina challenging the laws of God!'

'No, we are against the laws passed by the State Assembly.'

'Who is "we"?'

'The women of Bakaro.'

'Are you among them?'

'Am I not a woman?'

'All I know is she's troublesome and not religious.'

'No. She's a good Muslim. She prays and fasts ...'

'I don't believe that. People who receive a Western education aren't Muslims,' he said and left.

On their way back home, the three walked faster. Amina stumbled twice. She was not used to wearing high-heeled shoes. Alhaji Haruna was standing outside the compound with two men. Amina re-veiled herself, covering her face completely.

'Who are you?' Alhaji Haruna asked, as they were about to enter. Hauwa and Larai identified themselves.

'This is Rakiya, a new wife in the district, who wants to greet your wives,' Larai said calmly, pointing to Amina. The men turned away and they entered. Amina removed her shoes and veil and returned to eavesdrop on the discussion between her husband and the two men.

'Alhaji, her presence is a risk,' said the man in a white safari suit.

'I want to give her a surprise package for *Eid*. I've bought and furnished a house in the government reservation area, and bought a car, video and so on to give her after prayers,' Alhaji revealed.

'We're ready for the worst,' said a man in a T-shirt. 'The Mobile Police—that is the "Kill and Go" Squad—are on maximum alert. Soldiers of the Armoured and Infantry Brigades have been put on combat readiness. The airforce base has been informed in case we need air cover.'

'But the commissioner of police is against the use of force. He says that the women have a genuine cause, that the new laws are too harsh. He wants the law repealed and warns that he will not give orders to arrest the women should they meet and demonstrate. He strongly supports the Bakaro Women's Association's activities,' said the man in a safari suit.

'So what's going to happen?' Alhaji said.

'The deputy commissioner is against them.'

'The House committee on local governments,' Alhaji stated after a pause, 'of which I'm the chairman, has a meeting soon in Europe where we intend to study how they created and are running their local governments. I'll take her along, after which we'll perform the lesser Hajj and, on our way back we'll stop over in London so she can do some shopping.'

'Well, Alhaji, the ball's in your court,' the man in the safari suit said. 'Let's meet tomorrow evening.'

'*In Sha Allah. Barka Da Sallah*!' Alhaji Haruna said.

The night was calm and quiet. Amina stood up, walked to the window and looked outside. It was funny the way life continued throughout all this strife. Tomorrow the sun would shine, the wind would blow, the birds would fly and sing, and the people would be in festive mood, celebrating the most important Muslim festival. She lay down but could not sleep. If the rulers were prepared, so were the women. She would lead. They would protest tomorrow, come what may.

# 21

The next day, Amina woke up very early in the morning. Still in bed, she carefully reviewed her strategy for the protest. She was fully convinced that the protest was justified and that she was capable of leading it, but she weighed the chances of victory and possibilities of defeat. She could reach no definite conclusion, and got up to take her bath. During breakfast, Amina turned on the radio to listen to the state governor's traditional message of goodwill to the people of the state on the occasion of the *Eid-il-Kabir* festival.

'*Assalama Allaikum!* Good morning fellow citizens. On this occasion of Eid-il-Kabir, and with gratitude to Almighty Allah, I send my best wishes to all Muslims in the state. I also rejoice with Muslims throughout the world. Today is the day Muslims remember the cherished ideals of Islam and reiterate their faith in the Almighty. Today's celebrations remind us of sacrifice, tolerance and forgiveness, and demand from us untiring labour to build a just and a happy society. I am pleased to inform you that my administration has performed above average in meeting the demands of the masses, Almighty Allah is my witness. Let me seize this opportunity to appeal to all citizens to be law-abiding and peaceful. We need a peaceful atmosphere to live and progress. Islam means peace. It is for the grace and blessings of Allah, in our times, that we fervently pray! *Barka Da Sallah!*'

The broadcast was immediately followed by the state news:

'The state police command has appealed to the people of the state to be peaceful and law-abiding throughout the period of festivities. According to a statement, any person or group of persons acting against the interest of peace will be dealt with accordingly. All citizens are reminded that any meeting other than for religious purposes or those authorised by His Excellency, the state governor, will be dispersed, and troublesome people shot on sight.'

Amina switched off the radio and got dressed. She wore the "cooperative attire." The multicoloured outfit enhanced her natural beauty. She knotted the colourful headscarf firmly.

'They've all left,' Mairo informed her. Amina went out.

The turnout was high for the mobilisation, although some women were afraid. Many appeared with defiant and determined faces, demonstrating their support to Amina in the grand struggle. Some women even looked unconcerned and indifferent. The early morning sun picked out the brilliant colours of the women's clothes. Feeling its warmth, and comparing its brightness to the defiant faces of the rebelling women, one might have been tempted to ask which sight was the more brilliant, the rising sun or the rebelling women.

Amina thanked the women for coming. She did not immediately reveal the "zero option," but first touched on the laws and their effects.

'The taxes imposed on women are unpopular and harsh. Our country has adequate funds to cater for the majority of the people, if not all ... the truth is that the country's wealth is not justly and wisely distributed ...'

Amina was calm and spoke steadily, with no sign of nervousness, encouraged by the crowd. They were one in their support for her, in saying no to suffering, to injustice, to exploitation and to restrictions on their freedom. They were ready to listen, and Amina was inspired to speak with a confidence she had never felt before.

'Our experiences have shown that women can be involved and can actively work in almost all sectors of the economy. We can effectively carry out our duties and responsibilities. Women, like men, are intelligent and capable of being constructive, creative and efficient. If women were educated and encouraged; if they were not restricted by traditions and cultures, I'm confident that we would perform better than them. Let us ask our men these simple questions: What have you succeeded in doing to develop our society over the last century? Why are you afraid of women? If you really love and care for women, why can't you modernise things to alleviate their suffering? Men in other societies have gone a long way in satisfying the needs of their women, why can't you learn from them? Aren't you men ashamed of yourselves? A woman's anger is said to be like a volcano. Now that they have annoyed us, we will erupt.'

Amina told them her plan which she had code-named "zero option": 'We shall march peacefully out of our houses to the primary school and stay there until our demands are met. We are not fighting against our husbands, or against men. NO! We're protesting against harsh laws and injustice. Please, don't see it as a fight between husbands and wives, women and men. If they repeal the laws, remove the taxes, assure us that the ban on our association is lifted, give full assurance that any man who maltreats his wife, sister, daughter or any other woman will be punished if found guilty, we shall return.'

A young woman who disagreed walked up to Amina. She looked at Amina with disgust and hatred. 'You're a madwoman! You simply want to disturb the peace in Bakaro to achieve your own interests! If you're not happy in your husband's house, you're free to leave him for another.' She spat and left. Another group of women also left, some abusing and others threatening Amina. When they had left and calm was restored, Amina continued to speak to those who supported her.

'We shall take all the food and utensils needed from our houses. For example, I'll take two rams and a sack of rice from Alhaji's house. You should all gather in or outside Alhaji's compound, we'll start from there,' Amina said.

The whole of central Bakaro was charged. It was clear to the men that the women were in open revolt. It could be seen on their determined and defiant faces and movements. Everybody, especially the men, waited to see what would happen next. Amina positioned herself in the centre of the compound. A crowd of women stood behind her while others waited outside.

Alhaji Haruna appeared looking rumpled and concerned. 'What's going on?' he asked.

Amina stood squarely on her feet and answered him confidently. 'Many things are wrong! We've resolved to fight against the laws you sponsored and the ban on our association.'

'Today is the wrong day! Today is a holy day, a day when we should forget about our problems and be peaceful and happy,' Alhaji Haruna argued.

'We know it's an important religious day, but if you'd met our demands ...'

'What are you demanding?' Alhaji interrupted.

'Our demands are not new to you, you caused the problems.'

'The laws were passed to protect women,' he attempted to argue, before being drowned out by a chorus of women.

'No! No! No!' they chanted.

'We're not animals that you should decide on our behalf. We know what is good and bad for us. You should at least have consulted or listened to us, ' Amina stated.

Alhaji Haruna stood hesitating, looking at Amina and the other women with concern. He took a deep breath and tried again: 'When the state assembly reconvenes, I promise you that I will make sure the laws are reviewed ... and as your representative I promise to pay all the taxes for you women.'

'We thank you for your kind gesture but it doesn't solve the problem. We're against the law stipulating that women must pay taxes. If it's repealed, no woman in the state will pay. What if you can't pay next year?' Amina challenged him.

'These taxes are necessary to revive our economy and pay our external debts,' Alhaji Haruna asserted.

'That's not our problem. We didn't contribute to the bad state of the economy, so why should we pay for its revival. We haven't seen how these loans were used, so why should we pay?'

'You innocent women,' Alhaji started pointing to the women, 'are blindly following my wife who is seeking fame in her dangerous adventure. You are committing a very serious crime. Please, I beg you all in the name of Allah, please go away!'

'We also beg you in the name of Almighty Allah to repeal these laws,' Amina responded loudly. 'Let me remind you that our religion is opposed to exploitation, and oppression. The Holy Prophet Muhammad (*Peace Be Upon Him*) was totally against enslavement and bondage. He once said that "Allah wishes to ease your burdens not to make things more difficult." We call on you and other state officials, and traditional and religious leaders to follow both the letter and spirit of the actual teachings of Islam.'

In desperation, Alhaji took a step towards his wife. 'Keep quiet!' he commanded.

In the uneasy silence that followed, Amina wiped the sweat off her burning face. Alhaji stood like a statue, staring at his fourth wife. Moving calmly, she led the women out of the compound, leaving Alhaji standing there alone. Knowing she was in full control, for the time being at least, she ordered two rams, a sack of rice and other items to be removed from the house and told the women to assemble in the headquarters.

Some women had found reasons not to come and the turnout was not as large as for the earlier meeting, but Amina was impressed by the determination of those who were there.

'My dear women,' she said to them. 'Today we shall take a historic first step to freedom. If anybody among you doubts or does not believe in our cause, please stay behind. We're not forcing anybody, we want only dedicated people who'll fully support our cause. Fellow women, let's go!'

The procession started to move, with Amina in front. Old women, pregnant women, women with babies on their backs, girls and boys followed.

Larai organised a group of girls and boys to sing a song:

"Arise all those oppressed

Arise and fight for your right

The tricks have been uncovered

The freedom walk has started

Join! All those who're oppressed

The laws must be repealed

The taxes must not be paid!"

The procession moved uninterrupted through the main street of Bakaro and headed towards the town. People came out of their houses to watch, some with folded arms, and others with open mouths. Some women joined them while others insulted them. They reached the centre of the town where the traditional horse riding ceremony durbar was in full swing in front of the Emir's palace. Amina led the women past a wide field full of spectators watching the dramatic ceremony. Some people thought it was part of the ceremony and clapped. Those who were fully in the picture knew that at last the birds had flown out of their cages in Bakaro. A group of men charged towards Amina, shouting, 'What do you think you are doing? Heretics! Prostitutes! Go back to your houses!' Amina said nothing and continued to walk slowly but confidently. They crossed the wooden bridge over the Bakaro River and settled on the school's football field.

At last the women had arrived at their destination. They set about cooking, and while everyone was eating, Amina, together with Larai and four others, drew up a "Mode of Organisation." Five committees, for Food, Defence, Health, Housing and Negotiation, were set up.

Despite the circumstances, the women had made an effort to produce a delicious evening meal. After eating her share, Amina summoned a meeting in front of the headmaster's office. The sun was setting, and her face was lit with its gold radiance as she climbed onto the veranda and gestured for silence. Amina began to speak, 'We, the members of the Bakaro Women's Association, have moved out of our husbands' houses because we felt we were unjustly treated and that these injustices would continue if nothing was done. We've moved because we've suffered and we're still suffering simply because we're women. This might not be the best solution, but in a situation where our association was banned and other unreasonably harsh measures imposed on us, we feel we should show them we're human beings too.'

She asked for water. After drinking she called on a woman from the crowd. A woman carrying a child walked up to her. 'Look at this woman. She worked as a labourer in one of the houses my husband had built in Bakaro. She worked all day. Tell us, did you receive the same pay as the male manual labourers?'

'No. The men received more.'

'You see: equal job, unequal pay. My husband exploits all his workers by paying them low wages but exploits the women more. In this process he gets richer and the people poorer.'

Amina paused as if to let the importance of her words sink in. She felt they understood her and were enjoying the meeting. She nodded and smiled, inspired by the sight of the crowd listening to her. She continued.

'Denying women education condemns them to a second-class position in society. As long as they're not educated, they'll be forced to depend solely on men. As long as they depend on men they'll always be subservient to them. The first step to liberating a woman is to educate her, provide her with work and the necessary security.

'In this society most women are forced into marriage. We aren't against marriage as an institution but we should fight against forced marriages. Just as the man can choose his wife, the woman should have a choice. If a girl is forcefully married to a man she doesn't love she'll never be happy. If she's forcefully married to a man who maltreats her, and decides to seek a divorce, she can't stay on her own. If she does, she's called all sorts of dirty names. Most of these girls are not even educated to work anywhere. That's why a lot of them run away from their houses only to become prostitutes. When they've been sucked dry in the brothels, they're thrown out. Old and weak, such women are left with nothing to do other than sell things on the streets or beg in perpetual destitution, waiting for the day their flame will die. Now, even street trading has been banned. And to make it worse, those women who preferred to engage in domestic industries will now be taxed.

'We should make it clear that every human being in society should be free to work. Work should be a right, not a privilege. It's a shame to see thousands of women in brothels and millions idle in their husbands' houses. The government always says we lack skilled labour. But it will not fall from the skies. Experience has shown that women can be trained and skilled.

'As you know, there's no female legislator. So, we have no representation in the House of Assembly. We're totally excluded from politics.

'We voted during the election,' a voice interrupted.

'Yes, we did cast our votes, but after voting, have you been consulted on any serious matter affecting you? By voting, we the electorate gave the ruling class the legal power to dominate and rule us for four years. Instead of consulting us on matters affecting women, despite the fact that we had an association, they enacted unpopular laws to oppress us further. Is that democracy?

On the ban of our association, I'll say this to the Governor: If you think that by banning us you'll destroy us, then you've not succeeded. As the events of today show, you've strengthened us and we shall grow stronger and bigger in the future. My dear women, let us remain united and committed to our just cause. Let us build a very strong and powerful women's association. Only through this can we achieve our goals, can our voices be heard and heeded. No one is free until all are free! Thank you!'

# 22

The flames of the campfire leaped high in the quiet night. The wind was slight. The women sat round the fire, cracking jokes and dancing. A figure was sighted crossing the wooden bridge. The Defence Committee headed by Jummai charged in that direction. 'Stop there! Enemy or friend? Advance to be recognised!' Jummai stammered loudly. She questioned a woman and escorted her to the gathering. It was the Headmaster's wife, who brought the latest news and keys to the Headmaster's office.

'This is one of the only opportunities we have to know more about each other,' said Amina standing in the centre. 'Let's speak openly and honestly about our experiences so that we can enrich our knowledge ...

My name, as you all know, is Amina. I was born here about twenty-two years ago. My father is an Islamic preacher ...' she went on to describe her early life and linked it with how she got married, why and how she agreed to form the Women's Association and concluded: 'This is just a slice of my life story. Now come up here one after the other and tell us yours.'

An excited Larai leapt forward. 'I'm seventeen. I was born into a peasant family. I've lived from want to hunger, from sorrow to tragedy from lovelessness to childlessness. I was a street hawker and, just as my breasts started developing, I was forcefully married to a peasant who kept me in purdah.' She went on to describe how she was admitted to hospital and had a very traumatic childbirth.

'If you go to the General Hospital, you'll see many underage girls whose bladders have been damaged. The most painful thing is that their husbands abandon them without care or concern. The girl my husband married after me has been admitted to hospital. Last time I visited her, the doctors who operated on me predicted she'd end up like me. With God's help, and that of Amina, I was able to recover. I'm sure you all know Amina looked after me and restored hope and life in me. I remain eternally grateful for her help and support. But my greatest joy is that I took part in the activities of the Women's Association. I learnt a lot about life. I'm equally excited that I'm a participant in this heroic "stay-away" action.

Why should my former husband remain unpunished for physically harming others? Why should underage girls be illegally detained and brutalised in the name of marriage? Why can't the Assembly enact a law stating a suitable age for marriage to protect underage girls?

Now as I stand before you, I demand real compensation for illegal detention and the physical damage my husband has caused. I also propose that he and men like him be punished, as they're a risk to society.'

A slim beautiful woman with shining eyes and a pointed nose now came forwward. 'I'm also a peasant and live and work with my husband on the farm. I work daily from dusk to dawn on the farm, and at home I cook and wash his clothes. I've been doing this for over ten years. I'm very weak and tired. He cheated me and still cheats me. Every time the produce was harvested, he sold all of it and gave me nothing. When the Cooperative was formed, I refused to work for him and worked on our farm. Because of that he almost starved my children and me.

'Now let me tell you the story of my friend Lami. I'm sure you know she's permanently destitute. Her husband, as you must have heard, was killed in a land dispute a few months ago. He died fighting for the Emir, but immediately after the man was buried, the Emir ordered her to leave the house within three days. He claimed he'd bought the land and the house and had paid Lami's husband, and that now her husband was dead, the family should move out. Lami went to the area court to seek redress but the judge ruled that the Emir was right. Lami refused to leave and on the fourth day the police came in three Land Rovers. I was there and witnessed all that happened. They pulled down the doors and windows, sealed up the well and toilet and destroyed all the foodstuffs in the store and the kitchen. They were about to set the thatched roof ablaze when we all ran out.

'She now lives under a palm tree in central Bakaro with her three children and is terribly depressed and confused. Meanwhile, the house had been destroyed and a hotel is being built there. Is this Emir the representative of God here?'

Amina told the women to go to sleep but a girl shouted in opposition. She too wanted to tell her story. Amina left them to it and went to sit in the Headmaster's office.

'The whole town is in confusion,' said the Headmaster's wife who came in with Mairo and Jummai. 'Most men have not eaten since morning. They don't know how to cook. There was a rumour that the women who stayed behind were ordered to poison their husbands. Some men in Bakaro formed a "Bakaro Men's Association" and attempted to cook. They put some rice on a fire but while they were chatting it got burnt. Some men didn't know what to put in the pot first, oil or meat. A man admitted that, for the first time in his life, he'd sliced an onion today while another complained bitterly about smoke from the fire.'

The women laughed. 'This is one of the problems of over dependence,' said Amina. 'Do you know some men beat their wives for teaching their male children how to cook?'

'I also heard over the radio,' the Headmaster's wife continued, 'that the police are ready, but the Commissioner of Police has refused to give orders and has advised policemen in his religious sect not to take part in suppressing your uprising. He said the laws were too harsh and that the

Assembly was unrealistic. He threatened to resign if force was used. We also heard that mobile police units from the neighbouring state might be invited in case the conflict remains unresolved.'

Amina turned to Jummai who stood to attention with her palms on her thighs and stammered, 'Barricade raised on the bridge, checks conducted, situation normal. Permission to go and sleep.' The women laughed.

Amina remembered Jummai was the wife of a soldier and answered, 'Permission granted!'

'Yes ma'am!' she said with a laugh. 'My husband says these words daily when he comes home drunk.' She marched out of the room.

As the night progressed, Amina yearned for sleep but lay awake as different thoughts competed for a place in her mind. When she eventually dozed off, she was woken before dawn by the sound of raised voices.

'A girl is in pain. A girl is in labour,' some women were shouting. Amina woke up bewildered. Realising it was not a dream, she ran in search of Ngozi, the head of the Health Committee. Ngozi picked up her bag, checked its contents and ran to where the girl was lying. The girl, Zainab, was taken to the Headmaster's office. A few women who were awake assisted Ngozi.

Amina looked around at the dark, cramped space, and prayed that the delivery would go well. She waited outside with the others, and much later, Ngozi came out of the room, smiling radiantly. She whispered to Amina that a child had been safely delivered.

'Thank God,' Amina said after a deep breath.

'A boy or a girl?' some women asked.

'Guess,' said Ngozi.

'A girl.'

'No, it's a boy!'

'You've really saved us. Thank you,' Amina said to Ngozi.

'It's a pleasure. I'm a midwife by profession,' Ngozi disclosed with excitement in her voice. 'The mother and child need some rest. She's very weak.'

Some women could not wait to see the baby and entered the room.

'He looks like his father,' one said.

'No! You're wrong. He resembles his mother,' another one argued.

'Look, his nose and lips are like those of his mother.'

'May he live long enough to know his history so that he will help his mother,' one said.

'I'm sure he'll feel for her and help her.'

'You don't know men! Do you think all these Legislators, Emirs, Governors and others don't have mothers? Or that they were not once small and innocent like him?'

'Why do they change?'

'The way they are brought up.'

'Tell us, who's the father?' a woman asked Zainab after a brief silence.

'She'll tell you later,' Amina intervened and urged the women to go out. But they repeated the question. Zainab looked embarrassed.

'It's a long story,' she said in a low voice. 'I was a student at the Government Girls Secondary School some years ago. When my father lost his job he withdrew me from the school because he couldn't pay the fees. I then stayed at home and later started cooking and selling food ...'

'Where's your mother?' a woman interrupted.

'I don't know. I was told my father divorced her when I was five. One day late last year, when I had sold all my food and was returning home, a boy waylaid me near an uncompleted building called "Girl Free Zone." He seized my purse and ran into the building. I followed him but he overpowered me and raped me for about an hour.'

'Didn't you cry for help?'

# Chapter 22

'I cried out but he closed my mouth. When I realised I was pregnant I was confused, I didn't know what to do. I tried to hide my condition but my father found out and threw me out of the house.'

'Why didn't you tell him immediately?'

'At first I was afraid and ashamed. It was a terrible experience. I've no word to describe it.'

'What happened next?' another woman prompted.

'I told Amina and she took the case to court. I told her I wasn't the first girl this notorious boy had raped. He's still raping girls. No girl has ever won a case against him. The judge blamed me and freed the boy. I wanted an abortion but had no money.' She broke down in tears. The women looked at each other in disbelief. She wiped away her tears and said sadly; 'Today I even felt like dumping the baby in a bin, in the river, anywhere ...'

'Don't say that,' Amina hushed her.

'What else can I do? How can I take care of him? Imagine yourself in my position. He has no father, I've no helper. I'm blamed for something I haven't done. I thought it would be better to dump him, so that he would die young. This morning, I wanted to run away but I couldn't. I was too weak and you were around. I wanted to run to another town, start a new life there. When he held my hands and sucked my breast gently, I changed my mind. I saw he was mine, too innocent and young to be punished. He belongs to me. I assure you all, I'll take good care of him. He means a lot to me and us. This child is my life and when he grows up, I'll tell him everything!'

There was a moment of silence. Amina proposed that the child be named there and then. Zainab agreed with a nod. 'But first let's give them time to rest,' Amina suggested, motioning the others out of the room.

The women assembled after their breakfast for the naming ceremony. A ram was slaughtered. One of the boys said a long prayer and announced the name, Mainasara, a Hausa word for victor.

The naming ceremony was still in progress when an ambulance drove up slowly. Five women alighted and embraced Amina. 'Allah is never asleep,' she said, as she welcomed them. They were familiar faces, all actively involved in the health project and the adult literacy classes. One of them, a young, slim and neatly dressed lady called Dije, volunteered to address the women and Amina asked everyone to listen.

'We're from the Nurses and Midwives' Association and we've decided to continue our support. We were stunned by the government's action. We'd expected the government to encourage such projects everywhere. On Monday our association will embark on an indefinite strike in protest against the poor state of health in the state, against non-payment of salaries and continued laying off of well-qualified health workers.'

After her speech three of the nurses returned to the hospital with Zainab and her baby.

Later, a group of peasants came to persuade the women to go back to their houses. The leader of the delegation stepped forward calmly, arguing that a man and a woman must always be together. That was why when Almighty Allah created Adam, He created Hauwa; nowhere in the holy books was it written that women could revolt against men.

Amina appreciated their concerns and asked, 'Did you learn or gain from our activities?'

'Yes,' said a skinny man, 'and my wife too.' He pointed to a woman in the crowd. 'She learnt how to do so many things on her own. Her appearance even changed and she was happy. Generally our relationship improved.'

'My wife,' said another peasant stepping forward, 'gained a lot in terms of religion. Honestly, she'd not been praying properly but she learnt and now does it regularly. I watched your films and saw what the holy land looks like.'

'But you're against our association,' a woman shouted. 'I'm his wife. He threatened to burn our harvest and destroy our farms.'

'Yes, it's true, she's my wife,' the man said adjusting his position and smiling. 'It's true. My landlord first advised us to withdraw our wives from the association but when most women including my own wife refused, he advised me to burn your harvest or destroy the crops.'

'Why?' the same woman asked coming forward. 'Tell us! Don't be afraid. Strip the chicken of its feathers.'

'I'm not afraid,' the man said with a reserved smile. 'My landlord claimed you're growing similar crops and that if you're not discouraged it would damage his business. If you're allowed to continue and have more land, the prices of the crops would fall and he would lose. He then built a warehouse where he hoards his produce.'

'Is hoarding not a crime against humanity?' asked Amina.

'It is, but he's not the only one. Most rich farmers do it.'

'Are you willing to pay new taxes?' asked Larai.

'They're not new. We've always been paying different forms of taxes and levies.'

'Where will you get the money?' Larai pressed further.

'Almighty Allah, the Provider and the only Redeemer, will help. He who created us will give us the means.'

'You peasants,' Amina advised, 'should go and organise yourselves. It is from your sweat that these landlords are rich. If you do nothing, you'll remain in poverty. You must stand up and fight for a better life here on earth. With regard to our stay-away action, we shall continue until they meet our demands. Any woman who wants to go is free to do so. Just as men can't do without women, we can't do without men. That's a natural law. We do respect and love men.'

Members of the Support Group arrived later. Amina was excited to see them, and greeted Peter Akin, the suspended President, as he came up to her. Amina smiled at the tall, bearded figure, noticing his eyes were red and he was sweating. Her strong white teeth showed as she parted her lips.

'We went to the Federal Capital to protest against the introduction of higher school fees,' Akin told her.

'What happened?'

'The police threw tear gas and mercilessly beat us up and arrested and detained some students. Some of us managed to escape,' he explained.

'Where's Fatima?' Amina asked.

'She was taken to hospital but now she's recovering back at the university. A tear gas canister fell near her, she breathed some of it in and ...'

'And what?' Amina shouted, full of anxiety.

'She was beaten by some policemen but managed to escape.'

'What about Rebecca?'

'She was beaten and arrested. She's is still in detention.'

'... and Gloria?'

'She's in the hospital under police guard. She has a deep wound in her back,' Peter Akin explained with a smile. 'We expect them to be released soon. Some lawyers are working on their cases right now.'

Amina was appalled. 'It's unbelievable. This is madness,' she said.

'They claimed the meeting was illegal.'

'Were you injured?'

'Yes!' he said. He removed his black beret and showed her a wound covered with a plaster on his head.

'Sorry,' Amina sympathised with him.

'Don't worry! It's not so deep. We'll not give up fighting, that is for sure. We only arrived back yesterday. Fatima's too weak to come but sends her warm regards.'

Laila, the suspended vice-president and head of the support group, later spoke to the women.

'Comrade women, most of you must be aware of the case of the woman being tried for adultery in Funtua. She was said to have slept with a man and become pregnant. The local authorities arrested her after the child was born and charged her with adultery. Nothing was done to the man. The baby was presented in court as evidence of her immorality. The local court sentenced her to death by stoning.

'These rulers say it is Sharia law. That is not true. We have read the holy books and simply could not find any case where women were treated in such a barbaric way. On the other hand, we found many verses and examples where women were treated with dignity and respect. Our understanding of the religion is that during the time of Prophet Muhammad (*Sallallahu Alaihi Wassallam*), women were equal to men. His first wife Khadija (*May Allah be pleased with her*) was a prominent trader, who moved and traded freely. Another wife Zainab (*May Allah be pleased with her*) held an esteemed position in society. His last wife Aisha (*May Allah be pleased with her*) was a well-known poet and an accomplished military leader. If we were to apply the real Sharia law today, most of our rulers would have their hands chopped off for stealing public funds. Why is it that only poor women and men are punished under the law?

'Secondly, we protested because the federal government wants to increase school fees throughout the country. Naturally we are opposed to it. During our meeting, hundreds of armed policemen pounced on us, beat us and arrested some students. They claimed we'd no right to discuss matters affecting our own lives and future.

'These leaders cannot treat us as if we're from another planet. We all have the right to live and learn. Knowledge is not a privilege but a right which nobody can deny another. These leaders are illiterates ...

'Comrade women, let me explain what the loans are all about. For example, if without your knowledge and consent your husband goes to a rich Alhaji and borrows money from him, and spends the money any way he likes—for instance, he gambles and drinks with the borrowed money—if later,

# 23

Amina started feeling cold, and put on more clothes. Her saliva became bitter and her eyes smarted. By noon she felt dizzy and could hardly stand. She sat resting her head on the table. Five trade union officials arrived, and she heard their leader pleading with the women to go back to their houses, and offering them money. 'We'll soon have a meeting with the Governor and will appeal to him to repeal the laws, reduce the taxes and use his good office to create favourable conditions for workers and for women. The Governor is a good man but has some bad advisers. I'm sure he'll listen to us ...'

'We've listened to you,' Laila interrupted. 'Amina is ill, so Larai will speak on behalf of the women, but first, I'd like to make a few remarks. If you've failed to appreciate the positive lessons and genuine progress of the Women's Association in Bakaro over the last two years, then I'm sorry to say you're trailing far behind. There's a saying that "those who trail behind always get beaten." Unfortunately, the Governor is unlikely to heed your pleas on our behalf because we're not workers. We're women and our demands are different. As Amina has repeatedly emphasised, we're not against men but against the laws.'

Amina had started shivering and her teeth chattered. The nurses were called and they gave her some tablets and laid her on a makeshift bed with her body covered. Her sickness changed the mood of the women, who now looked disheartened and confused. The Students' Union leaders went into action to raise morale by organising discussion groups and plays.

After dinner, the women lit a fire again and Amina, feeling better after the tablets, sat with them. Larai volunteered to tell a story:

'Once upon a time, there lived a rich man in Dimbi village who had a very beautiful Shuwa Arab wife. She was so beautiful that she was called "queen." The man was a trader who travelled to different parts of the world. Before one of his journeys to trade and perform the holy pilgrimage, he called his best friend and entrusted him with the responsibility of taking care of his new wife.

'Three days after the rich man's departure, his friend visited the "queen" and, when it was dark, he made advances to her but she angrily refused. The friend smiled and said, "I was just playing with you. Don't you have such friendly games up there in the North?"

'When the rich man returned, he sent for his friend. In the evening while they were eating, his wife said she'd just remembered a funny incident that took place in her husband's absence. The rich man's friend quickly jumped up and ran away. The rich man and his wife were puzzled by the friend's behaviour. "Well," she continued, "in your absence a woman in the neighbourhood gave birth to an abnormal baby." They both laughed. After the meal the woman realised what had happened and told her husband that she knew why his friend had run away and that it was because he thought she was going to say what he had done to her. She then told him what his friend did. Up to today,' concluded Larai, 'the friend hasn't returned to the village.'

The women laughed. Laila came forward, thrusting her chest out and shaking her buttocks. She suggested the women continue with their stories of suffering.

'I'm from the eastern part,' stated Ngozi. 'I was laid off from the General Hospital recently. By profession I'm a nurse and midwife ...'

Feeling faint, Amina stood up and left, accompanied by a nurse who examined her and gave her some more tablets. She returned unnoticed and sat close to Larai who whispered, 'The more you hear, the less you understand how mean and cruel some people can be to others.'

'What happened?' Amina asked.

'Ngozi just told us about the conditions of women in the eastern part of Nigeria, mainly the high bride price and its effect on women. Women there are just like any commodity. The father's house is like a market where the sales and purchases are made. Girls are given away with price tags according to their education and the need of their family. This, she said, contributes to the high rate of prostitution among girls from the area.'

After Ngozi, a Yoruba woman, Mama Iyabo, spoke briefly on women in the western part of the country. She said that mutilating the female organs of girls was normal practice in her village. She said some parts were cut away so as to prevent girls from chasing men when they grew older. She revealed that it was a painful operation that often resulted in death.'

'Who's just finished speaking?' asked Amina.

'A prostitute from the part of Bakaro called "No Man's Land." The woman confessed she was forced into prostitution because she'd no alternative. She was happily married to a trader who became a party official. After the elections her husband married a girl who said she couldn't stay in the house with another woman. Her husband asked her, his first wife, to leave. She took the case to the area court. There, one Alhaji Aliyu, a man who owned brothels, cajoled her into agreeing to divorce and promised her a better place. Then he took her to one of his brothels where she stayed ...' Larai stopped to listen further.

'My name is Rekiya,' said a fat woman standing firmly on her feet. 'I'm a trader. My problems started when my father died a few years ago. When his property was being shared out, my brothers initially refused to give me anything. They claimed that under Islam, women are not entitled to inherit. I strongly disagreed and insisted they showed me where it was written in the Holy Koran. Although they showed me a verse, I didn't understand Arabic. I still insisted that as his child I was entitled to something. As a result of my determination, they gave me a small piece of land but refused me a share of his goods although I chose the goods rather than the land.

'One night thieves raided the market and burgled my shop. I then started selling goods for that woman called Kulu. As you all know, she's a smuggler and uses women to sell her smuggled goods. One afternoon, customs officials raided the market and seized all the goods. We were arrested. When we appeared before the Magistrate, I told the court the whole truth as requested, but when Kulu was summoned, she denied ever having done business with me. The Magistrate, a woman, said Kulu was a person of good character who, being educated and the wife of the Local Government Secretary, was aware of the dangers smuggling posed to the national economy. She concluded that I lied under oath and slandered a very important person. The Magistrate then sentenced me to three months' imprisonment without option of a fine. Amina knew about the case and even visited me in prison.

'How could this happen? Do they think that the market women are the smugglers? From that day I knew what they meant by justice in this society. Justice only for the rich and influential, and we the poor will have ours in the hereafter. I strongly believe in the day of judgement and on that day, I'm sure Almighty Allah will try Kulu. I'll testify and in his judgement there'll be no partiality.'

'I think although people struggle hard to survive, women here must struggle harder,' said Larai.

'You're right,' said Amina and nodded.

'Rekiya, what happened to your land?' a woman asked.

'While I was in prison I planned that after my release, I'd sell it and start business afresh, but to my greatest surprise, before I was released, this same woman Kulu connived with one of my brothers in the army and changed the ownership. I went there but was chased away. I took Kulu to court and tendered my certificate of ownership but Kulu produced a forged one that was accepted and the Magistrate claimed I forged mine. I was warned to stop blackmailing Kulu or else a heavier penalty would be imposed on me.

'I then started cooking at home and selling food in the motor park. Now street trading has been banned and taxes are to be levied on women like me if I continue cooking. Where do they expect us to get money to pay these taxes? My consolation is this: I believe in Almighty Allah, and one day there'll be justice.'

'It's time to go to sleep,' said Amina. 'There are challenges ahead. Tomorrow a delegation will go to town to address the press and, if the government is willing, to negotiate.'

#  24

For some reason, Amina could not fall asleep. The night dragged on slowly. When eventually she fell into a slumber, it was almost dawn and she had to wake up. Dawn itself was early. Amina tiptoed out of the headmaster's office and walked quietly out to the football field. Patches of cloud raced across the sky, chased by a cold, strong wind. The rising sun had not yet cast its warmth, and the air was full of early morning birdsong. Amina stopped and looked at Bakaro from afar. It lay before her like a carpet, endowed with beauty by nature, spoilt by human beings.

Amina returned to the camp for breakfast, and one of the nurses gave her a packet of pain relievers. She swallowed two and saved the rest for later. She painted her lips lightly and was spraying some perfume on when she was called to a meeting of the Negotiating Committee. As they were talking, the sound of sirens in the distance made them fall silent. The experienced ears of the students recognised it as "Kill and Go," the mobile police squad. Peter Akin shouted to the women to congregate quickly on the field.

'Fellow women,' Amina said, trying not to let her voice shake, 'they've finally sent the police, but please don't panic. I suggest the nurses, students, old and pregnant women, the lame, blind and the boys head for the hill and use another path back to the district. Go as quickly as you can before they appear.'

# Chapter 24

Those mentioned instantly scattered. At the same time, a convoy approached the wooden bridge. Amina could see one police car, a Land Rover and six lorries packed with mobile policemen. She took a deep breath and her heartbeat increased. The truth had finally dawned on her: That day would be the day of reckoning.

'Let's run and leave Amina to deal with them,' Mairo suggested to Larai.

'If you want you can go. I'll stand with Amina until the end. If we run, the police may chase us and arrest the pregnant women and others. It's better to stay and protect them,' Larai responded, moving closer to Amina.

Amina turned again to the women, who were clustered around her looking frightened. 'My dear women,' she said, 'this is our hour of trial. We have overcome so many hurdles, and we shall, by the grace of Allah, overcome this one.' Thick clouds now covered the sky, and the women's clothes fluttered in the wind. Amina tied her headgear more securely, as she said, 'We've not broken any law. We've no cause to fear. We're law-abiding citizens and the duty of the police is to protect citizens, not to kill them. Don't be afraid.'

Amina, Jummai and Larai raced towards the bridge and the other women sat down as requested by Amina. Some policemen effortlessly pulled down the barricade and crossed, followed by the dark blue Peugeot patrol car, the Land Rover, which was carrying a red flag and the six open lorries. They could see now that the policemen were all in anti-riot gear. A murmur went up, but nobody moved.

A tall man in a neatly pressed khaki uniform and beret walked towards them. He was wearing dark glasses, with binoculars strung around his neck, a belt tied across his chest and another holding a revolver around his waist. Amina took three steps towards him and stopped. 'You're welcome,' she said.

'Thank you,' replied the Superintendent. He did not sound friendly, and his hand went to the revolver as he added in a strained voice, 'We're here to maintain law and order.'

'We're lawful and orderly here,' Amina replied calmly.

He ignored her. 'We've come to arrest you for breach of the peace and rioting.'

'No one here is rioting,' Amina said steadily.

'Ignorance of the law is no excuse. Your association has been banned, you are a bunch of vagabonds, prostitutes and troublemakers!'

'Look, officer,' stammered Jummai from where she was standing. She pushed Amina aside and stood right in front of the officer. 'We're not afraid of your uniforms and guns. Why should you abuse us? If you are here to arrest us we'll not resist ... But if you say we're prostitutes, then your mother is one and you are a bastard.'

The officer became visibly infuriated, but Jummai stood her ground as he retorted, 'Fat ugly pig! Keep quiet before I have you shot. I warn you, don't make me lose my temper!'

'Lose it, nobody needs it. I'll face your bullets with a smile because I've got a strong heart,' and Jummai pounded her chest.

Amina touched her elbow and said in a low voice, 'Jummai, please keep quiet, don't provoke them!'

'I order you all to get up. Let's go,' the officer barked.

'Okay, I'll lead them,' Amina assured him and turned towards the women. Something in the faces of the women in front of her made her turn back quickly. She saw Jummai charge at the superintendent, grab him around the waist, pick him up, walk to the bridge and throw him into the flowing river.

There was immediate confusion. Two or three policemen dived into the water after him, while others sprang from the lorries and held Jummai. Amina watched in horror as she heard the sound of blows. The policemen dragged their officer from the river, minus his beret, binoculars and dark glasses. He removed his revolver and shook water from it. Another tall policeman marched forward with a loudspeaker and handed it to the dripping Superintendent, saying impatiently, 'We need orders.'

Amina ran to the women as the armed mobile policemen formed three lines facing them, the Assistant Superintendent in front. They could see his pockmarked face, red eyes and thick moustache. The policemen had shotguns, whips and tear-gas canisters. The officer commanded, 'I, the Superintendent of Police, Oscar Dangogoro, on behalf of the Commissioner of Police, hereby order you demonstrating women to disperse. If you fail to do so, you will be arrested. He paused and turning to the policemen, he said, 'I hereby order you, officers and men of the special squad, to move and arrest these vagabonds with immediate effect!'

The Assistant Superintendent roared an order that was followed by a volley of tear-gas canisters which dropped among the women. At first, they looked curiously at the strange objects emitting smoke. Then they started to cough and sneeze, tears streaming down their faces. There was panic as women screamed, and many of them fought to get out of the crowd. At a further order from the officer, the policemen charged towards the women. Amina couldn't see and struggled to wipe her tear-filled eyes. She felt something strike her on the head, harder than she could possibly have imagined, and staggered. A second blow caught her between her breasts. She shouted, 'Have pity!' but her voice was drowned in the cries that rent the air. Squinting through her tears, she made out a lanky, helmeted policeman directly in front of her, just as he raised his foot and kicked her with his heavy boot. Her legs gave way and she fell, but the policeman continued to kick her, shouting, 'Stand up!' Amina instinctively curled herself as small as she could and tried to roll out of his way, but she couldn't dodge the metal-tipped boot.

Around her, the pandemonium continued for some time, then suddenly the policemen retreated. From where she lay, Amina saw Larai struggling with a policeman, free herself and start to run. Then she heard a loud cracking noise which she realised was gunshots. As if in a dream, Amina saw Larai fling her arms up, take two slow motion steps, and fall.

The moment seemed to last forever. There was a wrenching, tearing noise somewhere nearby, which Amina realised was her own breathing. Then the Assistant Superintendent had her by the arm and had dragged her to her feet as he roared orders. The policemen charged forward again and arrested the women, herding them into the lorries. The Assistant Superintendent dragged Amina to where his still-wet superior was standing, stamped his left leg heavily on the ground and declared, 'Sir, Operation Hot Water successfully carried out! All bandits disarmed, arrested and in safe custody. No injuries on our side. Permission to lead the convoy to headquarters, sir?'

'Permission granted,' said the wet officer with a bitter look on his face.

Amina found herself pushed into the back of the Land Rover. There she found Jummai, bleeding through the mouth and nose and writhing in pain, but before she could do anything, she was ordered to lie on the floor. Policemen sat along the sides, and a couple of them deliberately put their boots on her stomach. When Amina protested, one of them laughed, 'Keep quiet! It's your own fault. You've not seen anything yet. You're going to scream until blood flows out of your eyes.'

The Assistant Superintendent peered through the glass window that separated the driver from the passengers in the back. Suddenly he ordered the driver to stop, jumped out and ordered Amina out. He escorted her to the front and helped her in, and then climbed in after her. As they drove to the police station, he continually gave her fierce glances, as if to reassure himself that she had not escaped.

At the police station, the Superintendent had a long discussion with the other officers and ordered that the women be taken to the Bakaro prison. After another ride, they arrived at the town's only prison. Amina was handed over to five warders who escorted her to a cell, pushed her inside and locked the metal door behind her.

Amina did not care to examine the room. She was suffering a level of pain she had never experienced before, even when Rasheed was being born. Her body ached as if the whole battalion of policemen had marched all over her. She lay face down on the bed, trying to empty her mind of the horror of what had happened. Instead, she thought about what might happen next, how she should face the challenges, how the trial would be, and how long it would last. She was still thinking when she fell asleep. She had no sense of how long she had lain there or what time of day it was, when a warder interrupted her sleep. She came to groggily, to hear that Alhaji Haruna wanted to see her.

'Tell him to come tomorrow. I'm too weak and sick to see anybody,' she said weakly. Amina thought she caught something like sympathy in the warder's expression as he turned to go, and added, 'When you're free, please come and see me.' As she lay there in the gloom, Amina felt as if she was floating somewhere in the small cell, looking down on the bruised and battered wreck that was her body.

By the time the warder returned, it was quite dark. At the sound of his voice, Amina felt herself return to her body with a rush of pain, and struggled to sit upright. He was called Gambo, lean, with a smooth face and a pleasant smile. He stood at the small opening in the cell door and called to her.

Amina told Gambo about the "stay-away" action and what had happened to the women. As they talked, he told her things about his job and working conditions, and she knew her instinct had been right–he was not her enemy, but a poor man doing a dirty job.

'I want to write to my husband,' Amina told him. 'Do you think you can get me paper and a pen?'

'But he's coming tomorrow,' Gambo said.

'Please do what I ask,' she said, smiling.

He winked and left. Within minutes he returned with several sheets of paper torn from an exercise book and a half-used pen. Jokingly, he said, 'Educated women are very troublesome.' Amina smiled and asked him to go and see the other women, and report to her on their condition. She decided to write to Fatima first.

"Dear Fatima,

From my cell in the Bakaro prison, I send my warm and sincere greetings to you and to all our supporters and sympathisers. A warder has been educating me about the horrible conditions of the prison, and in return, I've been telling him about our struggle and how he too can effectively fight for a better life. Warders, I have found out, are a group of forgotten workers, among the lowest paid in the civil service. I was told that some prisoners go about naked because they cannot buy prison uniforms or their relations do not send them clothes! Soon I guess prisoners will be told to pay for their food, and if they can't, then they will be free to starve!

I'm looking forward to Monday when our trial will commence. If, eventually, we are jailed, I'm confident that you and others will continue the struggle. The most urgent task before you is to try to recruit more women and other oppressed people to our cause. You would have been so proud of the enthusiasm and determination of the women during our stay-away action. I cannot tell you how they are because I'm in solitary confinement, but I expect to have news soon.

Convey my sincere greetings to all our supporters, tell them that although I am here behind bars I can feel their support, and it is keeping my spirit high.

Best wishes,

Amina

Bakaro Prison."

# Chapter 24

The next morning, Amina was told that the prison Superintendent wanted to see her in his office. She expected to see a fat, ugly, bullying man and had prepared for such a person and the statements likely to come from him. Instead she met a slender, good-natured old man who welcomed her with a smile. 'How are you, our special guest? Please sit down.' He offered her a cup of coffee, and though her reaction was instinctively negative, she accepted because she knew she had to keep up her strength. Alhaji Isa Dauda, the Superintendent, explained to her calmly: 'You women are actually not supposed to be here, but because the police cells in the town are full, you're here on a temporary basis.'

'Why am I in solitary confinement?' Amina asked.

'Oh no! Madam, you're not. You are there because you're our VIP—a very important prisoner. Actually, that's one of our rooms reserved for dignitaries.' He served her coffee with biscuits. As Amina sipped gratefully, he continued in his soft voice, 'I'm sorry to inform you that one woman died during the police operation. She was said to have resisted arrest and posed a threat.'

Amina blinked. He continued, 'A woman named Jummai is in critical condition in the hospital together with four others who aren't so critical. Soon the interrogators will visit you. Please cooperate with them so as to speed up the trial. Tell them the whole truth about those who influenced the uprising and how much you were paid.'

Amina was shocked. She jerked back and stared at him. Seeing her surprise, he repeated the last statement. 'I don't understand,' Amina protested.

'There are rumours,' he explained with a smile, 'about the actual cause of the uprising. Some people claim the opposition party gave you money to disturb the peace, while others even claim a foreign power sponsored you to destabilise the country.'

'That's certainly funny,' Amina responded with a smile.

'Yes. That's why your help is needed to clarify these issues. If you don't cooperate, you'll be charged for subversion and treasonable felony.'

Amina laughed aloud, and felt some kind of relief to know she hadn't lost her sense of humour. The Superintendent had one more piece of advice for her before she left. 'Your husband is coming to see you later. Please meet him this time. It's important, it might decide your fate here.'

There is a principle that someone who does not fear cannot be crushed. Some people freeze when others frown at them. Some shiver when others shout. Amina had been one of these, but she had changed. Now, nobody's frown frightened her, nobody's shouting made her shiver and nobody's words or sentences made her change her beliefs.

She confidently withstood the interrogation. She did not shiver when they shouted, nor was she cowed by their threats. She did not submit when they cajoled. She told them all she had done and what had happened. She accepted full responsibility. But when they left her cell, she was overwhelmed by her own performance, and started to shake.

Later, she was taken again to the Superintendent's office to meet her husband. Alhaji greeted her gently, but could not disguise his shock at what he saw. Amina thought ruefully of her bruised face and matted hair. She had not been allowed water or a comb since she arrived, and caked blood still clung to the cuts on her arms and legs where a metal-tipped boot had struck.

'I'm here to take you back home,' Alhaji told her. 'I've spoken to some people who have agreed to release you if you cooperate and tell the truth. You'll be freed for good if you answer the questions of the interrogators favourably.'

'We were told that your response was negative,' the Superintendent cut in. 'If you cooperate you'll be freed and only the women will appear in court. Your husband wants you home as soon as possible. This is not a place for a decent young woman like you. His influence has guaranteed your freedom. Just agree with the interrogators that the opposition party gave you money and told you to organise the uprising.'

She listened to their pleas and persuasion, half amused and half disgusted. After a while Amina cleared her throat gently and said: 'I cherish freedom, that's why I'm fighting for it, but I'm not ready to betray the cause or trade it for anything. What's the point of releasing me and detaining the women? As long as all of us are not unconditionally released, I'm going nowhere. Together we started it, together we shall finish it. On the other hand, you can keep me here if you'll only release the others. I'm going nowhere until this case has come to court.'

She stood up and thanked them. Alhaji Haruna held onto her and pleaded with her, but she did not yield. Instead, she pulled herself away.

Gambo brought her food in the evening in the usual prison bowl, but covered. She thanked him. She opened it and a strong wholesome smell filled the room. She looked at the rice and beans partly covered with well-fried tomato stew and slices of meat. 'This isn't prison food,' she commented.

'You're right!' Gambo confirmed with his usual grin, 'my wife cooked it for you. I told her you couldn't eat prison food.'

'Extend my sincere thanks to her,' Amina said gratefully.

'My wife is very worried! She strongly supports you. Please eat her food.'

'Don't worry, I'll eat everything,' she assured him. Amina handed him Fatima's letter and he immediately put it in his breast pocket. 'Please go to the university and hand it personally to her. Her name and room number are clearly written.'

'I'll deliver it tonight,' he promised.

# 25

As she waited for the court appearance, Amina worried about whether the women had a lawyer. She went over the possibilities: The police might apply for a long adjournment; they might be brought back to the prison; the trial might take months; and at the end of it they could all be jailed.

The iron door opened, and two warders escorted her, still limping, along the corridor. Outside, she saw that all the other women had already been loaded into a police van. A murmur went up as they caught sight of her, and Amina smiled at them. A tall, thin policeman came up to her holding handcuffs. She eyed him suspiciously as he approached. He ordered her to hold out her hands.

'No! Why should I be chained?' Amina protested.

'It's an order,' he replied.

'But I'm not running anywhere,' Amina objected again.

'It's an order,' he repeated expressionlessly.

'On what grounds are you chaining me?' she demanded.

'On this prison ground,' he asserted, pointing to the ground.

Illiterate zombie, she thought, suppressing a smile. She gave up, stretched out her hands, and was led to the front of the police Land Rover.

A crowd had gathered outside the Magistrate's Court. The area was being heavily guarded by units of plainclothes and uniformed armed policemen. As she alighted, she saw a crowd of students gathered in the street holding placards: STOP THE WOMEN'S TRIAL! FREE OUR PATRIOTS NOW! DOWN WITH NEOCOLONIALISM! DOWN WITH DICTATORSHIP! As they saw her, they clapped and shouted, 'FREE AMINA AND THE WOMEN NOW!' The police nearby moved threateningly towards them, and Amina raised her handcuffed hands above her head in greeting, but a policeman forced them down.

She caught sight of her husband with Kulu and other acquaintances on the steps of the Magistrate's Court, but just then, the police van carrying the other women appeared. The mobile police quickly made two lines, forming a narrow corridor from the van to the door of the court cell. The women filed through this corridor, Amina among them. She was glad to be back with the women again, but the cell was uncomfortably full so that they could hardly move, and the noise was deafening. Amina struggled over to the window and held onto its thick iron rods with her handcuffed hands for support. Through the bars, she saw Alhaji Haruna approach. His face was drawn and thin, and he said harshly, 'Look at the shame you've caused yourself.' Amina turned away from him and faced the women. A few minutes later, Peter Akin broke through the police line and ran to the window, where he removed his beret and greeted her. 'The nurses are worried about your health,' he said, his face full of concern.

'I'm fine. I've been taking the tablets,' she said.

'How are the conditions in the prison?' he asked.

'Bad,' Amina said.

'We heard one woman died,' Peter commented.

'Yes, it was Larai,' Amina confirmed.

He closed his eyes and bowed his head for some seconds. 'We're still unable to get a lawyer to defend you. Some lawyers wanted a very high deposit which we couldn't immediately get while others said it would be unwise for them to defend you.'

'Where's Fatima?' Amina asked.

'To be honest, we don't know,' Peter confessed. 'On Saturday morning she met Rabi, your lawyer friend, but I don't know the outcome. She came back to the university but we were told some plainclothes security men took her away in the middle of the night. We spent all day searching for her but have found no trace of her. I fear for her safety ...'

Peter broke off abruptly as a policeman grabbed him by the neck and dragged him away. The sight of Peter's eyes bulging as he struggled to release himself caused a group of students to charge through the police lines, angrily abusing the officer for maltreating their leader. Amina watched anxiously. Even from inside the cell, it was obvious that hostility was at boiling point and she feared a clash between the unarmed students and the police with their guns, tear-gas canisters and whips. Then she saw an elderly officer talking to the students, apparently persuading them to calm down. As they returned to their former position, Peter was among them, and she sighed with relief.

Just then, a sky-blue Mercedes-Benz pulled up not far from the window, and Amina saw two well-known lawyers, Sadiq and his wife, Rabi, alight from it. Despite herself, her heart lifted at the sight of Rabi. She and Rabi had been close at university, although they had lost touch since. She watched Rabi leave the car and walk towards the courtroom steps, radiating poise and calm self-confidence. In her dark, well-tailored coat over a white shirt and dark skirt, she looked born for the role of lawyer. Her husband, meanwhile, had parked the car, and was now talking with Alhaji Haruna. As she watched him in his conservative blue suit standing several inches taller than her husband, Amina recalled her relationship with the couple. It had been Rabi's influence that had made Amina choose to read law at university. Rabi,

Fatima and Amina had formed an alliance, and always studied together. Sadiq Usman had also been a close friend, and had even proposed to her more than once. She did not love him and had asked him to give her time to decide. Then one Friday night, walking back to the female hostel from the mosque, she had seen Sadiq's car with Rabi in the passenger seat. After that, Rabi's relationship with Amina had cooled, despite Amina's efforts to show her she felt no jealousy. Eventually, Rabi had left the hostel and married Sadiq, and now practised in her husband's chambers.

Amina was recalled to the present by the door opening, and she shuffled upstairs to the courtroom with the other women. She was surprised to see how full it was, with a police line separating the women and court officials from the public. There were two long tables facing each other, one for the court officials. At the second table, she counted five lawyers and two police Prosecuting Officers. Behind the court clerks' table, there was a raised dais with another table and a chair for the presiding Magistrate. Amina took up a position a little in front of the women, waiting for the proceedings to begin. As the Prosecuting Officer read out the charges, she felt detached, as though the whole scene were happening to someone else. Through the humming in her ears, fragments of sound reached her. 'Unlawful assembly...breach of the peace...undermining the legitimacy and authority of the state...riot...illegal meetings...class hatred...theft of husbands' property...trespass.'

It was the sound of her own name that brought her back to a consciousness of where and who she was. 'Amina Haruna, the first accused, incited peasants to revolt against payment of taxes and to assault a senior police officer. She is a subversive element. During interrogation, she did not help the police. Putting all the charges together, we conclude that she and her accomplices have to answer to high treason and sedition.' The voice paused before continuing: 'Sir, this case is only for preliminary trial. I urge your Worship to adjourn the case for at least three months without bail so as to enable us carry out full investigations. We have not yet obtained full statements from the witnesses. Some accused persons are on the run. Because the first accused has refused to cooperate with the police, we need time to make her help us. As the trial continues, we hope to add fresh charges.'

The Magistrate looked in the direction of the group of women. 'Do you understand the charges read by the prosecuting officer?' he asked, in a tone so neutral it was almost conversational.

There was murmuring and shuffling behind her as Amina responded, as firmly as she could, 'Yes, we do.'

Maintaining the same neutral tone, the Magistrate again: 'What's your plea? Guilty or not guilty?'

Amina drew herself up, mustering all the dignity she could. 'NOT GUILTY,' she replied, as if it hardly concerned her.

The Magistrate did not immediately write down her plea. He peered at her, adjusting his glasses, as if he could hardly credit her response. Eventually, he wrote something slowly on the pad in front of him. Immediately after he had recorded the plea, Rabi stood up, adjusted the cuffs of her coat and placed her palms on the table in front her. 'May it please your Worship, I'm the counsel for the accused,' she said, respectful but cool and clear-voiced.

Members of the audience smiled, some students clapped and a voice from the window shouted, 'VICTORY IS CERTAIN!' The Magistrate warned the audience to maintain absolute silence. Amina closed her eyes for some seconds in disbelief and took a deep breath. As she opened her eyes, her gaze met Rabi's. She smiled, and thought she detected a flicker of sympathy in her friend's expression. When Rabi resumed, however, she was all professional distance.

'Sir,' she began, 'before we begin, I request you to order the handcuffs removed from Amina. Handcuffs are justifiable in law only when the accused poses a threat to peace or has tried to escape. There are enough units of armed policemen both inside and outside the courtroom to restrain the prisoners. Moreover, I can vouch that she will not attempt to escape or cause a disturbance.'

The Magistrate bowed his head in acknowledgement, and with relief, Amina felt the handcuffs being removed from her wrists. From the whispering behind her, she knew the women had taken courage from this, and from the sight of Rabi.

The proceedings continued. Rabi Usman again stood up and declared, 'Sir, I've gone through the charges carefully and can submit that the accused persons can be tried for only one offence—unlawful assembly. Furthermore, I urge your Worship to rule that the whole case be determined today as further adjournment would cause unnecessary hardship to the accused, who, although not yet convicted, are being subjected to subhuman conditions, in overcrowded cells. I intend to prove beyond reasonable doubt that the charges against them are entirely lacking in substance.'

Following an objection from the prosecuting officer, on the grounds that only the High Court could give the final judgement, Rabi made a further submission: 'Bakaro is the *Locus in Quo*, that is, it's the place where the purported offences were said to have been committed. You as a Magistrate have the legal power to determine it: either free the accused persons or transfer the case to the High Court.'

The presiding Magistrate accepted her citations and gave examples of where he had determined cases of this nature, but insisted that Rabi must, 'conclusively convince the court that the women committed only the said offence.'

Without hesitation, Rabi continued: 'Contrary to the charges, the women did not in any way undermine the security and legitimacy of the state. There is no evidence and there can be no evidence to prove that they were subversive. A subversive element can be described as someone who consciously aims at destabilising a government and overthrowing it. First, the women hadn't that intention, they were not armed and it would be absurd to think that a group of defenceless and poor women in a single district of a small town could undermine the security and legitimacy of such a big and powerful country. I implore your Worship to please strike out the charge.'

The Prosecuting Officer looked around vaguely, his expression bitter and confused. The Magistrate waited, but the police officer remained silent.

'The charge has been struck out accordingly,' announced the Magistrate.

'Sir, these innocent women,' maintained Rabi, 'don't constitute a class, cannot constitute a class and as such cannot invoke class hatred.'

The Prosecuting Officer suddenly came to life, and roared: 'Objection!' flecks of saliva flying from his mouth along with the words. 'Amina said that there are two main classes in our society, the rich and the poor. She even told us boldly that she's organising the poor against the rich. She repeated several times that the ruling class must be overthrown and a new system put in its place. She maintained that her hatred and contempt for this ruling class is eternal.'

Rabi Usman was unperturbed. 'We don't have classes in our country,' she reasoned. 'The notion of class hatred is an inappropriate one, introduced into our legal system by the former colonialists. In our society we have tribes, clans, religious and ethnic groups. If one talks of some people owning more property than others, Amina is clearly from a property-owning family. If you agree with me, sir, that there are no classes, then logically there can't be hatred to be invoked. She and the women didn't invoke class hatred. I urge your Worship to strike out the charge.'

The Magistrate struck out the charge.

'A thief by simple definition,' said Rabi Usman, 'is someone who takes another person's property without that person's knowledge and consent. Going by that definition, the accused persons can't be charged with that offence. We admit that they took some household materials with them, but it was not stealing, because their husbands were there. It was daylight and no one stopped them. The husbands didn't even report it to the police. We submit that these items were taken with the knowledge and, by implication, the consent of the husbands. So the women are innocent of this charge.'

'The charge is struck out accordingly,' the Magistrate said.

Amina listened as though in a dream. After the nightmare of the assault, followed by the pain of imprisonment, it seemed impossible it could all be so easy now. She heard Rabi's evenly modulated voice continue without even paying attention to the details. The proceedings moved rapidly, and the Prosecuting Officer was dumbfounded when almost all of the charges were struck out. He had not expected it, had not expected a woman with the power of Rabi Usman to gainsay him in court.

'We admit,' Rabi continued, 'that the women assembled despite a ban, but it was not accompanied by a breach of peace, as the police officer stated. The women were peaceful—no clashes or fights were reported during their meetings. By the way, sir, in law a breach of peace can only be regarded as an offence when someone is harmed.'

'Objection!' the Prosecuting Officer said, this time in a subdued voice. 'These women disturbed their husbands' peace and denied them their rights ... I mean a man has a wife so that he can have some benefit from her,' he explained painfully.

There was laughter in the court. 'The issue of a husband's real or fringe benefits doesn't exist in our legal system,' Rabi posited, laughing too. 'If it does, then it probably exists only in the home. I implore your Worship to overrule the objection.'

'Objection overruled.'

'Amina,' Rabi contended, 'need not help the police in their investigations or even make a statement. Her silence cannot be held against her.'

The Magistrate nodded in agreement.

'The first accused cannot be charged for sedition because she never caused a public disturbance, did not undermine the state, its laws or the constitution of our country; never incited discontent.'

'*Haba!*' the Prosecuting Officer exclaimed, looking baffled and frustrated. He shook his head sadly, but nonetheless said emphatically: 'Amina on many occasions, and publicly too, called on the people to rise against what she called the agents of neo-colonialism and stooges of imperialism. She consistently maintained this position during interrogation. She and the students belong to a group that has foreign financial backing to overthrow our democratically elected government. She was even proud of being associated and linked with those opposed to the government. The defence counsel appears not to know the first accused very well.'

Rabi's eyes again met Amina's, and this time Amina was certain of their warmth. 'Sir,' responded Rabi, and for the first time something like passion entered her voice: 'I know Amina very well and what she is capable of doing. I had the good fortune of studying law with her at university. If counsel for the prosecution knew what he was here for, he should at least, out of respect for our beloved profession, show evidence to support his argument. I'd advise him to go back to school and learn how to prosecute before standing in front of any Magistrate or judge.

'Furthermore, and back to the case in hand, Amina as a citizen has freedom of speech, and the prosecution has failed to prove that her words were calculated to provoke public disorder and violence. We admit that the women were unlawfully assembled but, sir, I want you to judge them as first offenders. Similar cases abound in law where first offenders are freed, although in some extreme cases on a conditional basis. Permit me, sir, to say that treason is the most serious crime known to law. It occurs only when citizens vow to go to war with the state, and a treasonable felony charge is applicable only to a person who intends to overthrow a constituted government, which the accused persons never did.

'Moreover, the principle of legality states that nothing is criminal unless it is totally forbidden by law. We have proved that what the women did was within the framework of the law. In carrying out your judicial duty, I strongly urge you, sir, to bear in mind an important and fundamental ingredient of just law—that is, its acceptability. Justice,' Rabi Usman emphasised, 'is the correct application of law. I humbly and respectfully enjoin you to administer justice impartially. Let me respectfully remind you sir, that in some countries today people are being denied justice and it would be a judicial tragedy and disgrace if our country were compared to those. This is a democratic society.'

Rabi delivered these words with such authority and dignity that most of those in the courtroom were visibly moved. Only the Prosecuting Officer hunched his shoulders and stared at the floor.

'In conclusion,' Rabi announced, 'Amina maybe guilty of one minor offence but the prosecutors diminish our justice system when they accuse her of treason and felony, crimes that the facts do not support. I must state that since a *prima facie* case has not been established against the accused persons, I will urge you to pass a no case to answer verdict. That is, my clients should be discharged and acquitted of all charges.

'Do the police prosecutors want to speak?' asked the Magistrate.

The Inspector stood up and spoke with effort. 'This case is taking a dramatic and sensational turn which we think is a negation of law. We had wanted it adjourned for at least three months so that, while the women are kept in safe custody, we could continue our investigations and arrest those at large, including some Student Union leaders and nurses who fled from the school before the police operation. This would enable us to carry out proper, professional and deeper investigation into this case.'

While he spoke, Amina looked at the public gallery. She saw Peter Akin and Laila quickly walk out of the courtroom. She wanted to laugh but succeeded in restraining herself.

'I must say that we are not satisfied with the arguments and submission of the defence counsel. She eroded the path of law, mixed facts and placed all the principles of law upside down.'

For the first time, Rabi raised her voice as she jumped to her feet. 'Objection!' she shouted, looking daggers at him for some seconds. 'Sir, the prosecutor has no right under the law to comment on an issue already determined. He had a golden opportunity to object while the trial was in process but he didn't. Now that we have crossed that stage, I object to his statements.'

'Objection sustained,' the Magistrate ruled.

'Undoubtedly,' said the Inspector, 'you are to determine the case. I appeal to you to hand down the severest punishment to this gang of women. If you don't do this, then the law would be seen to have been thrown to the dogs. These women, and especially Amina, have committed very grievous offences against the state and if you set them free, then rest assured we can't have peace and stability. Such women are among the worst criminals in the country today, and it's our moral and professional duty to cleanse society of unhealthy and dangerous ideas. There is a saying that a mother who does not want her child to sleep will not sleep either. Sir, they do not want us to sleep.'

The Magistrate stood up, indicating that the court should remain seated. 'I shall retire to my chambers for a few minutes,' he announced. 'Let the accused persons remain here.'

# 26

As soon as he had left the room, Rabi Usman walked over to Amina. She smiled at her and her voice was sympathetic as she said, 'Don't worry, Amina, I'm sure you'll be released on bond. It's the way most first offenders convicted of unlawful assembly are normally dealt with. Though the Magistrate is known to be a tough man, I'm sure he'll be lenient with you.'

But as Amina had feared, it was not to be so straightforward. When the Magistrate returned, his first question was directed at Amina.

'Madam Amina, I want to ask you some questions, but be assured that it'll have nothing to do with the verdict. I just want to know some facts. What are your views on the role of women in society?'

Amina was taken aback, but struggled to maintain her calm demeanour. 'Women should be treated as responsible and should enjoy all the rights of a human being. They should neither be exploited nor oppressed. What is your own view on the role of women?' she asked.

'I'm not on trial,' the Magistrate said with a laugh. He put his pen down, laced his fingers and leaned back. 'Amina, I think you owe the court an explanation as to why you behaved as you did.'

Amina understood that she was being called on to justify herself, and by extension the women ranged behind her, and took a deep breath. 'I aligned myself with the poor women because I cannot ignore the fact that as a class they are exploited, and their rights and freedoms are violated daily.'

'What do you mean by their rights and freedoms?'

'Is our country not a member of the United Nations?'

'It is.'

'Is it not a signatory to the Universal Declaration on Human Rights?'

'In this court I ask the questions.'

'It's written there that every citizen has the right to life, freedom from torture and slavery, the right to liberty, freedom of thought and religion, freedom of association and movement, the right to work, education and social security. Tell me honestly, are these basic rights and freedoms not being flouted in our society?'

'Was that why you disturbed our peace and stability?'

'Peace for whom? stability for what? If it's peace for a minority to rule and dominate the majority, then there'll never be peace, and if it's stability for the oppression and exploitation of the majority, then that stability will never exist. Let me make it clear that ...'

'Listen, Amina,' the Magistrate interrupted. 'Don't turn the honourable court into a political lecture hall.'

'Politics determines everything ...' Amina said before Rabi interrupted her.

'Your Worship, I tender an unreserved apology on behalf of Amina. I urge your Worship not to take her statements literally. She's just carried away by her train of thought, which isn't unusual with people under conditions of stress. I'm sure you know why she's making such statements and will understand her.'

But Amina was not to be silenced. She knew she had one chance to say how she saw things, and she was going to take it. She continued, as calmly as she could. 'The police have committed aggravated assault on us, they've murdered, in cold blood, one of our young and industrious women and instead of bringing them to trial and punishing the murderer, we were brought to court. How can people who've committed crimes prosecute so-called criminals?'

Bursting with righteous indignation, the Prosecuting Officer jumped up to protest. 'Your Worship, we find this statement injurious to the well-being and good image of the police force. I insist that the first accused be appropriately tried and severely punished. Maybe she's mentally disturbed and needs a psychiatric test.'

'I think the first accused is in a normal state of health. I've a wealth of experience in handling such accused persons,' the Magistrate maintained and turned to Amina. 'The police only performed their duty. Keep them out of it.'

'But the police are in the case,' Amina asserted, pointing at the Prosecution Officer, 'they can't be neutral. They're the abetters of injustice, oppression and subjugation in our society. '

'Keep the police out of this case,' he insisted.

'What about the taxes?' she asked.

'Taxes are paid by everybody. I too pay,' he said with a smile.

'When taxes are unfair, women have protested before in this country. We're only following that tradition when we say we won't pay,' Amina declared. 'Why should the rich live on the taxes of the poor? The government says we have to repay our foreign loans, but when the government officials took these loans, we were not consulted and we can't see what they were used for. Instead, the standard of living of poor people has worsened. So how can we pay?'

'Are you aware it's an offence not to pay taxes?' the Magistrate asked.

'Of course I am, but what other means do we have to make our voices heard?'

'Was that why you were prepared to be violent?' he prompted.

Amina loved the question. As she looked from the women to the crowd, smiling slightly, there was absolute silence and all eyes were on her. She stepped forward and cleared her throat. 'Let me tell you my conception of violence. When young and innocent girls are married off at a very tender age and their bodies are mutilated, is that not violence? When girls are forced to marry men they've never come into contact with and without due regard to their feelings, emotions and sentiments, is that not violence? When a woman is sentenced to death for adultery and the man is set free, is that not violence? When people are condemned here on earth to abject poverty, and especially women are deprived of their fundamental human rights and treated as slaves, is that not violence? When men brutally assault their wives and girls are raped with pride, is that love? When women are debased and assaulted in the form of prostitution, is that not violence? When women are barred from work, while others are callously forced out of their houses, is that peace? When peasants are chased from their land and heavily taxed, what is it? When we peacefully move out of our houses in protest against exploitation, injustice and countless maltreatments and the police pounce on us, gas us, beat us and kill one of us, is that not violence?'

There was complete silence in the room as Amina stopped speaking. She stood with her head bowed, flushed and breathing deeply. Then she heard the Magistrate's voice.

'Well, I think you've said enough or should I say you've entertained us enough. It will not be in your interest to go any further. So tell me, do you undertake to go back to your houses peacefully?'

Amina turned and looked at the women. 'There is a saying that you can take a horse to water but you can't make it drink.'

There was laughter in the court.

'What if the horse is thirsty?' he asked with a smile.

'It'll drink,' Amina replied with a short laugh.

As laughter rippled round the court again, Rabi Usman stood up.

'Permission to speak?' she begged.

'Granted,' the Magistrate said with a smile.

'Your Worship,' Rabi began, 'before you pass judgement, I would like to point out that the accused persons in general and Amina in particular are sincerely and clearly repentant. I implore your Worship to please disregard Amina's statements. On behalf of my clients, I assure you it'll never happen again. As you can see yourself, these women are peace-loving and will live in peace from now on.'

The Magistrate drew his notes closer and started to read his judgement. 'Having objectively assessed the circumstances of the case, and being moved by the condition of the women; having taken into account that they have suffered considerable punishment, and the personalities involved, especially the first accused as the wife of an honourable legislator, a highly respected and member of the community, I find that the prosecution has failed to substantiate the charges brought against the accused persons. They have also failed to prove beyond reasonable doubt that the accused committed the said offences. I hereby discharge all the accused persons of all the charges against them but one. As regards the charge of unlawful assembly, the accused persons are conditionally discharged.

'I order the women to go back to their houses and live peacefully. I must warn them to be law-abiding and remind them that any offence of such nature in future will attract a heavy sentence. Let us all live in peace! May God help us. That is my verdict. Let the court rise!'

Rabi rushed over and hugged Amina, who hugged her back, laughing. It seemed to her that she left the courtroom an entirely new woman. Though weak, hungry, in pain and tired, she mustered all the strength she could and walked calmly but confidently into the crowd outside. The students and some women cheered as she walked past. She was glad she had not betrayed them as she looked into their faces.

Amina walked towards Zainab who was holding Mainasara. 'How are you?' Amina asked touching the boy.

'We're fine. I hear you are free,' Zainab said with excitement.

'Yes! When did you leave the hospital?' Amina asked?

'This morning.'

'Go home and wait for me,' said Amina. Suddenly, she felt dizzy and her legs became weak. The fine sand baked by the hot sun burnt her bare feet. As she bent down and placed her hands on her knees, Rabi Usman ran towards her. 'The whole legal procedure is over. I've signed the necessary forms on your behalf and you're free to go.'

'Thanks,' Amina replied faintly.

Rabi Usman looked at Amina with concern. 'Amina, you're weak and sick. You need a good rest. Please go home and recover.'

'I will,' Amina promised.

'When you've had time to rest, I want us to meet to file a case against the police, holding them responsible for Larai's death and demanding compensation. You're a key witness,' Rabi Usman stated.

'Compensation?' Amina repeated, and smiled. It was only the strangest aspect of a day that she could not have imagined.

# 27

Amina wondered what would happen to the women now. How would their husbands treat them? What would happen in the next minutes, hours, days, weeks, months and years? She looked around at the dispersing crowd. As the policemen moved towards the convoy of lorries, some of them shouted insults at her, but she was not concerned. The students were singing and dancing, taunting the policemen. She turned away, walking blindly along the rough sandy road, unthinking of her direction, conscious only of the hot sand burning her feet. She stepped onto the short grass at the edge of the narrow path, and pushed her way through the bushes.

Then someone was running after her, calling her name. The voice was familiar, and Amina stopped and looked back. It was her husband. He drew up, panting, and stopped in front of her. Amina waited, her mind blank. She was barely able to take in his words as he pleaded, 'Please, Amina, come back, I'll take good care of you. Let's forget about the whole incident. I've have already. Please let me take you home.'

Amina allowed herself to be led by Alhaji Haruna towards his car. He opened the door and she almost collapsed onto the front seat. They made their way along the road which was crowded with women and their well-wishers walking home. As they saw Amina, they shouted and waved, and she waved back. As they drove towards the centre of town, she realised they were not heading towards the compound.

'Where are we going?' she asked.

'To your new house,' he responded.

The car headed towards the northern part of the town on the dual carriageway. The driver turned left at a tree-lined road into the Government Reservation Area. Alhaji Haruna instructed the driver to turn right and park in front of a house.

'This is your new house,' he announced without excitement, as he led her inside.

'Thank you,' replied Amina, sinking gratefully onto the sofa.

'I'll give you some time to rest. We'll talk tomorrow,' he said looking straight into her eyes.

'*In Sha Allah,*' she responded faintly. Alhaji looked at her with concern.

'Hauwa is somewhere at the back. I'll go and get her,' he said, and left through the back door. He came back with Hauwa and after a few minutes bade them farewell.

Hauwa was very pleased to see Amina, but seeing her faintness, immediately served her food.

Amina ate ravenously, and felt strength coming back to her. Afterwards, she lay on the sofa, too exhausted to move. Behind her closed eyes, the events of last Friday began to play themselves out in slow motion. She saw herself applying lipstick and then spraying on perfume. She heard the sirens, saw the arrival of the police convoy and the faces of the Superintendent and his assistant; heard their orders, saw the ranks formed by the armed and helmeted policemen. She saw them charge forward, stamping their feet heavily, holding their shotguns and tear-gas canisters, into the ranks of defenceless, innocent women. Oh! She heard the first volley of tear gas fired…the women coughing, running, crying...the panic that ensued...the policemen chasing, beating, shouting, kicking and arresting her companions.

Mostly she thought about Larai, whom she hadn't had a chance to miss properly before now. She recalled their first meeting in the hut; how Larai had moved to her house; Larai's commitment to work; her love of knowledge; her musical talents, riddles and jokes; her expertise in cooking. The picture of how Larai died flashed before her. She distinctly saw Larai among the crying, coughing women, struggling with the attacking policeman, freeing herself as she attempted to escape his brutality. Finally, because she couldn't switch it off, she was forced to watch again as the policeman aimed at Larai, hear the shots, see how the bullets caught her from behind.

'Poor girl, it had been written that she must die young, poor and tragic. It's all over for her. No more thoughts of the struggle to live; no more days of hunger, torture and want; no more nights of neglect; no more worries, and no compensation. On the fallen walls of this decadent system, one day, on a bright sunny day, we shall proudly say at a school we open in your memory: This centre of learning is dedicated to Larai.

The next morning, Amina woke up very late. Her head had stopped aching but she still felt very tired when her husband called on her.

'What do you think of the house?' Alhaji Haruna asked, regarding her anxiously.

'It's a big house, thanks.'

'You've almost all you need here.'

'Thank you.'

'Amina,' he started, sitting down on the sofa, 'I'm giving you a second chance to live a normal life as my wife. This time around, no more friends from the university, no more meetings on campus, no more experiments with the women. You will settle down and perform your duties as my wife.' There was a moment of silence. 'Do you have any requests?'

'Can I have newspapers delivered to me?'

'Of course.'

Alhaji Haruna stood up to go. He looked down at her and asked gently, 'Tell me, how many months pregnant are you?'

'Just over three, I think.'

❖

Weeks later, the telephone rang. It was Bilkisu, who lived a few streets away from Amina and wanted to pay her a visit. She appeared at the gate moments later with a broad smile. 'My husband and I were in Dubai when the demonstration took place,' she explained. They settled down in the living room, and Amina told her what happened.

'What surprised you the most?

'I honestly did not expect the Magistrate to release us.'

'What about the police?'

'I didn't expect them to be armed with live bullets and to be brutal in a situation that did not call for it.'

'I was told you spoke courageously. Did you rehearse your speech before the trial?'

'No,' Amina said. 'I never thought I'd have the opportunity to speak.'

'How was life in prison?'

'Horrible.'

'I'm glad you're out of that place.'

'No, we're all in a big prison. Our society is a large prison where different types of institutional keys are used to lock up the people while the military and the police are the jailors.'

'Are you worried we've lost?'

'We've lost a battle, not a war. We've lost our property and a comrade but not our courage, so we're still strong. We've tested the strengths and weakness of the system. They've won this battle but their victory is temporary.'

'What will happen next?'

'I can't say anything now. I'll leave that for time to tell. The women will suffer more but now they know they can fight for their rights. We have to start afresh, to gather more strength, to develop stronger willpower and determination to resist and continue the fight. Our demonstration and stay-away action were just a dress rehearsal for more uprisings to come. I've realised that the masses don't want to live the old way, according to archaic laws, traditions and customs. The people are yearning for change, for law and order, happiness and prosperity, an end to need, disease and hunger. If our present rulers can't make these changes, we must dislodge them, build and defend a system that will be in all our interests.'

'What's the main problem bothering you?'

'It's how to organise for the new phase of the struggle. As a Muslim, I'm bound not to turn my back when I see any leader commit injustices. The Holy Prophet said, "Let him who sees a situation in which injustice is being perpetrated endeavour to change it." I think that justifies my position.'

'My husband says you're an idealist.'

'Not at all, I'm someone who believes in reality. In whatever I strive to do, I try to be real, to keep myself and those around me on a solid foundation. I believe in life, in the struggle and in Almighty Allah. It takes a lot to create a decent, normal and proper way of life, and every individual has a meaningful contribution to make. How can we keep quiet when all these problems face us? '

'What do you think we need in this country?'

'We must put things right, and to put things right we need a revolution.'

'What sort of revolution?'

'One that will change the whole structure of society, and usher in a new way of life; bring justice, freedom and equality, love, understanding and respect to all of us. A genuine revolution that will satisfy the yearnings of the people; that will give land, food and good living to peasants and their families; work and better life for the workers; hope and education to young people, and opportunities for women to take an active part in the development of society. Above all, we need a revolution that will modernise our society.'

They both lapsed into silence. As if uttering the conclusion to a prayer, Amina said softly: 'Although historical steps are normally almost silent, they are not completely noiseless. Those who have sharp ears can hear.'

❖

Three days later, Hauwa came in early in the morning and asked excitedly, '*Amarya,* have you heard the news?'

'No! What is it?

'There's been a change of government.'

Amina could not react with Hauwa's excitement, but she switched on the radio to hear the telltale military music. She listened until an announcement interrupted the music with the news that the civilian administration had been overthrown in a bloodless coup d'etat. A voice intoned the ritual procedures to which she was accustomed:

"The constitution has been suspended indefinitely.

A state of emergency has been declared.

Federal and State parliaments have been dissolved.

Military tribunals will be set up in each state.

All meetings – except for religious purposes have been banned.

The Police and Army have been empowered to fire at protesters.

A dusk to dawn curfew has been imposed.

The Police and Army can detain saboteurs without trial indefinitely. They can also enter homes without warrants and take any action they deem necessary to restore order."

Amina took a deep breath. A little while ago, the coup d'etat would have had a different meaning. Now, she was unaffected. Three days later, Lt Colonel Abubakar Usman was named as the State Military Administrator, while Alhaji Haruna moved from the Legislators' Estate to her house. She noticed that he was not worried about the change in government, but on the contrary, was in a good mood.

'These soldiers will not kill us,' he explained. 'And I don't think they'll confiscate our property either.' Amina simply shrugged. A week later, when Lt Colonel Abubakar Usman announced the members of his cabinet, Alhaji Haruna was the new Commissioner for Economic Development.

That evening, Kulu came in smiling. 'My husband has been made a Minister in the new Federal Military Government,' she announced joyously. 'Didn't I tell you that Fatima and her group were hopeless cowards? Where are they? They've all fled the country!' She laughed until tears started coming out of her eyes and she wiped them away.

'Amina, this is a great chance for you to start afresh. There are lots of opportunities to make money. Seize the time.'

Amina responded patiently, 'I'm pregnant and will wait until after giving birth to decide what to do next.'

The first time she felt anything at all about the coup was when Laila telephoned Amina that night. Her voice was shaky. 'The situation is very tense on campus. There are so many security men around. Some lecturers have been arrested while others were beaten up in their houses or offices. There is an atmosphere of fear and insecurity. Peter Akin is in detention. Some trade unionists that protested at the suspension of the constitution have been detained.'

'Where are you now?' Amina asked.

'I'm in hiding somewhere.'

'Where's Fatima?'

'She and Danbaki have fled the country. Bature got them out.'

'Where's Muktar?'

'I don't know. Lt Col Abubakar Usman has issued an arrest warrant for him.'

'Why?'

'Just before the coup, he had published an article saying that military dictatorships hinder progress, and the State Administrator considers it subversive. We think he's in a neighbouring country, from where he'll fly to Europe to seek political asylum. Bature has offered to get me out, and I'm afraid I may have to accept his offer and leave too. I'll keep in touch.'

This was the last Amina heard of her friends at the university until three months after the coup, when she went to the ante-natal clinic for a check-up. In the waiting room, she glanced idly at the newspaper, and saw a photograph that caught her attention. Her husband, Bature and Lt Colonel Abubakar Usman were shown, smiling. They had just signed a deal that placed all the state's mineral resources under an international consortium. 'This is a gigantic step towards sustainable development,' her husband was quoted as saying.

After her evening prayers, Amina was watching television when someone knocked at the door. Hauwa opened it and Bilkisu came in with two bodyguards. Looking radiant, she apologised for not calling her first to announce her visit. 'You're always welcome,' Amina said. 'Any news about Rebecca and Gloria? I haven't heard from them for some time.'

'They're both fine. Rebecca went to Zuru immediately after they were released while Gloria moved in with her boyfriend. I'm in touch with them and they send their warm regards.'

'Have you heard any news of Fatima?'

'Yes. I spoke to her last night and she promised to call you soon. She's got a very interesting project she wants to discuss with you.'

'What's it about?'

'I don't know.' After a pause, Bilkisu started with a shaky voice, 'Amina, I've come with a message from my husband, the Military Administrator of the state. His Excellency would like to invite you to serve in his cabinet as the first Commissioner for Women's Affairs.' Amina showed no emotion. She simply smiled and asked Bilkisu to repeat her proposal, looking closely at her and her bodyguards. Then she spoke. 'Listen, Bilkisu, thanks for the invitation, but I'm not that desperate. Please tell the Military Administrator that I can't take part in the systematic destruction of my beloved country.'

Bilkisu was visibly disappointed. She lowered her head. There was a moment of silence. The telephone rang. Amina picked it up and suddenly her pleasant face lit up with a distinct smile.

'Tiloti, what a pleasant surprise ... Fatima, I'm so happy to hear your voice again.' Fatima explained how she and Danbaki had escaped, and also spoke of their future plans. Then she turned to Amina's situation.

'I can understand your decision to lie low. But listen to this: I've been informed by an official at the United Nations that they want to present you with a Certificate of Honour at a venue of your choice.' Amina's initial reaction was to reject the award, but after a lengthy discussion, Fatima persuaded her to accept it. 'This is the best opportunity you have to show the world what is going on, to put Bakaro on the international scene, to raise the struggle one level higher. You must not waste such a golden opportunity,' Fatima argued. Amina ended by agreeing to receive the award and promising to write a speech. However, when Fatima wanted the ceremony to be held in London, Amina insisted it must be in Bakaro, 'where it all happened.'

Fatima and Amina talked for a long time, turning over ideas for future projects. Eventually, when Amina was too tired to talk any longer, she told her friend: 'I am with you, Fatima. We must continue the struggle! We simply have no choice. We have in our hearts a future that we have to bring to birth. I'm strong and ready for the next phase ... and I'm excited because I know we can succeed ... a better world is possible!'